VITTORIA COTTAGE

In the novels of D. E. Stevenson one is always certain to meet the most delightful characters, and there is a charm about the very pleasant people whom we meet in *Vittoria Cottage* which makes it certain that this entrancing novel will find a very wide public.

Books by D. E. Stevenson in the
Ulverscroft Large Print Series:

KATE HARDY · ANNA AND HER DAUGHTERS
AMBERWELL · CHARLOTTE FAIRLIE
KATHERINE WENTWORTH · CELIA'S HOUSE
WINTER AND ROUGH WEATHER
LISTENING VALLEY
BEL LAMINGTON · FLETCHER'S END
SPRING MAGIC · THE ENGLISH AIR
THE HOUSE OF THE DEER
KATHERINE'S MARRIAGE · THE FOUR GRACES
STILL GLIDES THE STREAM
MUSIC IN THE HILLS
CROOKED ADAM · THE TALL STRANGER
GERALD AND ELIZABETH
THE HOUSE ON THE CLIFF
VITTORIA COTTAGE · THE BLUE SAPPHIRE
SARAH MORRIS REMEMBERS

———◆———

This Large Print Edition
is published by kind permission of
COLLINS, LONDON & GLASGOW
and
HOLT, RINEHART AND WINSTON,
INC.
New York

D. E. STEVENSON

VITTORIA COTTAGE

Complete and Unabridged

ULVERSCROFT
Leicester

First published 1949

First Large Print Edition
published October 1977
SBN 0 7089 0057 7

© D. E. Stevenson, 1949

Published by
F. A. Thorpe (Publishing) Ltd.
Anstey, Leicestershire
Printed in England

Part One

1

THERE had always been Derings at Vittoria Cottage. Captain Mark Dering, having fought in the Battle of Vittoria and helped to drive Joseph Buonaparte out of Spain, retired from the Army — minus an arm — bought some ground near Ashbridge village and built himself a small house. It was the Regency Period of course and Baroque architecture was all the rage so the house was ornamented with turrets and other curious devices which delighted its owner's heart. Captain Mark had a son, and he in turn had several sons; there were plenty of Derings to enjoy the amenities of Vittoria Cottage. Time passed and tastes changed and, towards the end of the nineteenth century when Mr. John Dering came into ownership, he summoned a builder and gave orders for the turrets to be removed.

"Make a clean sweep," said Mr. Dering, waving his hand. "I don't like all these ridiculous excrescences."

"It'll look a bit bare, sir," objected Mr. Coney. "It will, really. It's the ex-crescents that give it character. I doubt if you'll like it when the turrets 'ave gone."

"Can you do it or not?" inquired Mr. Dering.

"Oh, I can *do* it, sir."

"Do it, then," said Mr. Dering.

Shorn of unnecessary ornamentation Vittoria Cottage became a long, low building without distinction but not unpleasing to the eye . . . and its bareness was gradually covered by the growth of a truly magnificent specimen of Virginia Creeper.

Mr. John Dering lived here for many years and, being a comfort-loving bachelor with money to spare, he made other alterations. He knocked down a partition and made a drawing-room which ran from the front to the back of the house with windows at each end — a beautiful gracious room with plenty of space to show off his fine old furniture. The dining-room was next door so he caused a large hole to be cut in the wall between the two rooms and he put in folding doors so that when he entertained his friends to dinner they could stroll from one room to the other without exertion. He built on a couple of bathrooms and put in electric light, he brought the kitchen premises up to date and remade the garden; eventually he died, full of years, and left the place to his nephew, Mr. Arnold Dering.

Mr. Arnold was quite different from his uncle; he had travelled widely and knew a good deal about history and architecture so Vittoria Cottage did not please his eye. He regretted the turrets . . . he had never seen them of course for they had been removed when he was an infant in arms, but it would have been amusing to own a genuine Regency Period Piece. He went so far as to summon Mr. Coney and to inquire whether the turrets could be replaced exactly as before.

Fortunately Mr. Coney knew his limitations. "Well, sir," said Mr. Coney in doubtful tones. "Well, sir, I don't say as what it couldn't be done, but it couldn't be done right — if you take me. All those ex-crescents — who's to remember 'ow they went?"

"You mean *you* don't remember," said Mr. Arnold Dering, crossly.

"I don't," admitted Mr. Coney. "An' if

4

I don't nobody does. It 'ud be a costly job, too."

Mr. Arnold Dering was thoroughly annoyed so he shut up the silly little house and went away. It was not until he found himself a wife that he returned to Ashbridge and settled down at Vittoria Cottage. He settled there because circumstances compelled him to do so, but having started with a prejudice against the place he could not be happy there. It is doubtful whether he would have been happy anywhere for he had a discontented nature. He liked travelling, he was a rover at heart, but it was impossible to travel about the world with a wife and family, so *there he was* firmly anchored to the silly little house which was neither the one thing nor the other.

"It is neither Vittoria nor a cottage," said Mr. Arnold Dering when some ill-advised person happened to admire his property. "The amusing characteristics of the Regency Period have been ruthlessly destroyed and it has been so pulled about and enlarged in all directions — without regard for symmetry — that nobody in their senses could call it a cottage. Rag-bag

5

House would be a better name for it," declared its owner, bitterly.

Discontented people are never popular with their neighbours and Mr. Arnold Dering was no exception to the rule. He was unpopular with his own sort of people, who thought him disagreeable and conceited, and even more unpopular with the villagers. The older people in the village remembered old Mr. Dering well. "*There* was a gentleman," old Mr. Mumper would say. "A fine gentleman *he* was, with a word for everybody. A big fine 'andsome gentleman; it was a pleasure to see him riding down the street on his big grey mare." And old Mr. Coney would chuckle and tell the story about how Mr. Dering had told him to remove the "ex-crescents"; and old Mr. Podbury would nod and say: "Ah, we shan't see his like again. Gentlemen are different nowadays. Mr. Arnold ain't a patch on his uncle — a poor creature with no 'ealth in 'im. 'E don't enjoy life."

He did not enjoy life, nor did he add to the enjoyment of life, so nobody in Ashbridge was particularly sorry when he died. Mrs. Dering continued to live in Vittoria Cottage with her three children;

she liked it and the absence of turrets did not worry her. She liked the peace and quiet of the country. Vittoria Cottage was very peaceful.

The road wound past, leading to the gravel-pit and the Roman Well. There was very little traffic upon the road. Occasionally a cart rumbled by to collect a load of gravel and, in the summer months, visitors to Ashbridge would visit the Well. These visitors often paused at Vittoria Cottage and looked up the flagged path, admiring the gay beds of flowers upon either side. All the cottage flowers bloomed here from tall hollyhocks and sunflowers and variegated lupins to tight little cushions of lobelia. Caroline Dering liked people to admire her flowers; sometimes, if she happened to be working in the garden, she would pick a bunch and hand it over the little green gate.

Most people who came to Ashbridge — even if they came from less than fifty miles away — were liable to remain "foreigners" to the day of their death, but Mrs. Dering had been accepted as a "native" quite early on. It was partly because of her husband's uncle and partly because of her own personality: she was friendly and tactful, she interested herself in the Girl Guides and the Women's Institute and she ran the Dramatic Club. The three young Derings were native by right of birth, the village had watched them grow up and what it didn't know about them wasn't worth knowing. It knew that Mr. James was out in "Malay" (though perhaps it was a little vague as to where "Malay" might be); it knew that Miss Leda liked pretty clothes — and why not? She was a pretty girl and you could only be young once. (Mr. Derek, the Admiral's son, had an eye on Miss Leda . . . Oh yes, the village saw that quite clearly) and of course the village knew Miss Bobbie. Any day in the week you could see Bobbie Dering dashing about on her bicycle, hatless and bare-legged, with Joss tearing after her. Bobbie always said Joss was a poodle, and nobody contradicted her, but those who knew about dogs — such as Mr. Shortlands who bred golden cockers and sold them for positively staggering prices — felt pretty certain that there was more than poodle in Joss; he was so big and strong and untiring. The vicar had been heard to say Joss was an enigma. This was a breed unknown to the villagers, of course.

It has been said that Mrs. Dering ran the Dramatic Club. She had been selected for the post of president because her sister was an actress which seemed to Ashbridge an outstanding qualification. Mrs. Dering's sister was none other than the celebrated Harriet Fane. Miss Fane sometimes came and stayed at Vittoria Cottage and you could see her in the garden or walking about the village just like an ordinary person. She was always beautifully dressed, slim and pretty with dark eyes and dark curly hair . . . just like her photographs in the picture papers. Miss Houseman, who kept the stationers' shop in Ashbridge, had all the picture papers and followed Miss Fane's career with the closest interest. She could tell you the plays in which Miss Fane had appeared and who acted in them with her and how long they had run; she knew when Miss Fane went to Australia; she found — and cut out — pictures of Miss Fane attending a first night at Covent Garden or talking to other celebrities at Ascot, or spending a weekend at

Cowes. Miss Fane was a good deal younger than Mrs. Dering but still it seemed funny that the two sisters should lead such different lives: Miss Fane (in her smart London flat) going about with all those interesting people and having so much fun and gaiety and Mrs. Dering content to remain quietly at Ashbridge, year in and year out, running her home and working in her garden.

Today Caroline Dering was not working in her garden. She had taken a basket and gone up the road to the gravel-pit to pick blackberries. There was a thicket of brambles, there, and Caroline knew it well. Every year she made this pilgrimage and every year she returned with her harvest of big, black, juicy berries to make into jelly and to bottle for the winter. It was curious (thought Caroline, as she began her task) how the years seemed to telescope when you looked back. Surely there were less than three hundred and sixty-five days between each picking! She remembered the first time she had come. She and Arnold had come together — they had just returned from their honeymoon and settled at Vittoria Cottage — but

Arnold had not enjoyed picking black-berries, he had got a thorn in his finger and had torn his trousers on a wild-rose bush and he had suggested that in future they should employ some of the village children to undertake the task. After that Caroline had come alone until James was old enough to help . . . and then the little girls had joined the party and blackberrying had become an event, a yearly picnic, which took place, weather permitting, upon James's birthday.

Now, once again, Caroline came alone. The girls had other things to do and Caroline had no use for reluctant assistants. Next year . . . would James be here? And if he were here would he want to come and pick blackberries on his birthday?

James was the best picker, thought Caroline as she looked back. She remem-bered James as a small fat boy, as a larger, thinner boy, as a schoolboy almost as large as herself . . . and then *suddenly* (or so it seemed) taller than herself with long legs and a gruff voice, but always black with juice and scratched with thorns, always climbing higher than anyone else and finding the biggest berries.

There was one particular picnic which remained very clearly in Caroline's memory; it might easily have been last year instead of twelve years ago. Twelve years! Yes, James was ten and Leda and Bobbie seven and five respectively. Caroline remembered it particularly well because it was her first "outing" for months; Arnold had been ill that summer and she had not been able to leave him. Then Arnold had recovered and had gone away for a holiday and Harriet had come to stay. Harriet had always preferred to come when Arnold was away, and Caroline preferred it too, for Arnold and Harriet had never hit it off and it had been extremely difficult to keep the peace between them. Arnold disapproved of Harriet, he thought her "flighty", and Harriet thought him dull and selfish . . . besides it was much more amusing to have Harriet to herself; they had fun together, they shared a bed and talked half the night, they tried on one another's clothes. Quite silly; of course, but tremendous fun.

The picnic had been arranged for James's birthday and fortunately it was a gorgeous day — just like today — fine and sunny and beautifully warm. The two Wares had come (Derek a little older than James, Rhoda a little younger) and Anne had been there: Anne Severn, the Vicar's daughter, a quiet little girl in a pink sunbonnet. It was interesting to look back and to think of all those children (she could almost see them, playing climbing, picking . . . and then sitting round the white cloth, eating buns and drinking milk out of large blue mugs; she could almost hear their light, shrill voices as they called to one another on the hill) they were all grown up now and most of them had set forth already upon the adventure of life.

2

BY this time Caroline's basket was three parts full of ripe, juicy fruit; her fingers were black and full of tiny thorns, her bare legs were scratched, her hair was in gorgeous disarray, and there was a large three-cornered tear in her old tweed skirt. The tear was the only thing that bothered her and even that did not bother her much. She weighed the basket in her hand; about five pounds, thought Caroline as she climbed down into the quarry to have her tea. When the children had come they had always made a fire — it was part of the fun — and they had spread a cloth and set out plates of scones and buns and little cakes — but Caroline contented herself with a much more frugal meal: she had brought a thermos flask and a sandwich of brown bread with cress in the middle.

She sat down and drawing up her knees put her arms round them . . . "Season of mist and mellow fruitfulness," said

Caroline softly. The words had come into her mind unbidden and she could not remember where they came from nor the context, but it didn't matter. The words fitted. The sun was warm and golden, the gravel upon which she sat was warm and golden, here and there the leaves were turning gold. The valley was full of a soft haze . . . smoke drifted lazily from the cottages in the village where the women were preparing supper for their families. On her right was the little grove of trees surrounding the Roman Well; it was a spring of clear water which bubbled out between rocks and fell into a stone basin. Arnold used to say it was not a Roman Well, "no more Roman than I am" but the Ashbridge people had always called it the Roman Well — and always would. Arnold had insisted that his family should refer to it as "The Spring" and for years they had obeyed him; but it is exceedingly difficult to go on calling a place by one name when every one else calls it something else — difficult and troublesome — and today Caroline had been thinking of it by the forbidden name. She was slightly shocked to discover that this was the case.

Was it worth the struggle, she wondered. Would Arnold know — and if he knew would he care? She believed people moved on to a higher plane — that was her idea of Heaven — and if this were true of Arnold such petty details would not disturb him . . . but if he were now above such trivialities he would not be Arnold at all; he would be somebody else, quite different.

The problem was interesting as well as puzzling, it went a great deal deeper than the Roman Well, and Caroline was still musing upon it when she saw a man emerge from the little grove of trees and make his way up the rutty road towards her. He was a stranger to Ashbridge for Caroline did not know him (she knew everybody in the district of course). She saw that he was tall and fair — the sun glinted on his sleek, brown head — she noticed that he was extremely well-dressed in a grey flannel suit with immaculately creased trousers . . . and noticing this she suddenly became aware of her own appearance, dirty and scratched, stockingless, hatless and untidy, but he had seen her so she could hardly get up and move away. He would think she was a tramp or a gipsy. Caroline smiled to herself and entertained for a moment the wild idea of acting the part. Harriet would have done it!

"Can you tell me if that is the Roman Well?" asked the stranger politely. He had reached her side by this time and stood, looking down at her.

"Yes," replied Caroline. "At least they call it that in Ashbridge. My husband said it wasn't Roman at all. He used to be quite angry about it."

She saw by his slight change of manner that he realised she was not a gipsy or whatever it was he had thought her.

"I've been picking blackberries," she added, indicating the basket.

He nodded understandingly.

"But — about the well," she continued. "I hope you aren't very disappointed. Some people are, if they've come a long way to see it."

"No, not a bit disappointed. I just came out for a walk. I'm staying in the village at the Cock and Bull."

"Oh, you're Mr. Shepperton," said Caroline, nodding.

He looked so amazed that she chuckled

involuntarily. "Ashbridge is like that," she explained. "If you wanted to remain anonymous you shouldn't have come here. As a matter of fact my daily help, who rejoices in the name of Comfort Podbury, is a cousin of the chambermaid at the Cock and Bull."

"Ah," said Mr. Shepperton, smiling. "That explains everything."

"Everything. You'd be surprised how much I know about you."

There was a moment's silence. Caroline had a definite impression of a shadow flitting across his face; the shadow was gone in a moment but the impression remained.

"It isn't really idle curiosity," she said quickly. "People are interested, that's all They haven't much to talk about, so it's an event when a stranger comes to Ashbridge."

"Yes, of course," he agreed.

"They're kind-hearted, you know. For instance if I were to sneeze violently in the High Street every one in the village would hear about it and people would call and bring blackcurrant cordial for me. It's the same sort of thing, isn't it?"

"Yes, of course," he repeated.

"Won't you sit down?" she continued. "I'm sorry I can't offer you some tea but I seem to have drunk every drop. You had better sit on my coat in case you get dirty."

He sat down beside her at once, refusing the coat.

"Of course, it works both ways," continued Caroline as she finished the last crumbs of her sandwich. "I mean if you want to know about any one in Ashbridge you have only to ask; in fact you needn't even ask, all you need do is to listen . . . but perhaps you aren't interested."

"I might be," he said thoughtfully. "Suppose you begin to enlighten me. What's that big house over there amongst the trees?"

"Ash House," Caroline told him. "It belongs to Sir Michael Ware. He was an admiral, but he's retired now. He owns most of the land round Ashbridge and he's very kind about letting people walk over his property, so if you're fond of walking you can go practically anywhere you like. My daughters have gone to Ash House this afternoon to play tennis. Derek

Ware is at Oxford, studying law, and Rhoda is at the School of Art in London. They're both here for the weekend — hence the tennis party."

"Go on," said Mr. Shepperton, smiling.

"Well, what else?" said Caroline, laughing and tossing back her hair. "Sir Michael is a widower. I liked Lady Ware immensely, she was a *real* person — if you know what I mean — very sincere and straightforward and warm-hearted but not terribly tactful and for that reason not terribly popular. Sir Michael is big — big in every way — rather like a bull. If you go to church tomorrow you'll hear him read the lessons."

Mr. Shepperton laughed. It was a very pleasant laugh and it made him look younger. Caroline had thought him a good deal older than herself but now she was not so sure.

"Have you been ill?" she asked.

"Yes," he replied.

There was a short silence.

"Then there are the Meldrums, of course," continued Caroline. "You can't see their house; it's the other side of Ashbridge. Mr. Meldrum is a lawyer, very clever and rather dry. Mrs. Meldrum is on the committee of the Women's Institute."

"You don't like her?"

"How did you know?" exclaimed Caroline in surprise.

"It wasn't very difficult," replied Mr. Shepperton, smiling.

"Oh dear — of course I ought to like her, and honestly I do try. I remind myself of all the kind things she does but the fact is we seem to disagree on so many subjects that I find it difficult. It's quite enough for Mrs. Meldrum to say one thing — I immediately find myself thinking the opposite," declared Caroline with a sigh.

"Very trying," said Mr. Shepperton, sympathetically. "Has this lady any family?"

"Two daughters. Joan is pretty and pampered, the joy of her mother's heart — Margaret is rather plain, but much nicer and more interesting. I don't know why I'm telling you all this . . ."

"Tell me more," said Mr. Shepperton. "I passed a very attractive little house on the way up. There were lovely flowers in the garden. Who does that belong to?"

"Me," said Caroline. "I'm so glad you liked my flowers. Sometimes when I'm working in the garden people stop and look over the gate and then I pick a little bunch of flowers and give it to them, but usually it's a waste. Quite often they carry the flowers for a little and then drop them in the road. I've found them lying there so I know . . . but I can't resist it."

"Why should you resist it?" inquired her companion.

"Because," said Caroline slowly. "Because it's wrong to drop flowers in the road and leave them to die — at least I think so — and by giving people flowers which they don't want, I'm encouraging them to do something that I think is wrong."

Mr. Shepperton considered the matter gravely. "But there must be a few people who like them," he pointed out. "There must be a few who carry them home and put them in water and enjoy them — enjoy them not only for their own sake but also for the graceful gesture — and those few are the important ones. The others matter less."

"I'm glad you don't think it silly," said Caroline thoughtfully. She rose as she spoke and picked up her basket and the thermos flask, but Mr. Shepperton took the basket and signified his intention of carrying it home for her.

"You've picked a lot," he said.

"Not enough. I shall have to come again. It takes longer when you've nobody to help you, but I don't really mind. The girls hate picking blackberries and, of course, you can't blame them; clothes are clothes, nowadays."

"But they eat them, I suppose," murmured Mr. Shepperton.

"We make jelly," replied Caroline, missing the point. "I want to make lots of jelly because James may be coming home in the spring. James is my son, he's been in Malaya for three years."

"You don't look old enough!" exclaimed her new friend.

"Oh, I'm quite old," said Caroline seriously.

3

THE girls had returned from their tennis-party when Caroline got home. Leda was laying the table for supper and Bobbie clattering about with pots and pans in the kitchen. Caroline decided to wash and change before confronting her daughters so she left her basket in the hall and crept upstairs. You couldn't pick blackberries without getting torn and dirty, but still . . .

She washed and changed and brushed her hair vigorously; it was light brown hair with a slight natural curl and was still bright and glossy. Her face had got a little sunburnt, her cheeks were flushed and her dark-blue eyes very bright with the exercise and the fresh air and sunshine. I'm still quite nice-looking thought Caroline in surprise as she regarded her image in the mirror. The reflection was a pleasant one and she went downstairs feeling quite pleased with herself.

"Did you weigh the basket?" she inquired as they sat down to supper.

"Yes," replied Bobbie. "Your harvest is five and a quarter pounds of fruit and a gent's chamois-leather glove, almost new. It was on the top of the fruit under your coat."

"What a pity you didn't find the other one!" Leda exclaimed.

"But I didn't *find* it!" cried Caroline.

The girls looked at her in surprise.

"It's his, of course," continued Caroline thoughtfully. "I suppose he must have put it in the basket and forgotten about it."

The glove was lying on the table; it was almost new — as Bobbie had said — but already it had taken on the shape of its owner's hand, rather a large hand with long fingers.

"Exhibit 'A', " said Bobbie, pointing to it dramatically. "Whose glove? That's what we want to know."

Leda said nothing, she seemed un-interested. Leda was very pretty, slim and fair with neat features. She was like Arnold, of course, thought Caroline looking at her. Bobbie was like — like a puppy, unformed as yet, plump and mischievous. (Having discovered that she, herself, was still not without a certain charm Caroline

25

was in the mood to look at her daughters objectively.)

Bobbie had dissolved into helpless giggles. "Come on, Mummy," she gasped. "Who was he? Where did he appear from? Why did he put his glove in the basket?"

"I expect he put it there to prevent it getting lost," said Caroline, smiling at her.

"Did he help you to pick?"

"Goodness, no! He looked more like Bond Street than blackberrying."

"It was Mr. Shepperton, I suppose," Leda said.

Caroline felt a trifle deflated. The joke had been rather amusing . . . but, of course, the mysterious gentleman could have been nobody else. The vicar never looked like Bond Street, nor did he wear gloves (except for gardening and this definitely was not a gardening glove) and these objections ruled out practically all the male inhabitants of the district.

"Comfort said his clothes were all new," added Leda. "Everything belonging to him."

"That's funny, isn't it?" said Bobbie. "I

mean most people's clothes are old and shabby. Wherever could he have got all the coupons!"

"Black Market," said Leda, helping herself to stewed plums.

Caroline found she wanted to disagree with this solution of the mystery but as she had no other solution to offer she held her peace. Fortunately the telephone began to ring madly so the subject could be dropped.

"It will be for me!" exclaimed Leda, making for the door.

"Derek, I expect," remarked Bobbie. "Do you think they're going to get married?"

This was the first time the idea had been put into words and Caroline's hand trembled suddenly as she poured out the coffee. She had wondered, of course, but Leda was very reserved and not in the habit of giving confidences. Now that she considered the matter squarely Caroline was troubled, she saw difficulties ahead. Sir Michael might object, he might want a better match for his only son.

"Do you?" urged Bobbie. "I mean, he's always here, isn't he?"

"He always liked coming here," Caroline pointed out.

"Yes, but he used to come to play with James, or just because he liked coming here. Now he comes to talk to Leda."

"Leda hasn't said anything, has she?"

"Leda never says anything. Oh, well," added Bobbie with a sigh. "I suppose we'll just have to wait and *bear* it. People in love are awfully silly, aren't they? So cross and disagreeable. I hope I shan't ever fall in love!"

There was no time to say more. Leda returned; and Caroline, looking at her with new eyes, was obliged to admit that Bobbie's stricture was true. Her expression was sulky. She had expected to hear Derek's voice when she lifted the receiver and was disappointed.

"It was a wrong number," said Leda as she sat down.

"All that time for a wrong number!" exclaimed Bobbie in surprise.

"No," replied Leda. "I rang up the Cock and Bull and said we had Mr. Shepperton's glove. Mrs. Herbert promised to tell him."

"Oh, thank you," murmured Caroline.

She had intended to ring up Mr. Shepperton herself but Leda's action had made this unnecessary.

Mr. Shepperton was in church the following morning. He was sitting in one of the front pews beneath the lectern. Caroline could see the back of his neatly-brushed head and his broad shoulders in perfectly-tailored brown worsted suiting. It was unnecessary for her to draw her daughters' attention to Mr. Shepperton, they had seen him, of course. Bobbie whispered, "We ought to have brought his glove," and Caroline nodded. They had left the glove lying upon the hall-chest.

Caroline's thoughts were always somewhat obstreperous in church, no matter how hard she tried to discipline them, and when the Admiral went up to read the lessons she could not help wondering if Mr. Shepperton thought he was like a bull. Perhaps she should not have said it, but she had not meant it unkindly. He *was* like a bull, thick-necked and shaggy looking, with strong, rather blunt features. Most people resembled an animal or a fish or a bird. Mr. Severn, the vicar, was like a cherub. He was exactly like one of the cherubs in the stained-glass window which Sir Michael Ware had donated in memory of his wife. Caroline had noticed this when the window was dedicated and before she had time to discipline her unruly thoughts she had imagined the cherub in a little crib in the vicarage nursery and old Mrs. Podbury looking at it with admiration and exclaiming, "There now, ain't 'e like 'is Dad!" Caroline was all the more ashamed of herself because she ought to have been thinking sorrowfully of Alice Ware, whom she had liked immensely and missed intensely (especially on the committee of the Women's Institute where they had had fun and games together) and because she knew that it was a grief and disappointment to the Severns that they had not managed to produce a son. Altogether it had been most regrettable and Caroline had suffered considerably from remorse.

There was usually a good deal of conversation in the churchyard after the service. People from outlying districts, having obtained petrol to come to church, seized the opportunity to talk to their friends and exchange family news. Caroline spoke to several people and then approached Mr. Shepperton, who was chatting to the vicar. She was just in time to hear Mr. Shepperton accept an invitation to tea at the vicarage on Wednesday afternoon.

"You got the message," Caroline said. "Your glove is safe, but it is rather dejected without its friend."

Mr. Shepperton smiled and replied that its friend was looking forward eagerly to the reunion. Having said as much as it was necessary to explain to Mr. Severn what had happened.

"Ah," said Mr. Severn, nodding. "A glove is a miserable object without its partner . . . which reminds me of rather an amusing incident. Some years ago I was in the train, travelling to London. The only other passenger in the compartment was a very well-dressed gentleman with a somewhat cantankerous expression. He was in possession of the compartment when I got in and obviously resented my intrusion. I remarked that the day was fine but he growled and buried himself in his newspaper."

"A boor!" commented Mr. Shepperton.

"Oh, definitely," agreed the vicar. "Definitely a boor — and choleric. I said no more, of course, and the journey was accomplished in silence. When we approached London and he began to collect his belongings he discovered he had only one glove. He looked around the compartment, he looked under the seat, the other glove had vanished. I noticed that the glove which remained to him was almost new, an exceedingly nice brown kid glove with a press fastening. Its owner looked at it in disgust and then, opening the window with a crash, he pitched it on to the line. A moment later he put his hand into his overcoat pocket and discovered the other one."

The vicar's stories were always amusing and this was no exception to the rule. Its hearers laughed heartily.

"I wonder what you did," said Mr. Shepperton.

"I left the compartment hastily and sought refuge in the corridor," replied the vicar. "It was the only thing to do; not only because I could not refrain from laughing but also because I was afraid the old gentleman would burst unless he gave vent to his feelings."

"Which he could hardly do in the presence of a clergyman!"

"Exactly," said Mr. Severn, chuckling. "Exactly."

4

COMFORT PODBURY came to Vittoria Cottage every day except Sundays to do the housework, wash up the dishes and help Caroline with the cooking. Caroline was so well-liked in the village that she could have had her pick of the women who went out to work, but she stuck to Comfort; she was fond of Comfort and, what was even more important, she knew Comfort was fond of her. It was true that Comfort was slow rather — she was so fat that she could not get about quickly — and she was not a very good cook. But Caroline, to her amazement, had discovered that she herself was an excellent cook and could teach Comfort to do things properly. Out of the meagre *ersatz* rations Caroline made stews that tasted quite different from ordinary stews; the meat tender, the gravy brown and smooth and savoury. Her puddings melted in the mouth. "Isn't it funny," she would say, "I never

34

cooked a potato before the war. I was utterly dependent upon my cook — *utterly*. I thought cooking was difficult. I thought you had to learn." And she would take a white-scrubbed wooden spoon out of the kitchen drawer and beat her mixture earnestly, beat it within an inch of its life. "You just have to do what it says in the book, that's all," Caroline would say.

It was important to Caroline to do things right, to do whatever she did to the best of her ability. She saw beauty in ordinary little things and took pleasure in it (and this was just as well because she had had very little pleasure in her life). She took pleasure in a well-made cake, a smoothly-ironed napkin, a pretty blouse, laundered and pressed; she liked to see the garden well dug, the rich soil brown and gravid; she loved her flowers. When you are young you are too busy with yourself — so Caroline thought — you haven't time for ordinary little things, but, when you leave youth behind, your eyes open and you see magic and mystery all around you: magic in the flight of a bird, the shape of a leaf, the bold arch of a bridge against the sky, footsteps at night and a voice calling in the darkness, the moment in a theatre before the curtain rises, the wind in the trees, or (in winter) an apple-branch clothed with pure white snow and icicles hanging from a stone and sparkling with rainbow colours.

Caroline's daughters did not know her of course. They loved her but they had no idea what she was like. She was their mother. She had always been the same and always would be. They accepted the fact that she was interested in their affairs, but it had never occurred to them that she might be interested in herself or that they might be interested in her. They had grown up from babyhood with her image before them so they never looked at it. Comfort knew more about her. Comfort adored Mrs. Dering — there was nothing she wouldn't have done for Mrs. Dering, literally nothing.

Sometimes, as she worked about the house, Comfort made up stories about Mrs. Dering and held long imaginary conversations with her. Mrs. Dering would say, "Comfort, I don't know what I'm going to do, I've lost all my money. I haven't a penny to pay the bills." And Comfort would go to the post-office and draw out her thirty pounds — her post-office savings — and give it to Mrs. Dering. "There, don't worry," she would say. "You pay the bills with that." Or Mrs. Dering would get ill and Comfort would nurse her night and day — it was scarlet fever, of course, so the young ladies wouldn't be allowed inside the room — and then at last the doctor would say, "Well, Comfort, she's getting better now. We'd never have pulled her round if it hadn't been for you." Or the house would go on fire and everybody would rush out except Mrs. Dering, who was lying insensible in the drawing-room, and Comfort would make her way in through the raging flames and carry her into safety. Comfort would be terribly burned, of course, and Mrs. Dering would come to the hospital and visit her. She would take Comfort's hand and with tears in her eyes she would say: "Oh, Comfort, you saved my life. You must get better for my sake; I can't do without you." Usually Comfort would get better, but sometimes not. Sometimes Comfort would die and there would be a marvellous funeral with wreaths of flowers. Everybody would be there. Everybody would forget she was fat and slow and ugly; they would remember only that she was brave and had saved Mrs. Dering's life . . . and Mrs. Dering would walk over to the cemetery on a fine Sunday afternoon and put a sheaf of lilies on Comfort's grave.

Of course Caroline had no idea of all this but she knew enough about Comfort to be very sorry for her. It was tragic. Within that mountain of flesh there dwelt a romantic, sensitive soul. Caroline remembered Comfort as a girl, plump and pretty, with merry brown eyes and a mop of unruly black curls. The village lads thought her extremely attractive but Comfort had eyes for nobody except Sid Houseman. He was a carpenter in his father's business. When he and Comfort decided to get married he announced his intention of going to Canada and bettering his position. Comfort said she would wait for him and the thing was settled. Caroline knew all about it because Comfort worked in the baker's and helped her with the Girl Guides and often talked about Sid. Several years passed and Sid Houseman made good; he had got a secure position, he had found a little house, he was coming home to marry Comfort and take her back with him to Montreal. By this time Comfort was fat. She was not just ordinarily fat, she was colossal. She was a figure of fun.

"D'you think Sid'll mind?" she asked Caroline.

"No, of course not," replied Caroline — but without conviction.

"Well, I don't know," said Comfort miserably. "I've told him of course, but what's telling? He hasn't seen me. I wouldn't blame Sid if he changed his mind."

Caroline hesitated and then said, "You know, Comfort, you should ask Doctor Smart. He would give you treatment — "

"Oh, I did," said Comfort. "He said it was my glands. He said I ought to have thyroid, but Mother said, no. That's monkey glands, Mother said. You're not having monkey glands except over my dead body, she said. You see, Mrs. Dering, there was a niece of Mother's that got fat like me and they gave her monkey glands. She went all queer," declared Comfort, looking at Caroline with round, scared eyes. "All queer, she went, Mrs. Dering."

Caroline said no more. She was aware that nothing she could say would overcome such deep-rooted prejudice. Perhaps it would be all right, thought Caroline hopefully. Perhaps Sid would realise that Comfort was still the same inside, and continue to love her in spite of her appearance.

Sid arrived in high spirits, he was full of good intentions. Comfort had told him she was fat but what did he care, he had always hated scraggy women . . . but when he saw her he could not hide his dismay; he could not — no, he simply could not go through with it. He went back to Canada alone. Everybody in the village knew about it — that was the hardest part — and a good many people blamed Sid. Comfort didn't blame him, she wouldn't hear a word against Sid.

It was after this that Caroline asked Comfort to give up her place in the baker's and come to Vittoria Cottage instead; she thought Comfort would be happier and Comfort thought so too. At Vittoria Cottage she saw nobody except the Derings; there was no need to go near the village, to encounter the pitying glances of her friends and the smiles of her enemies. She could not "live in" because her mother was afraid of being left alone at night, but if Caroline wanted to go away she came and stayed and brought her mother with her. Caroline, who had taken Comfort out of the kindness of her heart, found she had possessed herself of a treasure. Comfort was still slow, of course (she always would be slow), but she was thorough and reliable. She did what she was told and remembered to go on doing it and nothing was too much trouble.

Leda did not like her. "She's so repulsive," Leda would say. "I can't bear to see her waddling about the house. I don't know what on earth people think when she opens the door."

5

ON Monday morning Comfort arrived as usual at Vittoria Cottage and as usual she and Caroline debated the subject of food. Sometimes Caroline didn't mind thinking about food and arranging the meals, but at other times she felt the whole subject almost intolerable. Today she felt it almost intolerable. The larder was empty except for the remains of a stew which looked unappetising.

"It will do for Joss," said Caroline.

"Shall we open a tin of baked beans?" inquired Comfort.

Caroline assented with a sigh. "There are too many days in the week," she declared. "It's a pity we have to eat every day, isn't it? We'd have plenty of food for two or three days out of the seven."

"It's a pity we can't eat grass," said Comfort. "People *do* eat grass, at least one woman does. There was a film on Saturday night — Mother and me took the bus into

Wandlebury — a film all about a woman who eats nothing but grass. She lives in London and goes into the park and picks grass and eats it — cooks it first of course. It didn't 'arf look nasty."

Caroline laughed and Comfort laughed too. When Comfort laughed she shook all over like a jelly. "Oh, dear!" she gasped. "Oh, dear! There was a man behind us said 'Mrs. Nebuchadnezzar, that's who she is.' Oh, dear!"

Somewhat cheered by this incident Caroline took her basket and set forth for the village. It was less than half a mile, a pleasant walk on a fine day. The High Street was narrow and winding with little shops on both sides; most of the houses were old and many of them were slightly crooked. Caroline always felt there ought to be ladies in poke-bonnets and crinolines shopping in the village, chattering to one another in a leisurely manner and strolling in and out of the shops (buying bombazine by the dozen yards and ordering sirloins of beef and legs of mutton to sustain their large families); but those days had passed for ever and, instead of a crinolined lady, Caroline saw Rhoda Ware come

43

rushing down the street on a motor bike. Rhoda was dressed in corduroy slacks, her cream-coloured silk shirt was open at the neck and her golden hair was flying in the breeze. It was pure gold hair, gold as newly minted sovereigns, gold as the king-cups which grew in profusion on the banks of the Wandle . . . and today in the sunshine it was quite dazzling.

When Rhoda saw Caroline she stopped suddenly and almost fell off. "I haven't seen you for ages!" she exclaimed breathlessly. "Meet Blink! Isn't he a beauty? I've just bought him. He goes like smoke. I've always wanted a motor bike but Dad wouldn't give me one, so I saved up and pinched and scraped and sold a couple of horrible pictures — and there you are!"

Caroline admired Blink in suitable terms. "But why Blink?" she wanted to know.

"He makes me blink," explained his mistress. "I haven't got used to his speed. I suppose you wouldn't like a lift home, would you?"

"No, I wouldn't," said Caroline.

"I'd go very carefully — honestly, Mrs. Dering."

"No, Rhoda," repeated Caroline more firmly than before.

"Dad wouldn't either," said Rhoda sadly.

The idea of the Admiral perched upon the carrier-seat and clinging round his daughter's waist made Caroline laugh. She laughed heartily and Rhoda joined in.

"I suppose it *would* look funny," she admitted. "As a matter of fact I never thought of bringing him down to the village but just along the avenue and back. He said he was frightened."

Caroline was very fond of Rhoda, she was absolutely natural and forthright — just as her mother had been — there was no nonsense about her. Some people disapproved of her; they said she ought to stay at home and look after her father instead of living by herself in London and studying art; they said she was wild, she cared for nothing but having a good time, her parties were orgies and her clothes theatrical and absurd.

"I must come and talk to you," Rhoda was saying. "Can I come to tea or what?"

"You can come whenever you like; you know that, don't you?"

"Yes," admitted Rhoda. "Yes, and I *will* come. There seems to be so much to do, that's the trouble. Life's such a rush . . . and the truth is I always forget how nice you are until I see you again."

"Is that a compliment or not?" asked Caroline, smiling.

"It's true," declared Rhoda. "I've no use for compliments. Look here, Mrs. Dering, next time you're in town let me know and I'll throw a party for you."

"Your friends will find me extremely dull."

"They won't. They'll all want to paint you."

"Paint me!"

"Yes, but nobody is to paint you except me, and I'm not ready yet. No," said Rhoda, straddling her bike and preparing to kick off. "No, I'm not going to paint you for a year from now. It'll be my first Academy picture . . ."

She said more, but Caroline could not hear a word of it for Blink's engine had started and was making a din like a machine-gun in the narrow street.

"That awful girl!" exclaimed Mrs. Meldrum, emerging from the grocer's with a basket on her arm. "She'll break her neck — that will be the end of it — but as long as she doesn't break somebody else's neck it won't be much loss."

"I think it would be a great loss," retorted Caroline with spirit. "Rhoda may be a little wild but she's a real person and her heart is as golden as her hair. . . ."

Mrs. Meldrum smiled grimly and disappeared into the butcher's.

Caroline was left standing upon the pavement . . . and stood there for a moment or two before moving on . . . she felt remorseful for she had decided that she *must* try to get on better with Mrs. Meldrum, and here she was putting her foot in it again. Of course, Mrs. Meldrum was very trying — and quite wrong about Rhoda — but Caroline might have disagreed with her more politely, there was no doubt of that.

The village was full of friends. Caroline saw Mrs. Severn, the vicar's wife, ordering large quantities of buns (this reminded her that the Sewing Circle was meeting at the Vicarage in the afternoon) and she met Dr. Smart in the chemist's where he was having a professional conversation with the dispenser (at least it looked professional until suddenly they both dissolved into helpless laughter). Then she met Mrs. Burnard who was anxious to consult her about a proposed Hallowe'en party in the Girl Guides' Hut and to inquire whether there was a good crop of apples in Vittoria Cottage garden. "It's some time off," said Mrs. Burnard. "But I want to get people to promise apples," and she looked at Caroline hopefully. It always annoyed Caroline when people asked for things in this round-about way (why couldn't the woman say "Please give me apples?") but she swallowed her annoyance and said she would give twelve pounds of apples if that would do and escaped in the middle of Mrs. Burnard's protestations of gratitude. Finally she met Sue Widgeon buying fish.

Sue was Comfort's cousin. Her name had been Sue Podbury before she married Jim Widgeon; she was the eldest of a large and extremely happy family which lived in the middle of the village and took an active part in all that went on . . . the choir, the Boy Scouts, the Girl Guides and the Dramatic Club were all full of Sue's brothers and sisters and would not have known how to carry on without them. As a matter of fact Ashbridge was so full of Podburys (all of whom were Sue's relations) that if some unkind Fate had suddenly made a clean sweep of them village life would have come to a standstill. There were Podburys who baked bread and Podburys who sorted letters and delivered them; if your wireless went wrong a Podbury came and mended it; if your drains were blocked a Podbury cleared them for you. The butcher had a Podbury assistant, the grocer had two . . . Caroline sometimes thought that the village of Ashbridge should have been called Podbury.

Sue had been married last Christmas and all her brothers and sisters and cousins and aunts had attended the ceremony (for the Podburys were clannish and of such amiable dispositions that they were all on speaking terms with one another). She had married Jim Widgeon, a young ploughman on one of Sir Michael Ware's farms. The young couple lived in a little cottage near the gravel-pit and therefore not far from the Derings. Caroline knew Sue well, for she had been a leading light in the Dramatic Club. She was a chatterbox and somewhat indiscreet but so pretty and kind-hearted and unassuming that everybody liked her. She loved acting and had told Caroline that she could easily continue in the Club and come to all the meetings just as usual . . . but things had worked out differently from what Sue had expected.

"I suppose there's no chance of your being able to come to the Club after the baby arrives?" asked Caroline.

"I don't see how," replied Sue. "Of course Jim says I'm not to give up everything and stay at home and never go out at all. He says he'll look after the baby when I want to go out, but I can't see him," said Sue, smiling. "I can't see Jim looking after a baby — such great big hands, he has! The truth is Jim and me are so happy I don't ever seem to want to go out in the evenings, except p'raps just to run down and see Mother and all of them now and then . . . and I'm busy all day. Of course it's a bit lonely after home but you can't have everything, can you?"

Caroline agreed that you could not, but

she made up her mind to look in on Sue more often and to tell Comfort to ask her to tea.

"We went into Wandlebury on Saturday," continued Sue in her usual confiding manner. "We bought a pram — it's a lovely pram, Mrs. Dering, I'd like you to see it. Jim wouldn't have nothing but the best. He wants a boy, Jim does, I don't mind for myself. . . ."

They had both finished their shopping by this time so they walked up the hill together, talking as they went. Sue, having told her news, wanted all the news about the Club and Caroline amused her by describing the efforts of Beryl Coney to snatch the part of leading lady from Violet Houseman and of Violet Houseman's struggle to retain it.

"Silly — that's what they are!" declared Sue, laughing.

6

THE afternoon was gorgeous. It was exactly the afternoon Caroline would have chosen for picking another basket of blackberries, but unfortunately there was ironing to be done. Leda wanted her tennis shorts for tomorrow afternoon, there were two shirts belonging to Bobbie and a whole pile of underwear and table-napkins.

"I'll do them, Comfort," said Caroline . . . for Comfort was not particularly skilful with an iron and on one occasion had singed Leda's best pyjamas and they had not heard the end of it for days.

"Are you sure, Mrs. Dering?" asked Comfort. "Well, if you're *sure* I think I'll just take a run home and see Mother, she seemed a bit poorly this morning."

Caroline agreed to the plan. She could not help smiling at the thought of Comfort taking a run . . . and then she sighed, for of course it wasn't funny. Comfort was barely thirty and should be able to run and dance and have fun like other young women of her age. Doctor Smart had spoken to Caroline about her only last week and had declared that if Comfort would agree to have proper treatment her weight could be reduced and her health would improve. "I know," Caroline had said. "The difficulty is she's frightened," and she had explained Comfort's fears at length. "Go all queer!" snorted Doctor Smart. "She's more likely to go all queer if she doesn't have thyroid. She'll do it if you tell her, Mrs. Dering."

Caroline believed this to be true. She believed she could persuade Comfort to have proper treatment. But what a responsibility! Supposing something went wrong! It was all very well for Doctor Smart to say it was perfectly safe, he didn't understand Comfort's mentality. The problem was psychological rather than medical. Mrs. Podbury and Comfort were both convinced that the treatment was fraught with danger and, this being so, it was possible that Comfort might go all queer from sheer fright.

The iron was hot enough now — or should be — she wetted her finger and tested it; she spread a handkerchief on the board. At that very moment the front-door bell rang. It was an old-fashioned bell, so not only did she hear it but she saw it wagging absurdly, jangling to and fro amongst the line of bells high up near the ceiling.

"Bother!" exclaimed Caroline. "Oh, bother! But I don't care who you are I'm definitely going to finish my ironing . . . even if you're the Queen!" She switched off the iron and went to answer the door, and, as she went, her imagination ran away with her (as it so often did) and she thought, supposing it *is* the Queen! Supposing their Majesties were going to Sandringham and took a wrong turning and stopped at Vittoria Cottage to ask the way. The Queen would say, "What lovely flowers! Perhaps the people living in this nice little house would give us a cup of tea. . . ."

Caroline opened the door and saw Mr. Shepperton standing on the step. "Oh, it's *you*!" she exclaimed in surprise.

"Did you — were you expecting some-one else?" he asked.

"Only the Queen," replied Caroline, chuckling. "Don't mind me," she added.

"I often go slightly mad. Come in, won't you?"

"But perhaps you're busy."

"I'm ironing. You can come and watch me if you like."

She had half-hoped he would refuse the invitation, but he didn't.

"I thought I had seen you before," said Mr. Shepperton as he laid down his hat on the carved oak chest. "You wouldn't remember, of course; it was just a chance meeting. I couldn't think when or where, but now I know."

She led him into the kitchen and indicated the basket-chair. "It's more comfortable than it looks," she told him. "Comfort sits in it. She's more or less wrecked it, poor soul. Tell me where we met."

Mr. Shepperton sat down and watched her for a few moments without speaking; she was ironing handkerchiefs, he noticed.

"Tell me," repeated Caroline. "I'm awfully vague about people."

"In Denmark," he said. He was remembering more and more clearly. It was all coming back. He had been staying in Hillerod and had gone to see the Castle at Elsinore. There were about a dozen people going round the castle, following the guide from room to room and listening intently to all he said. Robert Shepperton had noticed the English couple and had wondered if they were father and daughter or husband and wife. She was a lot younger ... but no, she was not his daughter for she called him by his Christian name. "Are you sure it isn't too tiring for you, Arnold," she said. "Arnold" was behaving badly, behaving like a spoilt child. He commented unfavourably upon the exhibits, he wondered aloud what the devil that fellow was saying and why he couldn't speak some civilised language. The young wife tried to pacify him, she was embarrassed and ashamed. They had come to a large chamber full of finely-carved cupboards and chests and she lingered behind the others. "You're interested in carving?" he inquired. "Chests fascinate me," she replied, looking up at him (her eyes were deep blue — almost dark-blue, Robert Shepperton noticed). "Chests *are* fascinating," he agreed. "Almost frightening," she said a little breathlessly. "Perhaps because of the Golden Bough," he suggested. After that he had attached himself to the couple and had been able to translate some of the guide's patter for their benefit. Robert Shepperton understood Danish, he was a born linguist and expecially interested in Nordic languages.

That was all that had happened. He had forgotten the incident long ago, but he had remembered the girl's face. She hadn't changed much — not as much as he had, anyhow — and the carved oak chest in the hall had given him the necessary clue.

"In Denmark!" exclaimed Caroline. "But that was *years* ago. It must be twelve or thirteen years since Arnold and I went to Denmark."

"It was at Elsinore. There was a huge oak chest; you said it frightened you."

"But of course!" she cried, turning and looking at him. "You're the young man who spoke Danish! How queer! Oh, dear, that was rather a dreadful afternoon. Poor Arnold was so — so annoyed because he couldn't understand."

"It *is* annoying," said Mr. Shepperton hastily. He was almost sorry now that he had reminded her of something which was not a pleasant memory.

The iron went thump thump, for some moments before Caroline spoke again. She was remembering that wretched afternoon.

"Arnold was very clever," she said at last. "He saw how unsettled the world was — everything slipping downhill. He was sure there was going to be another war. Sometimes I almost feel glad he didn't live to see it. He said things were going from bad to worse and he was quite right, of course . . . but it doesn't *help* to be miserable; it doesn't make things right to keep on grieving over them. It clouds the sun, that's all. When Arnold spoke to people they used to get more and more worried, and they went away looking as if the cares of the world were upon their shoulders; their shoulders drooped under the burden. They were less able to carry on and do what they had to do — there was no heart left in them. I used to be sorry about it."

"Yes," agreed Mr. Shepperton. "I can understand — "

"People can't go on living without happiness — or at least without hope."

Mr. Shepperton nodded. He said, "A

58

merry heart goes all the way, a sad tires in a mile-O."

"Here have I been talking and talking," said Caroline, "and Shakespeare says it all in two lines!"

"He has a way of doing that."

"I've thought a lot about happiness," Caroline continued. "Perhaps because I saw what unhappiness did to Arnold. I've sometimes thought, supposing everybody — every single person — decided to do their level best to make one small corner of the world happier. Would that help?" She spread out a wrinkled pillow-slip as she spoke and smoothed it skilfully.

"Like that," he said.

She smiled. "You mean ironing out the wrinkles. That's easy."

"If you know how."

"I know how to iron out wrinkles," she admitted, folding the linen carefully. "If everybody did what they could . . . made a little happiness here and there, just to start with . . . and then the circles would spread until they touched and merged."

"Everything ironed out."

She took Leda's tennis shorts and spread them on the board. "It isn't impossible, she pleaded. "It isn't impossible if we started to go about it in the right way. We're going about it the wrong way. . . . Passing laws and trying to *make* people happy and good . . . there's only one way in which it can be done and that's from inside outwards; starting with the individual and spreading outwards to others. Some people have power in them and could do a lot, others could just do a little, but everybody could do something . . . even if they just made one house a happy place."

The thud of the iron as she pressed Leda's tennis shorts punctuated her remarks and Robert Shepperton did not interrupt. She was talking to herself really — or so he thought. He found it restful sitting in the bright kitchen, watching and listening. He needed rest and peace.

Presently she folded the last garment and added it to the pile. "Let's have tea," she said. "The girls have gone over to Wandlebury so I'm alone, and you certainly deserve tea after listening to all that. Tea is set in the drawing-room."

He rose at once and helped her with the preparations, lifting the shining aluminium kettle off the stove and pouring the boiling water into the teapot. Caroline went upstairs to tidy, and when she came down she found him in the drawing-room tending the fire.

"I've saved it," he said without looking up. "I haven't known you for seven years unless we count from Elsinore, but the case was pretty desperate."

"Let's count from Elsinore," she suggested. As a matter of fact, she was surprised to find him handy with kettles and fires. He looked so immaculate — as if he had never done a domestic chore in his life. "Your clothes are marvellous," she added with a sigh.

Robert Shepperton had no idea of the train of thought which had preceded Caroline's remark. "I have no old clothes, that's the trouble," he said. "I suppose these will get old in time."

"No old clothes?" she asked, sitting down and beginning to pour out tea.

He hesitated. She thought for a moment he was going to tell her why, and then she saw him change his mind. Well, if he doesn't want to . . . she decided, and began to talk of something else.

They were still having tea when the young people got back from Wandlebury. The Derings had brought Joan Meldrum and Derek Ware — or rather Derek had brought *them*. He had seen the girls waiting for the bus and had given them a lift. Introductions were made, more cups were fetched and the quiet room was suddenly full of chatter. Caroline was used to her daughters' friends and their conversation; she did not take much part in it. Usually she found it pleasant and amusing to sit back and listen. (Once *she* had been young and green, but she had known she was green and they didn't. Therein lay the difference. She did not presume to criticise them, not even to herself. She was sorry for them; they had so much to learn.) But tonight Caroline found their conversation almost intolerable. It was because of Mr. Shepperton, of course. Mr. Shepperton was sitting back, drinking his tea, smoking a cigarette and gazing at the fire (it was a delightful fire by this time); he looked quite happy and peaceful — he looked rested. She recognised him now and wondered why she had been so stupid about it. He had interested her —

all those years ago — and he interested her now. He had travelled widely and was full of interesting ideas, but there was no chance for him to talk, he was given no opportunity. Derek and Leda and Joan were doing all the talking, they were discussing their friends and their friends' affairs. Bobbie laughed and giggled and ate largely of buns and jam.

They were "showing off", thought Caroline, looking at them and wishing that they were all ten years younger so that she could tell them to be quiet. They thought they were being clever, but they were only being rude. It was outrageously bad manners to exclude Mr. Shepperton from their conversation; they were excluding him deliberately, talking of matters which he knew nothing about. She wondered what Mr. Shepperton was thinking; he had been kind and understanding about Arnold's bad behaviour, was he being kind and understanding about this?

Perhaps he sensed her discomfort, for all at once he pulled himself together and entered the fray. Derek was inveighing against the dullness of the country in general and of Ashbridge in particular.

"It is dull only to dull people," Mr. Shepperton said.

Derek looked at him in surprise. "But country people *are* dull. That's just the point," objected Derek. "Sometimes I go round the farms with Dad and it takes them about five minutes to answer a simple question."

"They're slow — not dull. It's quite a different thing."

"Oh, I agree with Derek!" cried Leda. "Country people are so dull that they don't even appreciate the beauty of the country."

"Are you sure of that, Miss Dering?"

"Good heavens, it's obvious!" exclaimed Derek. "Where would you find a farmer or a ploughman with an eye for the beauties of Nature? They're all as dull as ditch-water."

"That's rather sweeping," said Mr. Shepperton, smiling. "I grant you countrymen seldom write poetry about the country. Their hearts don't dance with the daffodils. They work in the earth so they know all about it — but in this case familiarity breeds respect. They don't see magic in a field of waving corn but they feel satisfacion and pride. The fact is they love the earth as a child loves its mother, not as a man loves his mistress." He hesitated and then added, "That's why the countryman is slow and wise."

"Oh well, you may be right," said Derek casually. "I don't pretend to know much about ploughmen except that they smell."

The girls laughed.

Caroline was incensed — this was beyond all limits of rudeness! She looked at Derek with flashing eyes. "If you don't pretend to know about ploughmen you've no right to say they're dull," she told him. "First you say one thing and then another; you can't have it both ways. I've always thought law students were taught to argue logically," added Caroline, ramming her point home.

There was an amazed silence.

"Come and see my garden, Mr. Shepperton," said Caroline sweetly.

Mr. Shepperton rose at once. He had taken out his handkerchief and was blowing his nose with unnecessary vigour to hide an untimely smile.

7

CAROLINE was sitting at her desk doing accounts. It was a job she disliked intensely. She disliked it all the more because her income seemed to dwindle and her expenses seemed to rise, and she had an uncomfortable feeling that if this went on much longer she would find herself in a mess. Arnold had left all his money in trust, for he had no opinion of Caroline's business capacity; he had left it in gilt-edged securities which were perfectly safe, of course, but which yielded very small returns. Arnold had foreseen the war but apparently he had not foreseen the increased income tax nor the rise in the cost of living. It was unfortunate that Caroline had no money of her own — unfortunate and somewhat unfair. Her parents had been well off; they owned a beautiful place in the South of Scotland, but they had four daughters, and when they managed to arrange an exceedingly good marriage for their eldest child they decided they had done all that was necessary for her. Caroline would be well cared for as the wife of Arnold Dering, so they could write her off and divide their capital between the others. Arnold Dering agreed. He had plenty of money and preferred that his wife should have none of her own. He felt safer. Caroline knew nothing of these arrangements, she was barely eighteen when she was told that Mr. Dering had asked for her hand and that her parents had accepted the offer. "You like him, don't you?" her mother had inquired. Caroline liked him. She was rather surprised that he wanted to marry her — he seemed older than her idea of a husband — but it was nice of him to like her so much. She was grateful to him. So Caroline had said "yes" to Arnold Dering and had done her level best to make him a good wife. She had sunk her whole personality to be Arnold's wife, but even that was not enough, he was still unsatisfied . . . he took everything and still wanted more. Sometimes Caroline had felt that a woman of stronger, tougher fibre might have made a better wife for Arnold, a woman who could have stood up to him and remained a whole person.

The other three Armstrong girls had been less docile than their elder sister and had chosen their own paths. Jean had married an American and lived near Boston. Caroline had not seen her for years but they corresponded regularly, and sometimes parcels of dried fruit, sugar and rice and large tins of shortening and bars of milk chocolate and boxes of candy arrived at Vittoria Cottage to gladden the hearts of its inmates.

Mamie had married a farmer and lived in the Scottish Borders, she had no children and (perhaps on that account) she took a lively interest in the affairs of the young Derings. They were invited to Mureth in the summer holidays and enjoyed themselves immensely; on one occasion they had all gone to Mureth for Christmas and had come in for deep snow and winter sports. James had always been an especial favourite . . . and Jock Johnstone had hinted to Caroline that he was thinking of making James his heir. "I like your laddie," he had said. "I'd like James to have Mureth when I'm gone. I like to think if Mamie had had a son he would have been just such another fine straightforward fellow." This was high praise (especially from Jock Johnstone, who was not given to flattering speeches), but Caroline had not known what to say in return for James had not decided what he wanted to do . . . and, besides, Caroline had felt that Mureth should go to one of Jock's own nephews, it had been in the Johnstone family for generations.

Harriet was the youngest of the Armstrong girls and the least docile. She had chosen her profession and pursued it in spite of all her parents could say or do, in spite of every obstacle they could put in her path. They broke with her completely at one time, but after a bit they "came round", for Harriet was their youngest and their dearest and they could not bear to be on bad terms with her. She had made good and they had lived to be proud of her — which amused Harriet a lot — they had even suggested that she should drop the fictitious name, which she had assumed for the stage, and allow herself to be known as Harriet Armstrong; but it was too late for that, she had climbed out of the ruck as Harriet Fane and intended to stick to it.

Mr. and Mrs. Armstrong died within a

few months of each other not long before the beginning of the Second World War, the place was sold up and the estate divided between Jean and Mamie and Harriet. It had all been arranged years ago, of course, and the Armstrongs had never thought of altering the arrangement. They had got it firmly fixed in their minds that Caroline was well off and did not need their money.

Caroline thought of all this as she added up her accounts. She did not blame her parents . . . but how nice it would have been to have a little money of her very own. What a difference it would have made! The only money she had which she considered her "very own" was the money she got for her honey. She kept it in a little box in a drawer in her desk. She could do what she liked with it, she could spend it on her own amusement, she could buy something she wanted — but did not really *need*. This year Caroline intended to go to London for a week and stay with Harriet. She had promised to go so often and always something had happened to prevent her. This year she would go — it was definite — and she would see Harriet in the new play, *Eve's Dilemma*. Harriet had got her a seat for the first night and an invitation to the supper-party afterwards. It would be fun.

Caroline smiled to herself. She lifted her head from the horrible account-book and, looking out through the french window, saw Leda and Derek coming up the path together.

They were engaged! Caroline was sure of it. She knew it as certainly as she knew her own name. Her heart gave an odd sort of flutter and seemed to turn over in her breast — it was not a pleasant feeling. Of course she had known it was coming . . . though now she became aware that she had not *really* known, for, if she had known, why should it be a shock? And why was it a definitely unpleasant shock? Derek was a nice lad in spite of the fact that he was a little too pleased with himself. He was good-looking and eligible and they were in love. I ought to be pleased, thought Caroline. Why am I not pleased? Will Sir Michael be pleased?

Caroline half rose and then sat down again. She would leave them alone. She would wait for them to come to her.

They came up the path, hand in hand, and paused at the window.

"Mummy," said Leda. "Derek and I — "

"We're engaged!" cried Derek. "Mrs. Dering, we're engaged! Isn't it wonderful!"

Caroline found herself speechless. She rose and put an arm round Leda and held out her other hand to Derek.

"It's wonderful," declared Derek. "I mean, we've always known each other but we never thought — did we, Leda? I mean, it's quite different now."

"You're both so young," murmured Caroline.

"Older than you were when you were married," objected Leda. "And not only older in years, Mummy. Nowadays people know more, and go about more, and have more friends."

"We want you to be pleased," added Derek. "But even if you aren't pleased . . . I mean, Leda and I know we're absolutely made for each other."

"But you are pleased, aren't you, Mummy?" said Leda confidently.

"If you're happy — "

"Of course we're happy!"

"And if Sir Michael agrees."

"Yes," said Derek with less confidence. "Yes, well — of course Dad may be a bit surprised at first. I expect he'll be like you and say we're too young, but that's nonsense, of course. We know our own minds. As Leda says, people are older nowadays; they aren't sheltered and pampered as they were when Dad was a boy."

"And we know each other so well," Leda put in. "It isn't like getting engaged to a stranger."

"When Dad sees we're absolutely determined . . ." continued Derek. "And of course I can tell him you're pleased about it, can't I, Mrs. Dering?"

"No," said Caroline. "I can't give my consent until I've discussed it with your father — "

They paid no heed to this pronouncement (perhaps they did not hear it) but continued to exclaim with rapture that it was wonderful, that it was the most marvellous thing that had ever happened, that they would be married quite soon. . . .

"Derek, listen," said Caroline firmly. "We must wait until we see what Sir

Michael thinks. You can't be engaged without his consent."

"But we *are* engaged," declared Derek. "I'll tell Dad tonight. It will be all right — honestly, Mrs. Dering — he's very fond of Leda."

"You'll stay to tea, Derek," Leda said, smiling at him. "Stay to supper, too. We've got plenty of food, haven't we, Mummy?"

"He can stay to tea but not supper," replied Caroline. "He must go home after tea and ask Sir Michael . . ."

"But, Mummy — "

"But, Mrs. Dering — honestly."

"And then I must see Sir Michael myself and talk it over," added Caroline.

8

DEREK stayed to tea and lingered on afterwards. It was only when the Derings' supper was actually on the table that he made a move to go. Leda accompanied him to the gate and returned with her hair in some disorder. Her mother and sister were finishing their meal.

"I suppose Derek has been kissing you," said Bobbie, looking at her critically.

Leda did not deny it.

The day had been so exhausting that the girls went off to bed early, and Caroline was not long after them; she had just finished her bath and was putting on her dressing-gown when the front-door bell rang. At first she decided not to answer it, for there had been several burglaries in the district and she was frightened — it was nearly eleven o'clock! But on looking out of her bedroom window she saw a car standing at the gate. There it stood in the bright moonlight with its sidelights shining dimly — the grey Rolls, rather aged, but still handsome and distinguished, which she knew belonged to Sir Michael Ware. It was rather a problem. If her bedroom light had not been lighted she might have pretended to be asleep, but . . .

The bell rang again. There was nothing for it but to go down, just as she was, and speak to him.

Sir Michael looked enormous, standing on the doorstep. He was a big man, of course, and tonight he looked larger than usual — perhaps because he was angry — Caroline felt very small and defenceless.

"I hear you're in favour of this ridiculous business," Sir Michael exclaimed.

"Come in, Sir Michael," said Caroline.

He came in without further ado and followed her into the drawing-room. She wondered if he noticed she was in her dressing-gown. Perhaps not, for it was a black silk kimono embroidered with white chrysanthemums (James had sent it to her from Malaya) and, when you came to think of it, the garment was not very different from informal evening dress. It *felt* different, of course, because all she had on beneath it was her nightdress and this made her feel at a disadvantage — and

76

cold. Caroline sat down on the fender-stool and tried to revive the dying fire.

"Don't do that for me. I'm not cold," said Sir Michael. "I shan't keep you long. All I've come for is to tell you I don't approve. To begin with, I'm not made of money, as Derek seems to imagine, and to go on with they're both too young. They're irresponsible. Don't know their own minds. If you think — "

"I'm not in favour of it either," Caroline told him.

"You're not in favour of it!"

"No, I agree with you."

"But I thought you were all for it. Derek said so."

"They wouldn't listen. I don't know whether you've noticed that young people don't seem to listen to what one says."

"Of course I've noticed," said Sir Michael crossly.

Caroline was beginning to feel better now. The fire was burning up nicely and Sir Michael was not really very alarming in spite of his immense size. As she watched him pace across her drawing-room and turn and pace back (as if he were walking upon his quarter-deck, or whatever it was admirals walked upon), she began to feel quite sorry for him. Even admirals, it seemed, were not listened to by their offspring, and it must be worse for them than ordinary people because they were used to laying down the law.

"Neither Derek nor Rhoda listens to what I say," he added.

"Mine don't listen to me, either. They're fond of me, but they think I'm rather silly. Sometimes I have a sort of feeling they may be right."

He stopped and looked at her. "Nonsense!" he exclaimed.

She smiled at him rather helplessly.

"It's all wrong," he declared. "If you aren't sure of yourself you can't expect them to listen."

Caroline almost asked him if he were sure of himself and if so why Derek and Rhoda did not listen to him, but being a wise woman she just shook her head sadly.

"I damn' well had to listen to my parents!" Sir Michael exclaimed.

By this time Caroline was feeling grand. "You know," she said thoughtfully, "I can't help wondering whether *they* will make *their* children listen to *them*. It will be interesting to see, won't it?"

Sir Michael failed to appreciate this problem of psychology. "They're irresponsible," he declared. "At least Derek is. What does he think he's going to live on? How does he think he's going to support a wife?"

"Nobody seems to have any money nowadays," said Caroline thoughtfully. "Somehow or other, people seem to be able to struggle along without it — I don't know how."

"Derek couldn't," Sir Michael said.

There was a little silence.

"I mean," he continued, starting to walk up and down again, "I mean Derek is — not exactly extravagant but — but unused to economy. He doesn't know what it means. He likes the best of everything; the best wine, the best clothes — his tailor is the best in Oxford — and he's generous and open-handed. That's all right if you've got the wherewithal, of course. It's taking me all my time to see him through the Varsity."

"Leda will have very little — " began Caroline.

"Leda is a nice girl," declared Sir Michael. "She's pretty and attractive. I've nothing against her. Dash it all, I *like* Leda! But Derek will have to make his own way in the world. It's no use his thinking of marriage in the meantime."

"That's what I thought," Caroline said.

"It's common sense. They wouldn't be happy if they had to pig it. I know Derek. He thinks I don't know the first thing about him but I know him through and through — "

Caroline nodded. "Leda is much the same. She likes nice clothes, she likes going about and having fun."

"That's settled then," he said.

"You mean you'll put your foot down?"

"I mean they can't be married until Derek graduates."

Caroline was surprised. She had never thought they could be.

"Oh yes," said Sir Michael, nodding. "That was Derek's idea — to be married at once and look for rooms in Oxford. I told him it was crazy. I told him he must work like hell and get his degree, and then we would see about it."

"Of course," agreed Caroline. She

hesitated and then asked, "Do you mean you're willing for them to be engaged, Sir Michael?"

He stood still and considered the matter. "That's for you to say," he replied. "To tell you the truth, I'm not in favour of it — long engagements are the devil — but would they listen to us if we said no?"

Caroline saw the point.

"I'm not in favour of it," repeated Sir Michael thoughtfully. "Knowing Derek . . . he gets tired of things . . . but it's for you to say. You're the girl's mother."

"What can I say?" asked Caroline.

"What do you want to say?"

Caroline hesitated. She wanted Leda to have what she wanted, and Leda wanted Derek. She wanted Leda to be happy, but Sir Michael's warning had not fallen upon deaf ears. Sir Michael might be like a bull, but he was not without intuition and intelligence. "I don't know what I want to say," said Caroline at last. "But that isn't the point, is it? If you're willing for them to be engaged I shall have to agree."

They discussed the matter further. Sir Michael ceased to pace the room, he sat down quite peacefully and smoked a cigarette. It was long after midnight when at last he rose and said he must go . . . even then he said it reluctantly.

"Yes," agreed Caroline. "It's terribly late. Come back some other time," and she saw him out of the front door and chained it behind him.

Leda was waiting for her on the landing. "What did he say?" cried Leda. "What on earth were you talking about all that time? Goodness, you're in your dressing-gown!"

"I don't think he noticed," said Caroline rather wearily. "He isn't a very noticing kind of man . . . and I could hardly keep him waiting on the doorstep while I dressed."

"He must have thought it most extraordinary," said Leda. "Anybody could see it was your dressing-gown. What did he say?"

"He says Derek must graduate before he thinks of getting married."

"But, Mummy — "

"And he's right," said Caroline firmly.

"Derek won't wait," declared Leda. "Besides, he could work much better if he didn't have to keep on coming over to Ashbridge to see me."

"Derek will have to work hard and come over to Ashbridge less often."

"D'you mean you aren't on our side?" cried her daughter in amazement.

"I mean Derek must do as his father says. He's dependent upon his father; he hasn't a penny except what Sir Michael gives him."

"But, Mummy, it wouldn't cost any more if — "

"That isn't the point," said Caroline, who was tired and therefore less patient than usual. "The point is Sir Michael is paying the piper and can call the tune. He says you can be engaged if you like. To my mind that's all you can expect."

"Oh, Mummy, you don't understand!"

"I understand that you're both very impatient," said Caroline, smiling to take the edge off the words, "but surely if you love each other you can wait. You want to do what's best for Derek, don't you?"

For once Leda seemed to be listening. She said, "Of course I want to do what's best for Derek."

"People can't live on air," continued

Caroline, pressing home her advantage. "It would be madness to quarrel with Sir Michael."

"Of course, but — "

"Do be sensible," urged Caroline, taking up her hair-brush and beginning to brush her hair. "Make up your mind to wait. Sir Michael is very kind, he says he likes you, but Derek must be in a position to support a wife (or at least to make *something* towards the support of a wife) before he marries. That seems very fair to me."

It did not seem fair to Leda, she flung herself face-downward on the bed. "I shall die!" she exclaimed in a muffled voice. "If I can't marry Derek I shall die — you'll be sorry then — other girls get engaged and every one congratulates them but of course it's different with me. I don't know why I should be so unlucky, why everything should go against me — always. It isn't fair."

Caroline stood and looked at her. It was no good offering sympathy or trying to reason with Leda; she knew that only too well. Leda was like Arnold, who had asked and asked for sympathy but had never accepted it. What could you do with people like that?

There was so much in heredity, thought Caroline. Leda was like Arnold, like him in appearance and in nature. In Bobbie she saw her own grandmother, who had come from Ireland and was impulsive and generous and full of fun. In neither of her daughters could she see the least resemblance to herself, but her son *was* herself — her better self, thought Caroline. It was worth while to have lived if only to have produced James. Quite willingly she would have lain down in the road and allowed a steam-roller to pass over her recumbent form if that would have done James any good . . . not so much because she adored him but because she felt that he was a more valuable person than herself, more valuable to the world.

9

MRS. SEVERN had invited Caroline to tea on Wednesday "to meet Mr. Shepperton". Caroline had met him already, of course, but she had no objection to meeting him again, so she put on her best hat and presented herself at the vicarage at the appointed hour. She found Mr. Shepperton had arrived before her; he was sitting in a shabby but comfortable armchair discussing world affairs with his host. Caroline sat down beside her hostess on the sofa and talked to her. Mrs. Severn was fat and cheerful and slightly lazy. She was not the bustling efficient type of vicar's wife, but in spite of this — or perhaps because of it — the village liked her immensely and so did Caroline.

"Is it true?" inquired Mrs. Severn in low tones. "I heard a rumour about Leda and Derek, and I could hardly wait until you came."

"Ashbridge is a dreadful place," said Caroline, smiling.

"It *is* true!"

"Yes, they're engaged."

"My dear, how thrilling! It's so much more interesting when you know them both. Anne *will* be excited."

"But of course they aren't going to be married for some time. The Admiral says Derek must graduate first and I think he's right."

"Of course," nodded Mrs. Severn. "They're both very young and it will do them no harm to wait. Things are so much more valuable if you have to wait for them. Jack and I waited nearly four years because he had no living and you can't keep a wife on a curate's stipend. We waited and saved," said Mrs. Severn with a sigh. "I did some dressmaking. (It was the only way I could make a little money.) It seemed a very long four years, but afterwards we were glad we had waited because we appreciated our happiness so much more."

Caroline was silent. Her own experience had been so different from Mrs. Severn's that she could find nothing to say.

"Anne ought to be back," said Mrs. Severn, glancing at the clock.

"Anne is late!" exclaimed Mr. Severn, taking a large gold watch out of his pocket and consulting it gravely.

"Perhaps the bus was late," suggested Caroline.

"Anne is our daughter," said Mr. Severn to his other guest. "She has a post at Miss Penworthy's school in Wandlebury and goes in daily. We are very fortunate to have her so near. Miss Penworthy is an admirable woman."

"Anne was there at school," put in Mrs. Severn. "So of course Miss Penworthy knows her. The Wares used to go to Miss Penworthy's and the Derings, of course . . . in fact, all the children from Ashbridge. Anne teaches music and dancing."

"I think Miss Penworthy is lucky to have her," said Caroline. "She plays so beautifully. I'm always glad when Mr. Forbes is away and we have Anne to play the organ."

They were still talking about Anne when the door opened and she appeared.

"The bus was late," she explained. "It's always late when I specially want to be home early."

There was something very attractive about Anne, she was not pretty but she was graceful and well-formed; her hair was dark and glistening — well washed and well brushed — her teeth were white and even, and her thin face was full of intelligence and humour. She had been a quiet little girl (Caroline remembered) and she was still quiet, but there was a twinkle in her dark-brown eyes which told of a capacity for fun. In spite of the fact that she was an only child and adored by her parents, Anne was quite unspoiled — perhaps she was unspoilable.

"There's some *very* interesting news," Mrs. Severn told her. "Leda and Derek are engaged."

"How lovely!" cried Anne. "Of course, I'm not exactly surprised — "

"Leda and Derek!" exclaimed Mr. Severn in amazement. "Why am I never informed of these interesting matters? Leda and Derek!"

Mrs. Severn smiled at him fondly. "Jack never sees anything," she said.

"I see as much as other people."

"No, dear, you don't. You know you're always surprised when babies appear at the font to be christened. For instance, when the sexton's wife — "

"Kate!" cried Mr. Severn in mock alarm. "Kate, I will *not* allow you to tell our guests that story!"

Mrs. Severn chuckled. "I think Mr. Shepperton would enjoy it," she declared. "The sexton and his wife live in a cottage just beside the church and Jack sees them every day — sometimes several times a day. One Sunday afternoon they appeared in church with two babies to be christened. Jack admired the babies very nicely. 'Dear little mites,' he said. 'They look like twins.' 'They *are* twins,' said Mrs. Spawl in bewilderment. 'Who do they belong to?' asked Jack with interest. Mr. and Mrs. Spawl were quite hurt."

"Kate," said Mr. Severn when the laughter had subsided. "Kate, I may be somewhat unobservant, but I cannot sit here and allow myself to be accused of faulty grammar. I feel sure I must have said, 'To whom do they belong?' "

"Of course you did, darling," Anne assured him.

"Talking of babies," said Mrs. Severn. "How are the Widgeons getting on? I ought to go and see Sue, but I never seem to have time."

"Widgeon!" exclaimed Mr. Severn. "He's the young fellow who lives in that very isolated cottage near the Roman Well. Spawl says he used to talk Socialism at the Cock and Bull, and he used to drink too much, I'm afraid, but perhaps he will turn over a new leaf now that he has a pretty little wife. I married them just the other day."

"Not the other day, Jack," objected Mrs. Severn. "You married them last Christmas. Don't you remember we left the Christmas decorations up for their wedding?"

"Of course, dear, I remember perfectly. Last Christmas, so it was . . . and I suppose I may expect a christening any moment now."

Caroline laughed and said not immediately but probably before very long, and then went on to talk about the Widgeons and to tell Mrs. Severn that Sue was feeling a little lonely.

"Poor Sue! Girls never think of these things when they go and get married," said Mrs. Severn with a sigh.

"My dear!" exclaimed her husband. "It sounds as though you had undergone a similar experience, but I was not away from you all day, so you could not have felt dull."

"Oh, but I did," Mrs. Severn told him. "I found it dreadfully dull not having my sisters to talk to."

Every one laughed and the conversation took a new turn.

When Caroline rose to go Mr. Shepperton said he must go too, and they left together. "I'll walk home with you," he said.

She realised that he must be lonely, living all by himself at the Cock and Bull. "Of course, come," she said, smiling at him. "Come and see us any time you like. Are you staying in Ashbridge for long?"

They were walking along together by this time. It was a misty, damp evening and nearly dark. Mr. Shepperton did not answer the question for a few moments, and then he said, "Yes, I think I shall be staying for some months. I'm very comfortable at the Cock and Bull — Mrs. Herbert is extraordinarily kind. You see, I've been ordered a complete rest, and as I have no home I may as well rest here as anywhere."

"No home?" asked Caroline.

"My house was burnt," he replied in a low voice. "My wife was in it at the time. I was abroad — it was during the war, of course — and I knew nothing about it until I came back."

"How ghastly!" Caroline exclaimed.

"It was," he admitted. "I came back expecting to find my wife and my son and my home waiting for me, and I found nothing. My son was sent to America and is still there, living with some very kind friends; I hope to go over and fetch him in the spring."

"Where was your house?" asked Caroline.

"In the Regent's Park district. I went out there the other day and had a look at it. There's a whole row of houses — a whole row of ruins with blackened walls and broken windows. When I think of what it used to be . . ."

"Can nothing be done?"

"Nothing except to pull them all down and rebuild them, and nobody seems to have the heart to begin the job. I meant to go into my house but the policeman on duty at the corner ran after me and warned me that it was unsafe; the walls are all crumbling and every now and then a big chunk of masonry comes rattling down. It's absolute desolation; the gardens are full of rubble and rubbish. I used to be rather keen on my garden."

"You didn't go in?"

"No, I didn't (not because I cared what happened to me but because I realised it would be a bother for the policeman; he seemed a nice young fellow). I stood at the gate for a few minutes and then came away."

It had taken Robert Shepperton some time to tell his story and they arrived at the gate of Vittoria Cottage as he finished it. Caroline could find very little to say — the tragedy was beyond words.

"That's all," he said. "I wanted you to know about it but we needn't speak of it again."

She had been going to ask where he was when it happened and why he had not heard of it before he came back, but he had made it impossible for her to question him.

"Good-night, Mrs. Dering," he said.

"Won't you come in?"

"Some other time," he replied, raising his hat and turning away.

10

THE "honey money" rolled in and was put away safely in Caroline's desk, it was a good year for honey, but in spite of this Caroline decided she would not go to London. Everything was too uncertain. She could not leave home; she could not spend "all that" on her own pleasure. If Leda were to be married next year they must set about collecting her trousseau, and the wedding would cost money. In addition to these considerations Caroline was unwilling to leave the two girls alone — even with Comfort to look after them — for Leda was being difficult and Bobbie was by no means tactful. Harriet would be sorry, of course, she might even be angry, but it could not be helped. Caroline wrote and explained matters to Harriet and awaited her reply.

Harriet replied in person. Her little car was standing at the gate when Caroline got back from the village after her morning's shopping and she herself was waiting

n the drawing-room. They hugged one
mother ecstatically.

"I've come to fetch you," Harriet said.

"But I told you in my letter — "

"I know, darling," nodded Harriet.
'I read the letter most carefully, it was
beautifully expressed. Your letters are
always interesting and so full of personality: I believe you could write a book
if you put your mind to it."

"But I told you why — "

"Yes, you told me. You told me *lots*.
I simply couldn't *begin* to reply — besides
I was much too tired and busy to write a
long letter — so I borrowed some petrol
from Marcus and came straight down.
I had a lovely run, the car went beautifully.
We had better start your packing directly
after lunch, it won't take long if I help
you."

"Harriet, listen — "

"No, my pet," said Harriet. "I haven't
come to listen. I hate listening. Besides
I'm so hungry. Is lunch nearly ready?"

"I can't leave the girls alone in the
house," said Caroline, firmly.

"No, but you can get Comfort to live in.
That's what you intended to do, isn't it?

The girls will be perfectly safe with Comfort. You aren't indispensable. When people begin to think they're indispensable it's high time for them to make a move. I know, because I think I'm indispensable."

"Are you going to make a move?"

"No, darling. I'm staying put. I simply hate my understudy, she's frightful. . . . And she just waiting for me to crock up. She's quite capable of putting something horrid in my coffee — nothing lethal, you know, but some sort of sleeping powder — something to knock me out so that she can step into my shoes. I can see the idea behind her eyes when she looks at me. Have you got anything to eat, darling?"

"Not very much, I'm afraid," declared Caroline, hastily reviewing the contents of her larder.

"How disappointing!" sighed Harriet. "I'm simply starving; it must be the air or something."

"Only eggs, I'm afraid — "

"Eggs!" exclaimed Harriet. "*Only* eggs I've forgotten what an egg looks like Lead me to them at once."

Caroline led her to them and, between them, they knocked up a savoury omelette (which — as Harriet declared — was fit for a Queen) and while they were so engaged Comfort cored some apples, stuffed them with chopped dates and put them in the oven. All this activity was accompanied by a running stream of conversation in which Comfort took the part of a highly interested and appreciative audience. She tried to remember every word so that she could retail it to her friends. . . . Comfort would be able to sup out on Miss Fane for some time to come.

Caroline had decided not to go to London, but she discovered that Harriet really wanted her — in fact needed her — for Harriet was not at all happy about the new play.

"It's a lousy play," declared Harriet in cheerful tones. "Thin as skim-milk. I thought at first it might go down quite well (the dialogue is amusing and Marcus and I are pretty good together) but Pinkie suddenly got cold feet and started altering everything, so now it's a mess."

Caroline was aware that Mr. Pinkerton was the producer. "How awful!" she exclaimed. "Couldn't you prevent him from — "

"Not without strangling him," Harriet replied. "Marcus wants to strangle him, of course, but I feel it's scarcely worth the risk. . . Oh, well, it's all in the day's work. No use worrying."

"But Harriet — "

"Worrying makes you ugly," declared the beautiful Miss Fane. "Worrying gives you horrid wrinkles. I never worry."

"I'll come," said Caroline.

"Of course you're coming! You don't suppose I'm going back without you? What a ridiculous idea! Comfort will look after everything while you're away — won't you, Comfort?"

"I'll fetch Mother up this afternoon," said Comfort, nodding. "It'll do Mother a world of good to have a little change of air."

The girls came in for lunch. Leda received her aunt's congratulations very graciously, but became less gracious when she discovered that Caroline was being spirited off to London.

"I don't see how you can go away *now*," objected Leda. "Sir Michael may want to see you again, or Derek may come over from Oxford."

"Sir Michael can wait," said Harriet. "And as for Derek — I suppose Derek comes to see *you*, doesn't he?"

"Comfort is so awful," continued Leda in a complaining voice. "She's much worse when you aren't here to keep her in order, and her cooking is appalling. Supposing Derek rings up and says he can come to lunch?"

"You can cook his lunch," Harriet told her. "It's a delightful task to cook delectable food for the man you love."

"Mother ought to be here," said Leda.

"You *are* a selfish pig!" exclaimed Bobbie.

"It's only for four days," Caroline reminded her. "Of course, if you really think I ought to be here — "

"The whole thing is fixed," declared Harriet in firm tones. "Fixed inalterably like the Laws of the Medes and Persians."

"I often wondered how they managed," Bobbie put in. "I mean, it must have been so awkward for them if they found the Law didn't work very well, or when conditions changed."

"I expect they did a good deal of wangling," said Harriet thoughtfully.

The little discussion into far-off history had changed the trend of the conversation and Leda was silenced, but she was still unresigned to her mother's abduction. After lunch, when Caroline had gone to speak to Comfort and to make arrangements with her about food, Leda pursued Harriet upstairs and found her in Caroline's bedroom. Harriet was busily engaged in removing garments from the wardrobe and laying them upon the bed, she looked up when Leda came in.

"We haven't much time," explained Harriet. "I thought I'd start packing. You might fetch a suit-case for me."

"Mummy isn't going," said Leda. "She can't go away *now*. It's frightfully selfish of you to try to take her away."

"Selfish! What about you? You aren't selfish, are you?"

"Mummy's place is here."

"Of course — slaving for you! Cooking for you! Ironing your clothes! She shouldn't ever have a holiday, should she?"

"She didn't want a holiday until you put it into her head."

"My goodness!" exclaimed Harriet. "I shouldn't like to be you!"

This was not what Leda had expected to hear; in fact, it was so different from what she had expected to hear that she was interested. "You wouldn't like to be me?" she inquired.

"Selfish people are nearly always unhappy," explained Harriet, taking a brown silk frock out of the wardrobe and examining it carefully before laying it over a chair. "Sometimes they go on for quite a long time before Nemesis descends upon them and knocks them flat, but Nemesis always gets them in the end. I'm sorry for you, Leda."

"I don't know what you mean."

"You'll know some day . . . or perhaps you won't," said Harriet, thoughtfully. "Perhaps you'll never realise that it's your own fault when you get knocked flat. Perhaps you're incurable."

"I think you're horrid," said Leda with complete calm. "I think it's you who's selfish. You want Mummy, so you're taking her. That's selfish, isn't it?"

"Have it your own way," replied her aunt with equal calmness. "I want Mummy

— so I'm taking her. The main thing is I *am* taking her, so will you fetch her suitcase, please."

When Caroline found herself sitting beside Harriet in the little car she had a sudden access of sheer panic. She had been *mad* to leave home . . . something awful would happen while she was away! One of the girls would develop acute appendicitis; Comfort would fall down the steps leading to the cellar and break her leg, or the house would go on fire.

"Harriet!" exclaimed Caroline in urgent tones. "Harriet I must go home. I must — honestly. It was crazy of me to say I would come. I simply must go home, Harriet."

"No, darling," replied Harriet. "I won't take you home, so you'll just have to make the best of it. High time you were dug out of your rut."

"Please, Harriet — "

"No," said Harriet firmly. "For one thing, it's too late — I haven't enough petrol to take you home and get back to London — for another thing I want you very badly. Last, but not least, it will be good for the girls to do without you for a little while. You spoil them dreadfully, especially Leda. Bobbie is slightly spoilt but not unbearable; but Leda!" said Harriet with emphasis. "Leda — really — is — getting — almost — unbearable."

"She's in love," murmured her mother. "You mustn't be too hard on her. She's like Arnold, you know. She isn't happy inside. People who aren't happy inside are always difficult."

They drove on for several miles without saying any more. Caroline's panic was passing off and she began to look about her and to enjoy the drive. She had not been in a car for months — the sensation of being whirled along through pleasant country was delightful — and there was so much to see. Here was the World. The World was full of people and all of them were important to themselves. Each had his or her problems (just as Caroline had) and each thought his or her problem the most important in the universe.

Harriet is right, thought Caroline. I was in a rut. My life was bounded by the village and things had become out of proportion.

They were approaching London now and the World was more full of people than ever . . . people with hopes and fears and troubles. That woman (for instance) standing on the edge of the path and looking up and down the road in eager anticipation, what was she waiting for? Some man, perhaps? Caroline would never know. They passed her and drove on. *Here* was a street with shops; a man was walking along, holding a little boy by the hand, he had a toy yacht under his arm and they both looked pleased and excited. *There* was a girl with a basket; she came out of a green gate and, shutting it behind her, turned and waved to a face at the window. Caroline saw a child playing in the gutter with an old tin, a dog bounding across the road to greet its master, two women greeting one another with cordial smiles . . . all these people — and many more — caught Caroline's eye and held it for a moment before she was swept on.

Houses slid past — hundreds of thousands of houses — and each one was a home, a secret place where people slept and ate and quarrelled and made it up again, where people were happy or miserable (or, even worse than miserable, were hopelessly resigned). Every house had its own peculiar atmosphere, its own peculiar smell, so that although there were dozens of houses, all alike to look at, they were all quite different.

11

HARRIET'S flat was luxurious, its
decorations were restful and easy
on the eye. Life with Harriet was
very dissimilar from life at Vittoria Cottage. Its tempo was more rapid: spiritoso
accelerato rather than adagio. Caroline
had noticed this before (everything was so
different that she herself felt like a different
person) but today she noticed it even more
than usual. Perhaps this was because it
started before she had time to get her
breath, before she had adjusted herself to
the changed conditions.

The telephone-bell was ringing madly
when they opened the front-door and
Harriet threw down her coat and Caroline's
hat-box and rushed to answer it. She was
still talking to some unknown friend (a
bosom friend judging from the endear-
ments which were falling from her lips)
when the door-bell rang. Caroline opened
the door — there was nobody else to open
it — and discovered a woman on the

landing. She was a very small woman and she was laden with several very large cardboard boxes. Caroline was helping her to pile the boxes in the hall when a young man came leaping up the stairs and dashed in through the open doorway.

"Who are you?" he demanded breathlessly. "Oh, you're Caroline, of course. She pinched all my petrol to fetch you. Where is she? I must see her immediately."

"I'm here, darling!" cried Harriet waving frantically from the sitting-room where she was still anchored to the telephone. "I'm here, Marcus! I'll speak to you in a minute."

Marcus plunged into the sitting-room, took the receiver from her hand and placed it firmly on its cradle. "You'll speak to me *now*," he declared. "This is important. This is absolute priority. Pinkie wants to cut the rocking-horse — our best bit of dialogue — the only decent thing left in the whole blinking play. You'll have to get hold of Pinkie somehow; he might listen to you. I don't know how you'll get hold of him of course, because he's as elusive as Old Nick, but you simply *must* get hold of him somehow."

"That was Pinkie," said Harriet, pointing to the telephone.

The young man flung himself into a chair and began to laugh hysterically.

"Have a drink," said Harriet.

"No, darling," said Marcus.

"A pink gin," said Harriet persuasively. "You can't say no to a pink gin."

"No darling . . . I mean, *no, I can't say no.*"

The very small woman was still waiting in the hall. She put her head round the door and said, "I thought perhaps you'd just slip on the yellow frock, Miss Fane. We've altered it as you wanted but I *should* like to see it on for a moment if it isn't a trouble."

"No trouble at all," declared Harriet with bitter sarcasm.

"If you aren't engaged, Miss Fane," said the woman diffidently.

"Definitely not," declared Harriet.

"If you've time . . ."

"All the time in the world," Harriet assured her.

Harriet went to try on the frock and Caroline was left with Marcus. She administered pink gin, gave him a cigarette out of Harriet's tortoiseshell cigarette-box and did her best to soothe him.

"Harriet will put it all right," declared Caroline, who had ample faith in her sister's capabilities.

"Nobody can put it right," said Marcus despairingly.

"Harriet will. You'll see."

He sipped his pink gin. "She's wonderful, of course," he admitted.

"Wonderful," agreed her sister.

"She's so full of vitality, isn't she?"

"Full to the brim," nodded Caroline as she refilled his glass.

"Full to the brim," repeated Marcus, watching her. "Darling Harriet could make anything go if she were left alone and not badgered and bullied — if she were left to do things in her own way. Even this damned spineless play had a sort of sparkle about it until Pinkie got on the job. It's dead now, of course. Isn't it hell?" said Marcus wearily. "Isn't it absolute hell?"

"It's frightful for you," Caroline agreed.

"You don't know, of course," he continued. "I mean you *can't* know what it's like, darling. How could you? I'd always wanted to act with Harriet — always — so of course I was in Heaven when Pinkie offered me the part — and now the whole thing has gone bad."

"No," said Caroline. "It will be all right — "

"It stinks," declared Marcus. "It stinks to high Heaven. I could strangle that man. Perhaps I *shall* strangle him before we're through."

"What a crazy beginning to your visit!" said Harriet when at last they had got rid of their troublesome guests and shut the front-door. "Things are not always so hectic; it's because we're getting near the First Night and people's nerves are on edge. Shall we go out and have dinner together — just you and me — somewhere quiet?"

They went out together and shut the door behind them and, as they did so, the lift appeared and the gates opened and a man stepped out. He was short and fat with curly black hair and a round, clean-shaven countenance.

"Harriet!" he exclaimed. "Thank heaven I've caught you! I must see you for a minute. Listen, darling, it's all right. It's absolutely all right . . . you aren't cross, are you?" He looked at her anxiously as he spoke.

Harriet did not answer.

"You *are* cross," he declared. "I knew you were when you suddenly cut off our conversation in the middle; so I rushed out and got a taxi and came straight here. . . . Darling, you mustn't be cross. If you want the rocking-horse, of course you can have it. *Of course* you can. You know that, don't you? I only thought it made the second act a teeny bit top-heavy — that was all — but if *you* want it . . . ."

"I was a little bit cross, Pinkie," admitted Harriet, showing a slight inclination to relent.

"I knew it!" he exclaimed. "I was sure of it . . . but you aren't cross now, are you?"

"I don't like all this chopping and changing, Pinkie."

"There won't be any more. Everything is all right now, isn't it?"

"Well," said Harriet doubtfully. "There are one or two things . . . for instance I don't like the way Daisy goes across in front of me in the last scene."

"Fancy you mentioning that!" he cried.
"I wasn't happy about that, either. I was
going to tell her about it tomorrow. You're
Eve, you see, so of course she mustn't
block you. You're absolutely the only
woman on the English stage who could play
Eve — "

"We must go, Pinkie," said Harriet,
cutting short his flattering speeches somewhat heartlessly.

"Of course," he agreed, following them
into the lift. "I won't keep you. I just
wanted to be quite, quite sure you weren't
cross . . ."

They got rid of him in the street and
walked off together, arm-in-arm and, as
they went, Harriet began to giggle feebly.

"Isn't it silly?" she said.

The movement and bustle of London,
the lights and the noise intoxicated Caroline. She felt excited and slightly dizzy and
was glad to cling to Harriet's arm. They
did not speak; there was no need, for they
understood one another without words.
Presently they came to a small restaurant
in Soho and Harriet opened the door and
walked in.

"This is the place," she said. "It's quiet

and pleasant and the food is good. I often come here."

Caroline was no longer the anxious mother of Leda and Bobbie, she was herself. She felt "herself" stirring within her. I'm still me, she thought with surprise. The idea was so strange that she felt moved to communicate it to her companion. "Of course, you won't understand," she added. "You're always you."

"Oh, I understand all right," declared Harriet. "I struggle all the time to hold on to myself. It's difficult to be oneself and not to become what other people think you are. Harriet Fane has a reputation of sorts and if I'm not careful I find myself becoming other people's idea of Harriet Fane . . . but never with you. That's why you're so good for me. If this play is a flop I shall come to Vittoria Cottage for a long holiday."

"Oh, dear, I almost hope — I don't know what I hope," murmured Caroline.

"I'm so sick of all the intrigue," continued Harriet as she took up the menu and studied it carefully. "It's such a strain. I can't afford to relax — I'm not good enough. The real out-and-out genius can relax but I'm not that by a long chalk so I've got to be up and doing all the time — acting on the stage and off it. Pinkie wears me down; he wears the others down even more because they're softer. When Pinkie is in one of his moods you can't do anything right. The other day things got to such a pitch that I thought Marcus was going to burst and the rest of the cast were in tears, so I just took up my fur coat and put it on quite slowly and walked out. I was acting, of course," said Harriet. "I was playing the part of the prima donna in a huff — but it worked all right."

"You played it again tonight," Caroline reminded her.

"Yes, that was funny, wasn't it?"

Harriet was silent for a few moments and then she continued: "Things go on and on. When you've lived in a play for weeks you forget there's any other life. You forget that some day it will be over and you'll be living and thinking quite differently. The only thing to do, to keep sane, is to get outside and look at the thing from a distance. That's where I have a pull over Marcus and the others. They can't get outside, whereas I can. Sometimes I go right outside and look at it and laugh. I don't know why I can do it — perhaps because I'm not really an actress, through and through. I'm me first and an actress afterwards. It could be that . . . or it could be because I've got you," added Harriet smiling at Caroline across the little table.

12

WHILE Caroline was enjoying herself in gay surroundings and giving very little thought to her home, Vittoria Cottage drowsed in the autumn sun. The cottage was old and had seen many changes. People came and went; they unpacked their belongings, settled down and sheltered beneath its roof and then they were gone like the wind leaving little evidence of their sojourn. The cottage did not regret the absence of its mistress, it had become philosophical in its old age. Its mistress would return.

Leda and Bobbie regretted their mother's absence, and Comfort of course. Life ran less smoothly without Caroline to direct its course. Leda and Bobbie quarrelled incessantly; they quarrelled over the food and they quarrelled over who should go to the village and fetch the fish. They quarrelled because Bobbie forgot to post Leda's letter to Derek and because Bobbie gave Joss the remains of a rabbit stew which

Leda had intended to heat up for supper. Leda usually got the better of the argument for she remained perfectly calm and shot her bolts with accurate aim, lodging them where she knew they would do most damage, whereas Bobbie would fly into a rage and hit out wildly in all directions without bothering where her blows fell. When the row was over, Leda would sulk for hours and Bobbie would retire to the kitchen and talk to Comfort and Mrs. Podbury and tell them all about it.

"It's a shame, that's what," Mrs. Podbury would declare. "Miss Leda didn't have no call to say that about Joss."

Comfort would nod and agree — she had no use at all for Miss Leda.

Thursday was Comfort's afternoon off; she and her mother decided to go to Wandlebury and do some shopping and see a picture. Bobbie volunteered to wash up the lunch dishes so that they could catch the early bus. Leda did not help, of course — *she* had not given the Podburys permission to go early — she took a book and sat by the fire while Bobbie cleared the table.

"I may as well set the tea while I'm about it," Bobbie said.

"You needn't set it for me," replied Leda. "Derek's coming. We're going out for a walk."

She had scarcely spoken when Derek arrived in his car and after some conversation the two set forth to walk over the hill together.

Bobbie was alone in the house. It was unusual and she didn't like it much; in fact she was thoroughly bored. The afternoon stretched before her like a wilderness. A pelican, that's what I am, thought Bobbie. I'm a pelican in the wilderness. She got out her stamps and spread them all over the table but somehow they failed to fascinate her. This being so, she was pleased when the telephone-bell rang . . . but not so pleased when she discovered it was only Mr. Shepperton.

"Mummy has gone to London," said Bobbie. "She's gone to see Aunt Harriet's new play. I'm here alone." She hesitated and then added, "Come to tea if you like; I'm doing stamps."

It appeared the Mr. Shepperton liked stamps. He had possessed a good collection but possessed it no longer.

"What a pity! We might have done some

swapping," exclaimed Bobbie in disappointed tone. "Did you sell your collection?"

Mr. Shepperton did not answer this, but said that if Bobbie really wanted him he would come; and Bobbie, being heartily sick of her own company, replied that she really wanted him.

Meanwhile Leda and Derek were walking over the hill. Leda liked walking but Derek didn't, he preferred to do his travelling by car. Unfortunately he was obliged to economise in petrol — he used it to come over from Oxford to Ashbridge — and there was none for unnecessary expeditions. It annoyed Derek to think of his car standing idle at the gate of Vittoria Cottage while he toiled up the hill.

"We could have gone to Wandlebury," Derek complained. "There's a good flick on there. It's sickening, isn't it?"

"We might have gone in the bus," said Leda.

"The bus!" exclaimed Derek in disgust. "I hate buses . . . it would have been more sensible to spend the afternoon at the cottage. Why didn't we think of that?"

"I did," Leda told him. "I thought a

walk would be nicer. Bobbie is at home so we couldn't have talked or anything."

"If we were married I shouldn't have to use up all my petrol coming over to see you," grumbled Derek. "Why shouldn't we be married? That's what I want to know."

"They're so silly," Leda agreed. "They've forgotten what it's like to be young. It wouldn't cost any more if we were married and had rooms together at Oxford. Think how lovely that would be."

"I know," said Derek, giving her hand a little squeeze.

"I could help you with your work," continued Leda. "We could live on very little, you know. Then you would get your degree and — "

"The only thing is," interrupted Derek. "The only thing is — I mean what's the use of getting my degree?"

"What's the use!" she exclaimed in amazement.

"To tell you the truth I'm most awfully fed up with Law. It's so damned dull."

"But Derek, I thought you wanted — "

"I did, of course. If I could have gone straight from school it would have been all right. I got out of the way of working when I was in the Army; it was such a different sort of life. Now it's just a grind. Grind, grind, grind!" said Derek impatiently.

"It won't be for long," soothed Leda.

"Won't it!" he returned. "Even if I get my degree next year — "

"Derek! Of course you'll get it."

He was silent.

"Derek, you simply must," she urged him. "It's the only way for us to get married. Your father says — "

"Not the only way," mumbled Derek. "As a matter of fact we could get married much sooner if I chucked the whole thing. I'm sick of Law. I'm sick of grinding away at books. What's the use of it, anyhow? It would be years before I could make enough money to live comfortably. Whereas if I went into business . . .''

They walked on for a few moments without speaking.

"What sort of business?" asked Leda.

"Any sort," he replied. "I'm not particular. All I want is a decent screw and plenty of holidays."

"But Derek, when you start a thing you

ought to finish it . . . all this time you've been working will be wasted."

"It's a waste going on working at something I hate. I didn't know I was going to hate it or I shouldn't have started, of course. Look here, Leda, I know a man who has a house near Oxford; it's a marvellous place with a swimming pool and tennis courts and everything you could want. He made all his money out of tooth-paste."

"Tooth-paste!"

"What's wrong with tooth-paste? Every one uses it. You've seen the posters advertising Bright's tooth-paste, haven't you?"

Leda had seen them — nobody could have helped seeing them for they were pasted upon nearly every hoarding — a brightly coloured picture of a girl with golden hair and two rows of magnificent teeth. SHE HAS BRIGHT TEETH, announced the posters. CLEAN YOUR TEETH THE BRIGHT WAY. THE BRIGHT WAY IS THE RIGHT WAY.

"That's Valerie," Derek said.

"Valerie?" asked Leda.

"Yes, Valerie Bright."

"You don't mean the girl on the posters is Mr. Bright's daughter?"

"Yes, Valerie has gorgeous teeth and she's always used Bright's tooth-paste."

"But Derek, how awful! They must be most extraordinary people."

"They aren't extraordinary at all," replied Derek with some heat. "They're very kind and hospitable. Valerie is rather marvellous, she's so . . . but that isn't the point," said Derek, swerving suddenly from his eulogism of Miss Bright and changing his tone of voice. "The point is they're very rich — and it's all tooth-paste — and I think Old Man Bright would give me a job in his factory if I asked him. He's got a huge factory, one of those modern factories with vita glass and little houses for all the work-people."

Leda showed no enthusiasm for the idea. "Your father would be furious," she said.

"Just at first, of course. I know exactly what Dad would say and how he would say it — extraordinary how easily I can see through Dad! There would be a hell of a row but he would come round in the end."

They had reached a sheltered spot. Derek spread his waterproof and they sat down side by side. It was almost exactly the same place where Caroline had sat and had her tea and talked to Mr. Shepperton, but today it was damp and grey instead of warm and golden.

"You ought to get your degree," said Leda. "It would be far better than making tooth-paste."

"You talk as if I were going to make it with my own hands!" Derek exclaimed. "I should have an executive post, of course, and — "

"It's still tooth-paste," Leda pointed out. "If you had your degree you could get a professional appointment."

"I've told you I shan't get it," said Derek crossly. "Oh, I suppose I *could* get it if I set to and worked like a black slave . . ."

"Of course you could," agreed Leda. "You *must* get it, Derek. Do it for me," she added.

Derek did not respond as she had hoped. He took up a handful of gravel and let it trickle through his fingers. "It would mean I couldn't come over here so often . . . but perhaps you wouldn't mind that."

"I should know you were working for me," Leda pointed out.

It was Derek's turn to be disappointed.

He was silent for a few moments and then he said, "I want a job. Let's go all out for that. Then we could get married."

"We can't go against everybody, Derek. Your Father would be very angry — so would Mummy — "

"They're silly — you said so yourself. You said they had forgotten what it was like to be young."

The argument had come full circle. They were back at the beginning.

"Yes," agreed Leda. "I said that — and it's true. If only they would let us be married everything would be all right. We could live in rooms in Oxford. You could get your degree quite easily if you worked hard and didn't have to come over to Ashbridge."

"We've said all that," said Derek, impatiently. "What's the use of saying it all over again! I've told you there isn't a hope of my graduating next year and Dad won't let us be married."

"Couldn't we persuade him? We could tell him we didn't want a penny more than you're getting now."

"It would be difficult for us to manage," said Derek doubtfully.

"We could live very cheaply," urged Leda. "It doesn't cost much more for two people to live together than for one to live alone — and you could sell your car, couldn't you?"

"I might lay it up," said Derek more doubtfully than before.

"If you sold it your father would see that you really meant to economise."

"But I don't want to sell it!" exclaimed Derek.

Leda was annoyed. She said, "Oh, of course, if you like your car better than me it would be a pity to sell it."

"Don't be a little silly! It's you I'm thinking of. We could have picnics on Sundays if we had a car . . . and all sorts of fun. As a matter of fact a car saves quite a lot of money in taxis and railway fares."

"What nonsense," cried Leda. "You know that's nonsense, Derek."

"All right, it's nonsense," replied Derek, turning his head and looking in the other direction. "You know much more about keeping a car than I do."

"I know it's expensive," she retorted. "The garage fees and the petrol and oil and — and everything."

"You don't seem to understand," Derek told her with an elaborate show of patience. "Don't you see that if I went into business and got a job with a good screw we could be married and have a car as well. There would be no need to scrimp and scramp and count every penny."

"It would be better to get your degree first — "

"Damn my degree!" he exclaimed.

They were silent for a little while.

"Oh, Derek, don't let's quarrel," said Leda at last in a shaky voice.

He turned at once and put his arm round her and they kissed each other. "There," he said. "We love each other, don't we?"

"Of course," agreed Leda, mopping her eyes. "Of course we do, Derek darling. That's all that matters, isn't it? But you won't do anything silly, will you?"

They rose and walked on, for it was too cold to sit there any longer.

Leda's mother could have told her that she had mismanaged her part in this important conversation (she had shown a complete lack of sympathy and under-standing and she had said things which Derek would remember and resent when she was not there to kiss and be kissed), but Leda thought her mother old-fashioned and silly. Leda was quite satisfied that she had played her part well.

13

DEREK intended to go straight back to Oxford that evening so he said good-bye to Leda and started off, but before he had gone very far he changed his mind. It would be much more sensible to spend the night at Ash House and have a talk with his father and sound him about the tooth-paste plan. I shan't say anything definite, thought Derek, as he turned in at the gate. I'll just sound him carefully and see what he says . . . then I could call in and see Leda tomorrow morning.

He had not expected that Rhoda would be at Ash House, for Rhoda worked hard and her visits were less frequent than his own, so he was surprised when he walked into the library to find her sitting there, reading the papers.

"Hallo, old stick!" she exclaimed. "What are you doing here? I thought you had your nose to the grindstone these days."

"What made you think that?" inquired Derek.

"The parent, of course. He told me little Derek had turned over a new leaf. It's astonishing what curious ideas he seems to get hold of."

"I'm working much harder," said Derek, huffily. "I can't work *all* the time."

"All work and no play makes Derek a dull boy," agreed Rhoda. "So you ought to be absolutely dazzling . . . but I don't mind telling you the parent won't be particularly pleased to see you."

Sir Michael was not particularly pleased to see his only son. "I thought you were going to stick in and do some work for a change," declared Sir Michael. "What's the use of me paying out hundreds of pounds of good money if you gad about the country instead of sticking in to your work!"

Derek hesitated. Here was his opportunity. He could say it was no use, that he was sick of the whole thing and wanted a job instead . . . but somehow he couldn't say it.

"I can't understand you," continued Sir Michael. "How d'you think you're going to support a wife if you won't work? When I was engaged to your mother I worked like a nigger for promotion. I wanted to have something to offer her; I wanted to show her what I could do. I never expected my father to support my wife; didn't want it . . . wanted to do it myself."

"I will," said Derek hastily. "I mean, of course. I'm working harder. I'm going back early tomorrow morning. I'm just going to call in at Vittoria Cottage for a few minutes on the way and then go straight back."

Rhoda looked up from her paper. "Going to the Cottage?" she said. "You can take me and drop me there. It'll save Blink's petrol."

Derek had intended to be on his way early, but by the time Rhoda was ready it was ten o'clock, and it was nearly half-past ten when they drove up to the gate of Vittoria Cottage in Derek's little car.

"It's a darling house, isn't it?" said Rhoda as she uncurled her long legs and got out. "We've had lovely times here. I always enjoyed the Derings' parties. Mrs. Dering is a pet."

"She's a bit silly and old-fashioned," replied Derek. "She doesn't move with the times — I wonder if any one is in."

"Won't Leda be in?" asked his sister in surprise.

"She isn't expecting me. I meant to go back to Oxford last night, but — "

"Mrs. Dering is sure to be in," said Rhoda confidently.

"Mrs. Dering has gone to London."

"Goodness, why didn't you tell me! I wouldn't have come."

"I thought you wanted to see Leda," Derek replied.

Rhoda did not comment upon this. She had no wish to see Leda, but now she was here she had better see her and get it over . . . if Leda were here to be seen. The house had an empty sort of look (Rhoda thought) and the front door was locked — a most unusual circumstance.

Rhoda rang the bell and they waited.

"Every one's out," said Derek impatiently.

"It looks like it," agreed Rhoda. "No, hold on! I hear someone coming!"

Comfort opened the door.

"Hallo, Comfort!" exclaimed Rhoda. "I haven't seen you for centuries — not since the Guides — how are you?"

"I'm all right, Miss Ware," replied Comfort smiling.

"Where is Miss Dering?" asked Derek.

"There now," said Comfort, her smile vanishing. "There now, isn't that provoking! The young ladies are both out. Miss Bobbie went off to the village to fetch the fish."

"I wanted to see Miss Dering," Derek told her.

"She's out, too. I don't know where she's gone."

"Didn't she tell you?" asked Derek. "Didn't she say when she'd be back? It's rather important."

"No, she didn't," replied Comfort. "Her and Miss Bobbie had a row and she went off in a huff. Goodness knows when she'll be back. I don't."

"How sickening!" said Rhoda, who was all keyed up to congratulate her future sister-in-law and was anxious to get the unpleasant task off her chest. "How perfectly sickening! Perhaps we could come in and wait for a few minutes, could we?"

Comfort welcomed the plan. She showed them into the drawing-room and, having tidied the cushions and made up the fire, she went away and left them.

Rhoda flung herself into a chair and crossed her legs. "Dear old elephant!" said Rhoda. "We loved her in the Guides. She was so good-natured."

"I think she's frightful," declared Derek. "It gives me a pain to look at her — and the idea of talking about Leda like that!"

"Leda often takes the huff," said Rhoda casually.

"She doesn't! I mean not nowadays. Of course she used to be a bit touchy when she was a child but she's quite different now."

"People don't change their natures."

"Rhoda," said Derek earnestly. "I do wish you'd be decent about Leda. I thought you were going to be decent or I wouldn't have brought you. I thought you were going to — to congratulate her and — and that sort of thing."

"I'll congratulate her all right. It's you I'm not congratulating. The truth is I never could stand Leda," added Rhoda with devastating frankness.

Derek was struck dumb.

"Oh, I know it's a pretty frightful thing to say about my future S-in-L," continued

Rhoda, leaning back and putting her hands behind her head. "But I never was much use at pretending things. It's mutual, of course, Leda can't stand me. You may as well know it, Derek."

"Rhoda!"

"It's because she *will* tell people what they ought to do, and she's always right," said Rhoda thoughtfully. "When we were children she was always held up as an example: look how good Leda is! Leda never tears her frock; Leda never loses her hair-ribbon; Leda never gets dirty or untidy . . . and it was too true, dear little Leda never did."

Derek was crimson to the ears. "You *are* a beast, Rhoda!" he cried.

"I know," agreed Rhoda. "I'm a beast — it's the way I'm made. Take no notice of what I say. After all, if you think she's perfectly marvellous, it doesn't matter a hoot what I think." She had taken out a long cigarette-holder and having fitted it with a cigarette, looked about for a light. Derek produced his lighter and lighted it.

"I *do* want you to get on well," he said persuasively.

"We never did."

"She's quite different now."

"Good."

"Honestly, Rhoda — "

"All right, let be. She's your choice. I shan't ask you to be bosom friends with my husband — when I get one. You'll hate him, most likely, but I shall expect you to be polite to him, that's all. I'm quite prepared to be polite to Leda as long as she doesn't keep on telling me what I ought to do. Perhaps you like being told what you ought to do — it drives me mad."

"I think you're absolutely foul," said Derek gloomily.

"Dash it all, what have I said?" asked Rhoda smiling at him in a friendly manner. "You'd think I'd said she was a thief or something. I only said she's always right and loves telling people what they ought to do."

It was almost impossible to quarrel with Rhoda, besides Derek didn't want to quarrel with her . . . and, of course, there was a good deal of truth in what she had said. Leda had told him he ought to work harder, that he ought to stick to his guns and, last but by no means least, that he ought to sell his car.

"I'd better be getting along," said Derek. "It's no use waiting, and I'm going to a tennis-party at the Brights' this afternoon."

"The Tooth-Paste King," nodded Rhoda, who had been told about the Brights. She hesitated and then asked, "Why don't you tell Dad you want to make tooth-paste?"

"There'd be such a row."

"Not if you did it properly," said Rhoda. "Dad's all right if you take him the right way. He would understand if you explained the whole thing and told him what you felt about it. He would be a bit fed-up, of course — who wouldn't — but he would see the sense of it, especially if you told him you haven't a hope of graduating next year — you haven't, have you?"

"Not a hope," agreed Derek in gloomy tones.

"I thought not," said Rhoda, nodding. "Only brilliant people can afford to slack and you aren't brilliant, are you, ducky? So the best thing is to cut your losses and get down to something useful — like tooth-paste. Would old Bright take you?"

"I haven't asked him."

"Why don't you ask him?"

Derek was silent. The fact was he couldn't make up his mind. When he saw Mr. Bright it seemed to Derek that it would be better to ask his father first — before he spoke to Mr. Bright about it — and when he was with his father it seemed better to do it the other way about.

"There are other things besides tooth-paste," Rhoda continued. "I know someone whose father makes cement; I could pull a string there, if you like. Dad might prefer cement to tooth-paste. He might think it more respectable." Rhoda chuckled to herself, for the idea amused her.

"It's no laughing matter," said Derek with an offended air. "It's important. I'm standing at the cross-roads."

"I should move," Rhoda replied. "Cross-roads are dangerous. You may get run over if you linger there too long . . . Oh, yes, I'm sympathetic, all right, but it seems odd to me that you can't make up your mind. I always know what I want."

"You always get what you want," said Derek bitterly.

"That's why, you ass!" exclaimed Rhoda. "I know what I want and I go all out for it .. I don't stand at the cross-roads and wait for somebody to give me a shove. Why don't you get a move on!" cried Rhoda impatiently. "If you want to make tooth-paste, go ahead and make it. If you want to marry Leda, marry her!"

Derek was silent. It was all so difficult. Rhoda didn't realise how difficult it was. What was the sense of burning your boats before you had made up your mind whether you wanted to advance or retreat. He wanted to marry Leda — of course he did — but he had begun to realise that marriage with Leda wouldn't be all honey and jam. It would be pretty rotten to live in cheap digs, to have no car and no money for fun and games . . . you dropped out of things pretty quickly when people discovered you were short of cash.

14

CAROLINE had enjoyed her visit to London but she was very glad to get home and her welcome was more than satisfactory: Leda, Bobbie and Joss were waiting for her at the front door when she arrived, Comfort's smiling face was in the background. Caroline hugged her daughters, patted Joss and returned Comfort's greeting . . . everybody was talking at once.

"Why did you go away!" Bobbie cried. "It's been absolutely deadly without you!"

"I went away so that I could come back, of course," laughed Caroline.

"What about the play?" asked Leda.

"I thought it was marvellous," declared Caroline. "I enjoyed every moment of it, but apparently it isn't a tremendous success. . . ."

Supper was ready so they sat down and Caroline continued to tell them about *Eve's Dilemma* and about the supper-party which had followed it. All the cast had been present . . . it had been tremendous fun.

"Now for your news," said Caroline at last. "What has been happening here?"

Quite a lot of things had happened in Ashbridge during Caroline's absence. Leda had been to see Miss Penworthy and it had been arranged that she was to go over to Wandlebury daily with Anne Severn and help in the school. Miss Penworthy had seemed very glad to have her and had asked her to start on Monday.

"And Derek came over one day," continued Leda. "He's working very hard, of course, and he won't have any more petrol till the beginning of next month."

"He came again yesterday morning," said Bobbie. "He and Rhoda looked in for a minute but we were both out."

"Yesterday morning!" cried Leda.

"Didn't Comfort tell you?" asked Bobbie in surprise.

"No, she didn't — oh, what a beast she is!"

"It's because you're a beast to her," retorted Bobbie. "And anyhow what does it matter? They only called for a minute and you were out."

"But I wasn't out!" cried Leda. "I was in the garden. Why didn't she come and tell me they were here?"

"You never said where you were going," declared Bobbie, becoming heated, "It was after that row about the fish and you just walked off with your head in the air. I didn't know where you were going, so how could Comfort know?"

"She knew perfectly well," stormed Leda. "She did it on purpose — "

"She didn't!" cried Bobbie. "Comfort isn't that sort!"

"Leda! Bobbie!" Caroline exclaimed.

They relapsed into silence.

"It's dreadful," said Caroline. "It is really quite unbearable. You do nothing but argue and quarrel. I suppose you've been quarrelling ever since I went away."

"Not really," mumbled Bobbie. "I mean not all the time."

"I don't like it," Caroline said. "I'm not going to stand it. Why should I have to sit and listen to you quarrelling all day long?"

It was so seldom that Caroline took a strong line that her daughters were quite alarmed. They gazed at her in amazement.

They looked so astonished that she had some difficulty in hiding a smile for she had far too lively a sense of humour. The fact was Caroline had been brooding over Harriet's imputation that her daughters were spoilt and that she was to blame for spoiling them . . . but they were not to know this, of course.

"Mr. Shepperton came to tea one day," said Bobbie, changing the subject hastily. "We did stamps together; he knows a lot about stamps."

"She shouldn't have asked him, should she?" Leda put in.

"Why shouldn't I? Everybody was out—"

"That's why," Leda told her.

"I suppose you'd have liked me to sit here all alone the whole afternoon!" cried Bobbie with mounting rage. "You didn't care if I was lonely—not you! You and Derek went off together so why shouldn't I have Mr. Shepperton?"

"It's quite different," said Leda with infuriating calmness. "Derek and I happen to be engaged. Mr. Shepperton is a stranger, we don't know anything about him and—"

"I like him!" cried Bobbie.

"I don't," retorted Leda. "Derek doesn't like him, either. There's something very queer about him, you can't deny that. Why does he live at the Cock and Bull? How does he manage to have such marvellous clothes?"

Caroline had listened to all this in silence but now she thought it was time to interfere. She knew a little about Mr. Shepperton and saw no reason why she should withhold the information from her daughters. Bobbie was horrified to hear of her new friend's misfortune but Leda was less sympathetic.

"It makes him more mysterious than ever," Leda pointed out. "Where was he all those years and why didn't somebody write and tell him that his house had been bombed? If he had been in the Army, somewhere abroad, he would have heard about it officially."

Caroline had wondered about this herself, but she liked him and was willing to take him on trust.

"Of course, he may have been in prison," added Leda.

"Leda!" cried Bobbie indignantly.

"Ask him," suggested Leda with a superior smile. "You're such friends he might tell you . . . or he might not. There's no harm in trying."

"That's enough!" exclaimed Caroline, putting her foot down again.

"Oh, well, I was only warning you," said Leda.

After that things went more smoothly, the subjects discussed were less controversial. Bobbie had received a letter from James who held out strong hopes of coming home in the Spring.

"He's coming on Python," said Bobbie handing over the letter. "Goodness knows what that means."

"Python is a ship — " began Leda.

"No," said Caroline (who had heard about Python already). "No, Python isn't a ship, it's a — it's just a name for — for — I mean when men come home from FARELF after doing their three years they say they are *coming home on Python*. And if you want to know what FARELF means," added Caroline cheerfully, "it means Far Eastern Land Forces."

Her daughters looked at her in surprise. Bobbie put their feelings into words.

"You seem — you seem in terrific form, Mummy!" said Bobbie in puzzled tones.

Living with Harriet in the whirl of London there had been no time to write letters and Caroline had a sheaf of letters waiting to be answered. She must write to Jean and thank her for a parcel (which had arrived at Vittoria Cottage during Caroline's absence) and of course she must write to James. The others could wait.

It was easy to write to James. Even when there was no news at all except tittle tattle from the village and the chronicle of everyday life at Vittoria Cottage her pen ran on and on, for she knew James liked hearing about all she did. When he was quite a little boy and she had been away from him for a few days she always had to tell him the whole story. "Tell me from the very beginning," he would say. "Tell me all your ventures." Tonight Caroline had plenty of news for James and, unlike the famous Lady Bertram, she was fortunate in having the telling of it all to herself without any one else to spoil it. She could spread herself over Leda's engagement and Sir Michael's midnight visit — that would amuse him vastly — and then she could tell him about her visit to London and the play, and Harriet's queer friends and various "ventures" which had befallen her in the Big City.

It was late when she started her letter; the girls had gone to bed and the house was very quiet. The clock ticked industriously. Writing to James was almost like talking to him, it made him seem very near. She could almost feel his presence in the room . . . but he wasn't in the room, he was thousands of miles away. What was he doing at this moment? Caroline laid down her pen and gave her imagination free rein. She had worked out the difference in time so she was aware that if it was midnight in England it was half-past seven in Malaya. James would be awake — he always woke early — perhaps he had wakened in his room at the base in Kuala Lumpur, or perhaps he had spent the night hunting bandits. She knew a little about the country, not only from James's letters but also from books which she had obtained from the library; it was hot and damp, there were low-lying belts of land, mangrove swamps and rice fields, and there were mountains in the interior clothed with forests. She tried to imagine James in this sort of land . . . but somehow she couldn't. It was impossible to imagine James in a place she had never seen.

Caroline sighed and took up her pen.

"The First Night was marvellous," wrote Caroline. "I felt almost sick with excitement, waiting for the curtain to go up. It seemed hours — and then suddenly up it went when I wasn't expecting it and *there* was Harriet on the stage, sitting at her desk, writing . . . and the odd thing was it was just Harriet, Harriet herself, looking exactly as I have seen her look a hundred times. All through the play it was the same — it was just Harriet, Harriet doing and saying Harrietish things, talking and laughing quite naturally. The others were not really so like themselves (of course I knew them all because, as I told you, they kept on coming to the flat at all hours of the day — and night — and throwing themselves into chairs and almost weeping and having to be revived with pink gin). Marcus wasn't a bit like himself. You could see he was acting. There is one scene where he and Harriet have a duologue all about a rocking-horse, and there had been a frightful fuss about this because, at the very last moment, the producer wanted to cut it out (fortunately Harriet took a strong line about it and pretended to be annoyed so it wasn't cut out). What happened was this: Marcus had bought a magnificent rocking-horse for his nephew and, at the same time, he had bought a hand-bag for Harriet, and the shop made a mistake and sent the rocking-horse to Harriet. (Of course they are called Eve and Freddie in the play but I just went on thinking of them as Harriet and Marcus.) Harriet unpacks the rocking-horse on the stage — it is all carefully packed in a crate and it was most amusing to see her unpacking it. She wonders why Marcus has sent it. Has it some hidden meaning? She gets on to the rocking-horse and rides it and sings, 'Ride a Rock-Horse to Banbury Cross' and Marcus comes in and watches her — and then suddenly she sees him and they have a conversation about it, all cross purposes and crooked answers. It sounds silly telling you like this but it really was very good and amused me a lot. I thought the whole play most amusing.

Harriet (or I suppose I ought to call her Eve!) gets involved in all sorts of dilemmas; she has two admirers and can't make up her mind which to have, and she also gets involved in a frightfully complicated Black Market ramp in home-cured bacon. It is even *more* complicated because one of her admirers is called Mr. Bacon and Harriet never knows whether they are talking about the man or the pig! But apparently other people didn't like the play as much as I did. The reviews are poor and it may be withdrawn quite soon. It seems dreadful after all their hard work. Fortunately Harriet takes it philosophically and she says if the play is withdrawn she is coming to Vittoria Cottage for a long holiday. I have got more hens, now. We are all being told to Grow More Food so I thought I would grow eggs! It is rather a bother having so many but I feel I am doing something to help the food shortage. I think I told you about Mr. Shepperton in my last letter, he is still at the Cock and Bull and says Mrs. Herbert makes him very comfortable. I think you would like Mr. Shepperton, he is interesting and unusual and has seen a lot of the world . . ."

Caroline paused again. Would James like him? She found that she attached quite a lot of importance to this question . . . but why? By the time James came home — on Python — Mr. Shepperton would have gone. He certainly would not stay at the Cock and Bull for ever.

She took up her pen and finished the letter hastily — it was after one o'clock.

15

MR. HERBERT, the landlord of the Cock and Bull, was a roundabout fellow and merry at heart; his nose was small — or perhaps it only looked small because his smile was so broad — his eyes were dark and twinkling; he was always ready for a joke and to him old jokes were best. The name of his inn was a constant source of amusement to Mr. Herbert. "Don't you tell me no Cock an' Bull stories 'ere," he would say, chuckling. "This ain't the place for Cock an' Bull stories." His favourite joke was to assert that he had married "the missus" because nobody could make a better apple-pie. "Nobody in England," Mr. Herbert would say. "An' that means nobody in the world, That's why I married 'er — see? Because of that, an' because of the bed — a fourposter what belonged to 'er great-aunt Em'ly — that's the most comfor'ble bed in England, that is." He would begin to shake with internal convulsions, his whole ample girth would shake. "Ha, ha!" he would shout. "Ha, ha, ha — apple-pie an' a comfor'ble bed — what more do a man want!"

Mrs. Herbert would smile quietly for she knew quite well why Herbert had married her. He had married her because she had made up her mind he was the man for her — he and no other. Apple-pie indeed!

In addition to the bed, Mrs. Herbert had brought some very nice pictures to the inn as part of her dowry. There was Drake playing bowls, with the Spanish Armada coming up over the horizon; there was a coach and four labouring in deep snow; there was a hunting scene with pink-coated horsemen and the hounds streaming before them in full cry; there was young Queen Victoria receiving the news of her accession to the throne . . . and many more. Mrs. Herbert noticed that people liked her pictures, people would stand and look at the pictures while they waited for their dinner to be brought in. That was as it should be (so Mrs. Herbert thought), for pictures were painted for people to look at, and the more there was in a picture to interest people the better it fulfilled its purpose. Sometimes when strangers came to the inn she would point out the details of her pictures in case they should be overlooked.

The inn itself was an ancient building, old-fashioned and rambling. There were oak beams and wide chimneys and long passages leading nowhere in particular, and unexpected flights of steps. It was exceedingly difficult to manage, but Mrs. Herbert managed it admirably. Her staff consisted of a few very old, experienced servants and a few very raw young girls; there was constant friction between them and scarcely a day passed without "words". Mrs. Herbert was always being summoned to arbitrate in some ridiculous quarrel . . . and occasionally she got so fed up with the whole thing that she would have liked to take the combatants by the scruff of their necks and knock their heads together.

Robert Shepperton liked the Cock and Bull; the food was good, the rooms were clean, and his bed — though only the second-best bed in the house — was extremely comfortable. His jovial host amused him a good deal and his hostess was a gem.

Robert Shepperton had come to Ashbridge as a refugee from the noise and bustle of London. He had hated London — it was so different from the London he remembered. He could not help comparing his present circumstances with the life he had led before the war. In those days he had had a wife, a son, a comfortable home with his own furniture round him; he had had his books, his garden, his friends, who lived near and with whom he could chat and exchange ideas. *Now* he lived in a hotel where nothing belonged to him, he had no books and no friends — there was not a creature who cared whether he was ill or well. It was little wonder that Robert Shepperton looked upon London with a jaundiced eye. Robert saw no graces in this post-war London. It seemed to him that there were no amenities, not even the ordinary little courtesies of everyday life. The houses were shabby and unpainted, there were ruins and rubble, there were crowds everywhere. It seemed to Robert that the difficulty of existing made existence hardly worth while . . . the difficulty of obtaining a decent meal, of buying a pair of shoes, of getting your watch mended . . .

nobody cared whether you got what you wanted or not, take it or leave it was the general attitude. The difficulty of transport was even worse; tubes and buses were crammed to overflowing and people scrambled to enter them in much the same way as panicking people in a shipwreck might scramble for the boats. *Sauve qui peut!*

Robert had been very ill, and although he had now recovered he still felt wretched and miserable. His memories tortured him but he decided that he must face up to them — it was not his nature to run away — so he had gone and looked at his house, or what remained of it, and he had gone and looked at Chelsea Old Church, where he and Wanda had been married. Chelsea Old Church . . . there was not much of that left either.

I was a fool to come, thought Robert.

Perhaps he had spoken aloud or perhaps his attitude betrayed his misery and despair, for at that moment a girl, who happened to be passing, stopped and spoke to him. She was hatless and her hair was pure gold, like a halo framing her lovely face. She was carrying a large flat parcel under her arm.

"It's no good crying over spilt milk, you know," the girl said.

This girl was the first person in London who had taken the slightest interest in Robert, and although her words were somewhat crude her smile was kind.

Robert hesitated for a moment. "It's difficult not to cry over spilt milk when you've no milk left," he told her.

"None at all?" she asked.

"My house was bombed," he replied. "My wife was in it at the time. This was the church where we were married."

She did not say she was sorry nor commiserate with him, but somehow he felt her sympathy. "You should go away," she said.

"Do you think so?" he asked. "I'm trying to face up to it —"

"What's the use of moping about amongst ruins?" said the girl sensibly. "Turn over a new page. Go away. Go anywhere. Go to Ashbridge, it's quiet enough there in all conscience." She smiled at him and turned away and was lost in the crowd.

Robert had never heard of Ashbridge and there was no reason why he should pay the slightest attention to the words of a passer-by, but he was in a fatalistic mood. The girl had been kind; she had seemed to care what happened to him; she had listened to him and had taken the trouble to give him her advice. He went back to the hotel and looked up Ashbridge in the railway time-table; he packed his clothes, paid his bill and shook the dust of London off his feet.

At first Robert found very little solace in the peace of the country; it was almost worse than town, for he had more time to brood over his troubles, and the intense interest which he evoked in the village embarrassed him . . . and embarrassed him all the more because he could not return it. He felt isolated from life, as if there were a pane of glass separating him from his fellow-men and women.

Then he met Caroline Dering. Caroline and Vittoria Cottage seemed to possess the graciousness of life that he remembered. The house was not really run on pre-war lines, for its mistress did far more work, but the atmosphere she created was a survival from that other life, it was an atmosphere of peace and kindness and simple gaiety. You could almost forget the war when you sat in Caroline's drawing-room. Robert had walked in a dream but now he began to awake, he began to feel life flowing round him. He began to take an interest in the place and the people. He had turned over a new page and was beginning to write a new story.

The story began with Caroline Dering, her name was first on the page, but gradually other people came into it — Mrs. Herbert, for instance. Mrs. Herbert talked to Robert and brought him her problems, and he discovered that the problems of the Cock and Bull were very like the problems of the Big World, only seen through the wrong end of a telescope. Here, in this old-fashioned rabbit-warren, the war of personalities and conflicting ideas was waged without ceasing; the Socialist and the Tory, the Idealist and the Materialist, the Worker and the Idler fought and squabbled and argued from morning to night. Mrs. Herbert poured oil upon the stormy seas or sometimes raised a storm on her own account and rode the hurricane.

One evening Robert strolled into the

bar and took part in a game of darts
and he was so well amused that he went
again and made a habit of it. At first he
was a restraining influence (the talk died
away when he appeared and the habitués
were on their best behaviour), but soon
they left off bothering. They decided Mr
Shepperton was a good sport; he was
quiet and unassuming and fond of a joke
and he was always ready to stand a round
of drinks to keep the ball rolling. He was
neither very good at darts nor very bad, a
circumstance that added greatly to his
popularity. Young Mumper was the best
performer, but Silas Podbury ran him
pretty close — Silas was one of Comfort's
many cousins.

"You should see Jim Widgeon," said
old Mr. Coney confidentially. "Jim could
beat 'em all left-'anded, but 'e's married
now and don't never come no more."

Mr. Coney had hardly finished speaking
when Jim Widgeon walked in, looking a
trifle self-conscious. He was received with
shouts of welcome and jeers of derision
from the assembled company. The assembled company wished to be informed
what Jim did with himself in the evenings

. . . various amusements were suggested. The humour was coarse and Elizabethan and quite unfit to record, but it did not offend the ears of Robert Shepperton for it was natural and unaffected and this was the right time and place for it. Young Widgeon took it in good part and returned measure for measure.

"Yes, I like Sue better'n darts," he declared. "What's more, I like 'er better'n beer."

"Sue likes you better'n toffee-apples, I s'pose," jeered young Mumper.

"Better'n you, any'ow, Tom Mumper," returned Widgeon with a grin.

This brought down the house, for it was well known that young Mumper had been high up in the running for Sue until Widgeon had cut him out.

Widgeon had a few games of darts and several pints of beer, but he went off early, and as sober as a judge, saying he must fetch Sue from her mother's, where she had been spending the evening, and escort her home.

"Changed, that's what," was the verdict of the company. "It's marriage what does it." "Sue's got 'im under 'er thumb."

The younger men lamented the change in their boon companion, but the older and staider were loud in their approval.

Robert played darts if he were wanted, but he really preferred talking to the older men and hearing about things that had happened in Ashbridge long ago. Their memories went far back into the dim past and sometimes they told and retold stories of events which had occurred long before they were born and of which they must have heard from their grandfathers . . . and these events got muddled up in their ancient minds with events in which they had participated.

"Ah! Ye should 'ave seen the bonfire we 'ad when Queen Victoria were coronated," said old Mr. Mumper in his squeaky voice, which always reminded Robert of an ungreased wheelbarrow. "That there bonfire on Vee Jay Day weren't a patch on it. Great logs, we'ad, soaked in tar, an' piles of brushwood fifty feet 'igh. That were a sight, that were. Squire lent 'is 'orses to pull the stuff up the 'ill an' us young ones went from 'ouse to 'ouse collectin' rubbidge. On Cock 'ill, it were. Up there by the gravel-pit, it were, just above Vittoria

Cottage. Well, that were a good place an' not in nobody's way. But then the wind got up an' the bonfire got out of 'and — there it were, blazing like a furnace, an' the bits of blazing wood went whirling down on Vittoria Cottage till I thought every minit the cottage would be set alight an' a fine old bonfire that would 'ave been."

"That would be when the cottage still 'ad its ex-crescents," Mr. Coney remarked.

"Ah, it were before you 'ad a go at 'em," chuckled Mr. Mumper.

"Ex-crescents?" asked Robert.

"Wooden ornaments, prime to take afire," explained old Mr. Podbury.

"The kind what you see on the pier at Brighton," explained Mr. Mumper.

"Baroque ornaments?" suggested Robert.

"That's right, barracks," agreed Mr. Coney with a smile which showed his toothless gums. "There now, I got it. I bin tryin' to remember the name Mr. John Dering called them there ex-crescents, an' I couldn't; an' now this gentleman comes along an' says it right off — there's a funny thing! I knowed it 'ad something to do with soldiers but I couldn't get it nohow."

"You tell the gentleman the story," said Mr. Mumper generously.

"So I will," nodded Mr. Coney. "It were like this . . ." and he launched forth into his story about how Mr. John Dering had told him to remove the "ex-crescents" and Mr. Arnold Dering had wanted them replaced.

" 'E were a fule," declared Mr. Mumper.

"A poor thing," commented Mr. Podbury.

"A complainin' man," nodded Mr. Coney. "Always complainin' 'e were — an' what 'ad 'e to complain of?"

The verdict was that Mr. Arnold Dering, far from having grounds for complaint, was an exceedingly fortunate individual since he had possessed a good wife, three fine children, a comfortable house and as much money as he needed.

"Ah!" agreed old Mr. Podbury, who was Comfort's grandfather and therefore considered himself an authority on the Dering family. "Mrs. Dering's all right — a fine lady she be."

"An' Mr. James," put in Mr. Coney.

"Mr. James is a fine young gentleman. 'E were too young for 'itler's war, but 'e's fightin' now in foreign parts — "

"Fightin' bandits," agreed Mr. Podbury. "Comin' 'ome in the spring, Comfort says."

16

ONE morning when Caroline got up and looked out of her window she felt a distinct nip in the air . . . the sun was rising from behind Cock Hill amongst banks of golden-lined clouds, but the rest of the sky was a clear pale blue. Winter was coming, but Caroline did not mind winter now. She had dreaded it when Arnold was alive. "There's gorgeous sunshine in Egypt," Arnold would say. "Do you realise that, Caroline? Now, at this very moment when this wretched country is shrouded in fog there are places where the sun is shining." He would shiver ostentatiously and add, "If it were not for the children and this ridiculous little house, hanging round our necks like a millstone, you and I could be basking in gorgeous sunshine." These complaints and others of the same kind used to distress Caroline — in fact they frightened her — for she felt it was wrong to complain of the children and the house. Supposing they were taken away! Supposing some awful fate befell the children and the house went on fire and was burnt to the ground! Fortunately the Powers that Be were kind and had not listened to Arnold.

It was such a lovely day that Caroline decided to give herself a holiday, she would start off directly after lunch and have a long walk over the moor. The girls were going to Wandlebury to spend the day with friends, so Caroline was completely free. She took a stick in her hand and set forth with a swinging step . . . up the hill, she went, past the gravel pit and on to the moor . . . and as she went she thought about all the things that were happening. Some of the things were pleasant, others slightly worrying.

Life goes on monotonously for certain periods of time and one gets the feeling that it will go on just the same for ever, and then suddenly a whole lot of things begin to happen all at once and the monotonous period is over. There was Leda's engagement, for instance; that was one of the slightly worrying things, for Caroline could not see the future clearly and it was not very satisfactory for Leda to be engaged without any definite prospect of marriage. Robert Shepperton was another event in Caroline's uneventful existence. He had become her friend, and it was pleasant to have a new friend — especially one with whom she felt so comfortable. He had been wretchedly unhappy when first he came to Ashbridge, but lately his spirits had improved; Caroline had noticed this and was very glad about it. Then there was Harriet. *Eve's Dilemma* had been withdrawn, so Harriet would be here tomorrow. Caroline wondered how Harriet was feeling about it . . . but it would be delightful to have her for a long visit. Last, but not least, it was now practically certain that James was coming home in the spring.

Caroline enjoyed her walk in spite of the fact that a cold east wind got up and the sky became grey and overcast. She was on her way home and had reached the top of the hill when she saw a man come out of the little wood and begin to walk slowly towards her. He was carrying a gun and he had a spaniel with him. It was Sir Michael, of course, and this was Sir Michael's ground. Although he had told

Caroline a dozen times that she might go anywhere she liked, she felt a trifle uneasy in case she had disturbed the game. Perhaps she should turn and go back, thought Caroline, hesitating. At this moment a covey of partridges rose, almost at her feet, and flew straight over Sir Michael. He threw up his gun and got a right and left . . . and two brown balls of feathers came tumbling out of the sky.

Well, he can't complain! thought Caroline, smiling to herself. She waited where she was until the spaniel had found the birds and taken them to his master.

Sir Michael waved and came towards her. "Good!" he cried. "Good work!" He looked fit and ruddy and cheerful . . . and somehow less enormous than usual; perhaps it was because he was in his proper surroundings. He was wearing brown leather gaiters and an exceedingly old suit of plus-fours which had faded to a moory sort of colour. "Good work!" he repeated as he came nearer. "Well done, Caroline! Couldn't have been better if we'd arranged it."

Caroline was amused at this undeserved praise; she had done nothing — absolutely nothing — but he was as delighted with her as if she had been extremely clever. He was so enchanted with her performance that he had called her Caroline, which he had never done before in all the years she had known him . . . but perhaps it is because we are going to be related by marriage, thought Caroline vaguely.

"I've been stalking that covey all afternoon," he told her. "Nearly gave up — and then I thought I'd have one more try. Just shows, doesn't it?"

"Yes," she agreed. "Your perseverance was rewarded."

"A nice brace," he said, holding it up. "You must have the birds, of course — that goes without saying."

She tried to refuse graciously but he would take no denial. "You've earned them," he declared. "I never saw a neater bit of work in my life. Here they are! You don't mind carrying them home, do you?"

Caroline did not mind in the least; a brace of partridges would be a very welcome addition to her ill-filled larder.

"That's right then," he said with satisfaction. "Sensible woman! Don't go and eat them too soon. They ought to hang for a week at least in this weather . . . cold, isn't it?"

"But very pleasant weather for a good walk," said Caroline. She was amused when she found herself making the platitudinous reply.

"Yes," he agreed, nodding. "Better than yesterday. I had Shepperton out with me yesterday — that fellow who's staying at the Cock and Bull. D'you know him?"

Caroline said she did.

"Nice fellow," Sir Michael continued. "A bit of a puzzle in some ways. Doesn't say much about himself, does he? He doesn't seem to have a gun — I lent him one of mine — but he's a damned fine shot all the same. We didn't get a record bag but it was very pleasant, very pleasant indeed."

Caroline murmured that she was glad.

"The fellow's been ill — I only found that out at the end. I wouldn't have taken him so far if I'd known about it to start with. You shouldn't overdo things when you've been ill," said Sir Michael gravely. "I'm never ill, myself, of course. How is everybody? Good news from James?"

"Yes, he seems quite fit — "

"And Leda? Is Leda all right?"

"Yes, thank you."

"Derek seems a bit more settled. He's working better — hasn't been gadding about so much."

"Leda has settled down, too," said Caroline . . . and then she wondered if this were true. Leda was so secretive, you never knew what she was feeling; some days Leda seemed fairly happy and other days not. Caroline guessed that her ups and downs depended upon Derek's letters, but it was only guesswork of course.

"You can tell her it's fixed," Sir Michael said.

"Fixed!" exclaimed Caroline.

"Yes, my lawyers have agreed to take Derek into the firm when he gets his degree. It's an old-established firm in London and it should give him a decent start. I'll have to stump up some money, of course, and it means selling Betterlands Farm, which has been in the family for generations, but we can't help that, the important thing is to get the boy well settled. I've written to Derek and told him, so you can tell Leda. She'll be pleased, I expect."

"Of course she'll be pleased," said Caroline warmly. "It's very generous of you, Sir Michael."

"Oh well," he mumbled. "Must get them fixed up."

"Leda will have a little of her own. It's all in trust, but I've been into it with my lawyer and she'll have about two hundred a year."

"Better than nothing. They ought to manage if they're careful . . . Rhoda's coming," he added, changing the subject abruptly. "She's coming down on that frightful contraption of hers. Going to stay for a bit and have a rest. Rhoda works too hard and Derek doesn't work hard enough. Odd, isn't it? We're having a party for Rhoda's birthday, you must all come."

"That will be lovely," Caroline said.

It was time to go home now. Sir Michael handed over the partridges and said good-bye. She watched him walk away across the moor and thought how kind he was — how good and solid and generous beneath his somewhat awe-inspiring manner — and she thought he must be lonely living all by himself in Ash House with nobody to talk to and only the old couple to "do for him", but he never complained or worried other people with his troubles. She had noticed a button missing from his jacket and an undarned tear in his elbow. How distressed Alice would be if she knew! thought Caroline.

17

THE light was fading when Caroline got to the top of Cock Hill; the sky was grey, the wind was very cold, the village seemed to cower beneath its cruelty . . . and then suddenly, as she went down the path by the side of the gravel pit, the darkness overcame the grey light. One moment it was a cold grey afternoon and the next moment it was gloaming. The lights sprang up in the village, first one and then another — then three — four — seven — ten — until nearly every little cottage boasted a square of faint amber light and the village was no longer a bleak, deserted, cowering village but a whole encampment of little homes . . . warm comfortable homes with tea laid out upon their kitchen tables and a friendly kettle singing on the hob. Caroline's own lights were especially welcoming. She saw them from afar off and hastened her steps.

Tea was ready in the drawing-room, the fire was burning brightly and the curtains were drawn. Robert Shepperton rose from an armchair as she went in.

"I hope you don't mind," he said. "Comfort insisted that I should come in and wait for you. She found the girls were out and you would be glad of company."

Caroline was glad, not because she minded being alone — it was rather pleasant sometimes — but because she liked her uninvited guest; he was a comfortable companion and she could be silent with him or chatter, just as she felt inclined. It was because he was comfortable with her of course, for these feelings work in both directions or not at all. She sat down and began to tell him her news — the great news that Derek and Leda were to be married next year.

"You're happy about it," said Robert, nodding.

Caroline hesitated for a moment. "It's what they want," she said. "I want Leda to be happy."

"Of course," he agreed. "We all want our children to be happy. I feel the same about Philip. One must just hope they will choose right."

"You don't like Derek?" she asked.

"That doesn't matter, does it? If Leda likes him — if he's the right person for her — but I'm afraid I was thinking of my own child when I made that remark. The fact is I've had a letter from Philip which has given me rather a shock. He says . . . but perhaps you would read it."

Caroline took the letter and unfolded it and read it through; it was well written in a round schoolboy hand:

DEAR FATHER,

I was very pleased to hear you are better and it will be good to see you when you come over here in the spring, but I would rather stay here and not go back to England. I like America very much and I like Mr. and Mrs. Honeyman very much. It would be quite different in England and I would feel strange after being here so long. The school would be different, too. I would not get much food, would I? I get very good food here and Mrs. Honeyman says I am growing fast and I need it. We went for a picnic last week, it was the Sunday School picnic. First we ran races and I won second prize, then we had two hot dogs and buckwheat cakes with butter and maple syrup, and then we had ice-cream and ice-cream soda with chocolate on the top, and we had fruit and marsh mallows and whipped cream and candy. It was a very good picnic. Mr. Honeyman wants me to stay and he says he will pay for everything. He says he is going to write and tell you. I hope you will let me stay as I do not want to leave Mr. and Mrs. Honeyman and I know I would not like England and you have not got a home or anything. Please write soon and say it is OK.

Love from

PHILIP.

Caroline was horrified for she knew how much Mr. Shepperton had been looking forward to having Philip home. Philip was all he had in the world . . . she was so shocked that she could find nothing to say.

"It's a blow, of course," said Robert quietly. "Somehow I never expected this; I thought Philip was looking forward to coming home, just as I was looking forward to having him. It was foolish of me, of course; I ought to have seen it from his point of view. He has been with the

Honeymans for years — ever since he was eight years old — and they have treated him as if he were their own child, so it would be unnatural if he were not fond of them."

"You're his father!"

"Yes, but he scarcely knows me."

"It's terribly hard!"

He thought she meant it was hard to decide what to do and replied at once, "Oh, Philip must do as he wants — and as they want — I don't feel I have any claim. Besides, how could I bring him over here when he doesn't want to come? It would be an impossible situation. And of course I see, now that I think of it, how difficult it would be for him to adjust himself to life in England."

"It certainly would be very difficult to feed him," said Caroline with a lift of her brows.

He smiled quite cheerfully in return. "You've said it," he agreed. "Philip sounds a little greedy, doesn't he? I dare say I was greedy when I was twelve."

Caroline had thought at first that it was a cruel letter, but now she took it up and read it again more carefully. It was not cruel, it was just child-like. Children are ruthless because they have not learned pity, they are inconsiderate because they have never experienced pain. When Philip had written the letter he had not seen his father receiving it, Philip had just sat down and written exactly what he was feeling with absolute honesty and, as Robert had said, you couldn't blame him. You couldn't blame the Honeymans either; they had taken care of Philip for four years and obviously were devoted to him, and — also obviously — could not bear the idea of their precious foster-child being taken away to austerity conditions and deprived of his proper nourishment. You could blame nobody, you could only be sorry for Robert . . . how could he bear it? Caroline was thinking of Philip in terms of James and she decided that if James did not want to come home to her but preferred somebody else as a parent, she would just — she would just lie down and die.

"Robert!" she exclaimed, "I don't know what to say. It sounds ridiculous to say I'm sorry."

"Don't worry too much," he replied.

"It's a great disappointment but it isn't a grief. It would have been much worse if I had known Philip and lost him. Philip is an abstract idea to me rather than a personality. Of course I have been looking forward to having him and making friends with him and enjoying his companionship. I thought it would be tremendous fun to show him round and give him presents, to take him down to Marlborough . . . but it can't be helped. It would be no use at all unless he enjoyed it."

"Yes, I see that," agreed Caroline. "But I must say I think you're taking it very well, Mr. Shepperton."

"You called me Robert a moment ago," said Robert, smiling.

"Oh, it was a mistake!"

"I thought it sounded friendly."

Caroline laughed and blushed. "It's old-fashioned to stand on ceremony," she said. "I found that when I was staying with Harriet; none of her friends possessed any surnames — or, if they did, I never heard them! But they all called me Caroline straight off, which made it easier."

"I'm quite willing to make it easier," said Robert smilingly.

They said no more on the subject, in fact Caroline changed the subject rather hastily. "You're looking much better," she told him. "Ashbridge is doing you good . . ."

Robert agreed that it was. They discussed Ashbridge and the people — especially the Podbury family — and Caroline tried to explain the ramifications of the Podburys to her friend but without much success, for in fact the ramifications were so far-reaching and so complicated by inter-marriage that unless you had lived in Ashbridge all your life there was little hope of understanding them.

"I'm afraid it's beyond me," declared Robert as he rose to go home. "I could never get them straight without pen and paper, but I've learnt one thing about them. Old Mr. Ebenezer Podbury had seventeen children and they all survived and settled in Ashbridge."

"That's enough to go on with," said Caroline, laughing.

Robert had learnt one thing about the Podburys but he had also learnt something about himself which — though less important to Ashbridge — was more important to himself. He had realised quite suddenly that he was happy. He had lost Wanda and now he had lost Philip; he ought to be miserable . . . but he was not. Being honest with oneself is often a startling experience, and as Robert walked back to the Cock and Bull he tried to be completely honest with himself and was considerably startled at the result. He discovered that he had ceased to yearn for Wanda; he still grieved for her, of course, but the grief he felt was for her untimely death and not for his own loss. He had passed on from that part of his life and left it behind him. Life is transitory, thought Robert as he strolled along in the dark. Nothing in this world is permanent — neither sorrow nor joy — and only a foolish person would ask for permanence. We don't stand still, thought Robert. We are travellers upon the path of life. No traveller can bathe twice in the same stream. He bathes and goes on his way and, if the road is dusty and hot, he may look back longingly and think of the clear cool water with regret . . . but presently he may come upon another stream, different of course, but equally delightful to bathe in.

Part Two

18

HARRIET arrived at Vittoria Cottage the next day. Caroline and Bobbie were waiting for her, they had spent all morning clearing out the garage to make room for her little car. She drove it into the space allotted to her and got out.

"Darling Aunt Harrie!" cried Bobbie flinging herself upon her aunt and enveloping her in caresses.

"You're bigger than ever and *much* stronger," declared Harriet when at last she could speak.

"Not fatter, am I?" inquired Bobbie anxiously. "I don't want to get like Comfort. I do exercises every morning and walk miles with Joss, but the worst of it is it makes me hungry. What do you think I ought to do?"

"Live in London on one person's rations," said her aunt without hesitation.

They went into the house together talking and laughing.

Caroline had been worried about Harriet (the failure of *Eve's Dilemma* must have been a disappointment); she looked for signs of discouragement or dejection but none were visible. It was a great relief but also extremely puzzling, for Caroline judged others by herself and she knew that she would have felt disheartened if she had been in Harriet's shoes.

"It will be lovely to have you," Bobbie was saying. "You'll stay for ages, won't you? You *must* meet Mr. Shepperton. I've told him all about you and he's never known a real-live actress before."

"Who is Mr. Shepperton?"

"Oh, a man," replied Bobbie. "His house was bombed so he's staying at the Cock and Bull and he likes stamps."

"A philatelist," nodded Harriet.

"No," said Bobbie doubtfully. "At least I don't think so — not specially — he's quite sensible to talk to and he goes to church every Sunday morning."

"That proves it," declared Harriet gravely. "I've known philatelists who were quite sensible to talk to — except about philately — but never one who went regularly to church."

She doesn't mind a bit, thought Caroline, hiding a smile.

It was a misty afternoon, and as time went on the mist closed down and thickened into a damp white fog, blanketing the country and dulling every sound. The Londoner was inured to fog, of course, but not to silence.

"I feel as if I had suddenly gone deaf," declared Harriet. "There's something positively uncanny about it," and she shuddered involuntarily.

Her relations were sympathetic, especially Bobbie. "Poor Aunt Harrie!" Bobbie exclaimed. "Would it help if I went out to the garage and kept on blowing your horn? You'd feel more at home, wouldn't you?"

Harriet agreed that this might help quite a lot but refused the offer on account of her batteries.

It was more comfortable when the curtains were drawn and the fog and the silence shut out, and Harriet soon recovered from her slight attack of depression and became her usual cheerful self. After supper she taught them Liar Dice (a game which is played with poker lice and which necessitates telling the most outrageous lies with an innocent expression); the Derings took to it like ducks to water and spent a noisy and hilarious evening. Caroline won quite easily — a circumstance which surprised herself and astonished her relations.

"I don't know how I did it," she declared as she counted her chips.

"Neither do I," replied her sister. "You would make your fortune at one of Pinkie's parties. Your talents are wasted in Ashbridge."

"It's because nobody *expects* Mummy to tell lies," said Bobbie as she put away the dice.

"That certainly gives her an unfair advantage," admitted Harriet.

The girls went up to bed and, as it was still quite early, Caroline made up the fire and she and Harriet sat down and prepared themselves for a good talk. It was an old-established habit for them to talk far into the night. You could talk more freely when you knew you ought to be in bed and asleep. Sometimes their talk was serious and sometimes extremely frivolous, depending upon their mood.

They had not many childhood memories to share, for Harriet was a good deal younger than her sisters (she was only eight years old when Caroline was married) but the difference in age which had seemed so great had now ceased to matter, and to all intents and purposes they were contemporaries . . . in fact, Harriet felt older and wiser and more experienced than her elder sister, for she had had a more varied life and a wider view of the world.

"Who and what is Mr. Shepperton?" Harriet asked.

"A philatelist," suggested Caroline smiling.

"Yes, I know all that . . . but honestly and seriously who is he? He sounds rather mysterious."

"Mysterious!" echoed Caroline, somewhat taken aback.

"Definitely mysterious," nodded Harriet. "Bobbie seems to dote on him and Leda hates him like poison. I wondered what your reactions were."

"Oh, I like him," Caroline replied.

"Mildly?" inquired Harriet in interested tones.

Caroline hesitated. She and Harriet

were so close, so devoted to one another, so much in harmony. Should she tell Harriet how much she liked Robert — almost too much for her peace of mind — and ask Harriet's advice? There was still time to draw back from this increasing intimacy with Robert, she could draw back now if necessary, but if things went on as they were doing it would soon be too late. Harriet would know whether she ought to draw back, whether she was just being silly . . . at her age . . . with three grown-up children. All this passed through her mind in a flash and she was just leaning forward to speak when a log rolled out of the fire.

"Let me!" cried Harriet, flinging herself on her knees and seizing the tongs. "I love your log-fires, they're so nice to look at and so cosy. I can't have fires in the flat except horrid electric ones."

The moment passed, and when Harriet looked up and demanded more information about the mysterious stranger, Caroline had changed her mind (not now, she thought, perhaps I'll tell her some other time) and, instead of revealing her own personal feelings about Robert Shepperton, she merely gave Harriet an account of his misfortunes.

It was long after midnight when Caroline suddenly saw the clock and decided that they really *must* go to bed. Harriet was less a slave of time and there was still talk in her, but she agreed that if you had to get up to breakfast it was better to be in bed before two.

"You mustn't get up," Caroline told her. "We can easily bring you a tray, so don't — "

"What's that!" cried Harriet in sudden alarm.

"Did you hear something?"

"Yes, somebody walking about outside." They stood still and listened. It was very quiet.

"I can't hear a sound," declared Caroline

"Not now," agreed Harriet in a low voice. "But I'm sure I heard steps on the path — " She stopped suddenly for somebody was tapping gently on the window-pane.

Caroline turned. "Who can it be?" she said.

"Don't go. Don't answer," whispered Harriet.

Somebody tapped again and then tried the handle of the french window, but it was locked.

"I must see who it is," said Caroline.

"No," whispered Harriet, catching her by the arm and holding her back. "No, it might be a tramp! It might be a burglar!"

Caroline was surprised to find that her sister's hand was trembling, for she had always thought Harriet as brave as a lion — "Good, great and joyous, beautiful and free" — who but a brave woman could stand upon a stage before the eyes of thousands without shaking in her shoes ?

"Burglars don't tap on windows," said Caroline reasonably.

"They might — "

The outsider tapped again more urgently and called out, "Mrs. Dering! Mrs. Dering, are you there ?"

"It isn't a burglar," said Caroline, trying to release her arm.

"Don't go," whispered Harriet, clinging to her more tightly. "How do you know it isn't a burglar ? They're up to all sorts of tricks. It's a man . . . and there isn't a man in the house."

"Nonsense!" said Caroline. She released herself, drew back the curtain and opened the french window.

The light, shining out, disclosed a young man with a white face and staring eyes. He had no collar nor tie and his hair was straggling over his forehead . . . in fact, he looked so strange and disordered that it took Caroline a few moments to recognise him.

"Widgeon — it's you!" she exclaimed.

"Yes," said Widgeon. "Oh, Mrs. Dering, I *am* glad you 'aven't gone to bed. I thought p'raps you'd gone off to bed an' left the light on by mistake. It's the baby, Mrs. Dering."

"The baby! But it isn't due till next month, is it?"

"She fell on the stairs," said Widgeon miserably. "We was going up to bed. It didn't seem much of a fall, but she gave 'erself a sort of twist or something. She's awful bad, Mrs. Dering."

"You want to telephone to the doctor, of course," exclaimed Caroline, opening the window wider.

He came in and stood there, cap in hand. "It's no use telephoning," he said. "Nurse is in bed with flu an' doctor's gone to Chevis Green. Mrs. Smart says they can't get 'im nohow."

"There's another doctor, isn't there?" Harriet said.

"Not now," replied Widgeon.

"He's left Ashbridge," explained Caroline. "We're only allowed one doctor under the new Health Insurance Scheme."

"But that's ridiculous!" cried Harriet (for Harriet was a Londoner and was used to London amenities, including a doctor round the corner and several others in the next street). "It's positively wicked. Do you mean to say there isn't a doctor within hail?"

"That's right," said Widgeon bitterly. "We've only one doctor now, an' 'e can't be in two places at once. The Gover'mint don't care about Sue — don't care if she dies — an' it's supposed to be a working-man's Gover'mint. They don't get me voting for them again, not if I knows it."

"There's Dr. Wrench at Wandlebury," said Caroline doubtfully. "I don't know him, of course, but — "

"Sue's mortal bad," said Widgeon, twisting his cap in his hands. "I don't know what to do. That's the truth." He looked at Caroline with brown-spaniel eyes and added, "I thought you'd know, Mrs. Dering. I saw your light — so I came."

Caroline was not surprised at having the responsibility shifted on to her shoulders, for she was used to these country people and understood them pretty well. They were very independent when things were going smoothly, some of them affected the creed of Socialism and pretended to despise "the gentry", but when they were in any sort of trouble they turned quite naturally to people like herself. ("I thought you'd know," Widgeon had said. "I saw your light — so I came." It was as simple as that.)

"Yes," said Caroline, accepting the responsibility. "Yes, Widgeon. This is what we'll do: I'll come with you myself, *now*, and my sister will ring up Dr. Wrench and see if he can help us."

Widgeon smiled. "That's right," he said. "Sue'll be glad, Mrs. Dering."

Harriet went to the telephone at once and Caroline ran upstairs to get her coat and to collect a few things which might be useful. She had accepted the responsibility because there was nothing else to do, but she was anything but happy about it. She had helped Dr. Smart once or twice, so she knew just enough to know that she knew very little. If all went well she could manage, but it was most unlikely that all would go well. It was an eight-months' baby . . . Sue's cottage would be clean, that was one comfort.

Caroline had wondered how Dr. Smart was going to manage the whole district single-handed. (It was not really a very large practice — in numbers — but it was widely scattered, embracing several villages and a dozen outlying farms.) She had spoken of her fears to Dr. Smart and he had shrugged his shoulders and replied that he would do his best, nobody could do more, but that if two babies elected to arrive at the same moment at opposite ends of his practice, one of them would have to arrive without his assistance. Fortunately, Nurse Petersham was reliable and experienced, they would have to manage somehow. Now, here they were, in exactly that predicament and Nurse Petersham was ill.

Harriet was waiting in the hall. She had

got hold of Dr. Wrench and he had said he would come — had said it quite cheerfully and without the slightest hesitation.

"Doctors are wonderful people!" Caroline declared. She was thankful to hear he was coming . . . she realised that it might take him hours to come over from Wandlebury in the fog, and quite a lot might happen before he could get here, but the mere fact that help was on its way cheered her considerably.

"Don't wait up; I've got the key," added Caroline as she followed Widgeon out of the french window.

19

THE fog was still quite thick and it was very dark. Caroline was never very good in the dark and, having just stepped out of a lighted room, her eyes were completely blinded, so she seized Widgeon's arm and put her own through it. She was aware by the sudden stiffening of Widgeon's arm that its owner was reluctant to lend her its support (he was shy, and it did not seem the correct thing to walk arm-in-arm with Mrs. Dering); but Mrs. Dering had no intention of relinquishing its support and clung firmly. She did not want to twist her ankle in a rut, nor to walk straight into a tree.

"I can't see anything at all," she explained.

"'Tis a bit dark," he replied. "I did ought to 'ave brought a light, but there, I was so taken all of a 'eap, I never thought."

"But you can see, can't you?" (It was obvious that he could see, for he was walking along quite confidently and guiding his blind companion round unseen obstacles.)

Widgeon admitted he could see a bit. "I'm used to it," he said. "It's dark as pitch in the mornings when I go out to feed the beasts. I'll be glad when Summer Time comes off — they ought to take it off sooner, but they never think of *us*, not them. It's people in towns they think of."

Caroline agreed that "they" were inconsiderate, she was just as fed up with "them" as Widgeon and even more so than usual at the moment, because she had got into trouble over her hens. "They" had told her to GROW MORE FOOD, so she had increased her hennery to fifty birds and sent the eggs to the packing station to feed the henless . . . but occasionally she sent some eggs to Harriet. It had never occurred to her that any one could possibly object to her sending a few eggs to her sister; in fact, her conscience was so clear, and she was so innocent of intent to deceive, that she sent the eggs by post in a box marked "Eggs With Care" in large black letters. Nobody was more surprised than Caroline when she discovered she had committed a crime.

As they walked along through the darkness she revealed her troubles to Widgeon and found him sympathetic.

"I'll tell you what," Widgeon said. "You keep less than twenty-five — then you can do as you please. You don't need to send no eggs to the packing station then."

"You mean to sell the other hens?"

"No," replied Widgeon. "That'ud be a pity — such lovely 'ens they are! Just you send 'em up to my place, I'll keep 'em for you, see? I can get corn from the farm an' you can let me 'ave some of the eggs for my trouble, then we'll both be pleased."

"But that would be against the law, wouldn't it?"

"Don't you worry," Widgeon told her. "They'd never know nothing about it."

Caroline was slightly taken aback (shocked would be much too strong a word to describe her feelings). It was difficult to know what to say to Widgeon. The whole affair seemed so topsy turvy, so typical of the topsy turvy conditions of modern life. She had tried to help her country by Growing More Food, and all she had got for the trouble involved was more trouble. She had received countless forms to fill up; she had been visited by inspectors who seemed to think it was within their province to be rude to her, and who treated her as if she were trying to defraud the authorities of their just and lawful due, and she had been fined quite heavily for doing something she did not know was wrong. Somewhat naturally Caroline felt annoyed and the opportunity to break the law without any risk at all tempted her considerably.

"But I don't think I could, Widgeon," said Caroline at last.

"Why not?" he urged. "What's the 'arm? You wouldn't be doing nobody no 'arm, you'd be doing a lot of good. You could give the eggs to people what needs 'em. You could let me 'ave eggs for Sue; she'll need eggs an' I can't afford to buy 'ens — not good ones like you've got. I'd buy 'em from you if I could, but I've 'ad a lot of expenses lately an' I 'aven't got the money, so 'tisn't any use saying I 'ave. You let me keep 'em for you, Mrs. Dering. You think about it."

She thought about it. She was still

thinking about it when they arrived at the Widgeon's cottage.

Inexperienced though she was, Caroline saw at a glance that Sue was seriously ill . . . Caroline had wondered once or twice if, perhaps, it were a false alarm and she had summoned Dr. Wrench from Wandlebury only to discover that his midnight drive through fog and darkness was unnecessary . . . but this was no false alarm. Sue was in pain, she was panic-stricken and hysterical, she wept and wailed and flung herself about in the bed and clung to Caroline with hot, damp hands.

"Oh, Mrs. Dering," moaned Sue. "Oh, my baby! My little baby — it won't live, I know it won't! Oh, I'm frightened! Oh dear, what shall I do! Oh dear, I'm so frightened."

Caroline was frightened too, but she hid her feelings and busied herself about the house, and she sent Widgeon to the cross-roads with a lantern to watch for the doctor so that he should not mistake the turning. This plan had a double advantage for it would hasten the doctor's arrival and it took Widgeon out of the way. Now, having done all she could and made all the preparations she could think of, Caroline sat down beside Sue and held her hand and prayed.

She had been frightened and miserable, her nerves tense with apprehension, the responsibility weighing upon her like lead, but gradually all the fear and anxiety ebbed away and a flood of love and courage poured into her heart. She could feel it flowing through her and into the suffering girl like a warm comforting stream. Caroline did not move; she sat there quietly and let it flow — it was as easy as that — and presently Sue's trembling hand relaxed and her moans ceased and there was silence in the room.

"What are you doing to me, Mrs. Dering?" whispered Sue.

"Loving you," replied Caroline gently. "Shut your eyes, Sue."

Sue sighed and shut her eyes.

It was very quiet now. A little breeze had sprung up and was whispering through the leaves of the ivy with which the cottage was covered (perhaps it would blow away the fog); there was a drip from the roof, a tiny splash as drop after drop gathered and fell; there was a mouse scratching in the wainscot; Sue was breathing quietly and rhythmically.

Minutes passed — or hours — Caroline did not know how long she sat there holding Sue's hand. She felt peaceful and happy, she felt rested, there was no tension any more. She had ceased to strain towards the arrival of the doctor; she knew he would come and all would be well. Presently, in the stillness, she heard the sound of a car (a throbbing sound in the far distance). It came nearer. She heard it coming up the hill . . . it was stopping at the gate. She heard steps on the gravel path and the grumble of lowered voices; the cottage door opened and shut quietly and there was the sound of feet upon the stairs.

Caroline had never seen Dr. Wrench before, but she had heard various descriptions of him; some of his patients swore by him, others said he was dictatorial and unsympathetic. He had been described to her as a funny little man with a wizened, monkey-like face and surprised eyebrows, but although this might have been true enough in one way it was untrue in another. Dr. Wrench was small in stature but his personality filled the room. Caroline trusted him at once. She stood up as he came in but he did not look at her; he walked across to the bed and looked at his patient.

"She's quiet now," said Caroline in a low voice. "Perhaps we might have waited till the morning, but I was frightened about her."

"You were right not to wait," he replied. He threw off his coat, rolled up his sleeves and began to give directions in a tone of authority. Dr. Wrench had taken charge and Caroline was only too glad to shift all the responsibility on to his shoulders. She moved about the room doing what she was told, unpacking his bag and fetching the kettles of boiling water which she had prepared.

Until now Dr. Wrench had not looked at her at all, but now, suddenly, she felt his eyes upon her. They were keen grey eyes beneath the curiously-shaped eyebrows.

"Can you help me?" he asked. "It's going to be pretty bad but I want to save the baby if I possibly can. It's their first, isn't it?"

"I can do what you tell me," said Caroline soberly.

"That's all I want," he told her. "Lock the door — we can't have that man coming in and making a fuss at the critical moment."

Caroline drew back the curtains and the grey light of dawn flooded the little room; it was all tidied up. Sue lay in bed, fast asleep, her hair straggling over the pillow in damp strands; the baby, wrapped in shawls, lay in the moses-basket. It was the smallest atom of humanity Caroline had ever seen . . . it was alarmingly small (so Caroline thought) but Dr. Wrench was quite pleased with it — and Caroline had absolute confidence in Dr. Wrench. She had trusted him at once and as the night passed she trusted him more, and admired him profoundly; she had never believed any one could be so patient, so strong and sure and skilful. Certainly he was dominating, but Caroline did not mind that — she was glad to be dominated.

He joined her at the window and they stood there together looking out at the cold, grey morning. The fog had gone but there was white frost on every twig, on every blade of grass, and the whole world seemed to have been outlined with a pure white pencil.

"You're not worrying, are you?" said Dr. Wrench in a quiet voice. "They'll be all right. The baby is small but she's a perfectly healthy little specimen; she'll be bigger than you one of these days."

This was the first time he had spoken to her in an unprofessional manner, and Caroline realised it was because their job was done. She smiled at him. His eyes were on a level with her own. If Sue's baby grew to be bigger than Caroline, she would be bigger than Dr. Wrench.

"You must rest," he added. "I suppose there's a neighbour who can come in and look after them; there usually is."

"I've sent Widgeon to fetch Mrs. Podbury — Sue's mother."

He nodded. "That's right," he said. "Mothers are useful people."

"I've never thanked you for coming, Dr. Wrench."

"We'll cut that out," he replied. "We've done a good job of work between us. Have you had any training — professionally, I mean?"

"No," said Caroline. She smiled and added, "It's just a hobby."

Dr. Wrench chuckled. "Who are you?" he asked. "It seems a silly question when we know one another so well, but it would interest me to hear your name."

"I thought you knew! I'm Mrs. Dering. I live a few minutes' walk from here. You'll come and have breakfast with me, won't you?"

"Breakfast sounds good. I'll just wait and see the old lady when she comes and tell her what to do, and then we'll push off. It will suit me splendidly because I'd like to come back and have another look at them before I go home. I suppose the old lady is fairly sensible?"

Caroline gave Mrs. Podbury an excellent character . . . "and here she is," added Caroline.

They watched Widgeon and Mrs. Podbury coming in at the gate; Mrs. Podbury was hurrying, she was breathless and red in the face from her exertions; Widgeon was carrying her suit-case.

"She looks all right," said Dr. Wrench. "I'll go down and talk to her."

Mrs. Podbury took charge of the situation without turning a hair. She had had seven of her own and had helped at the arrival of numerous other Podburys. The only thing that worried her was the fact that she had not been here to help in the arrival of this, her first grandchild. She had had a feeling last night, declared Mrs. Podbury, a queer sort of feeling — all shivery — and she had told Daniel she was sure it meant something, but Daniel had been most unsympathetic and had put it down to pickled onions . . . and what with the fog and all . . .

"Yes, yes," agreed the doctor. "But that's over. Please attend to my instructions, Mrs. Podbury."

Mrs. Podbury attended. She was apt to be a little too chatty (like Sue) but she was no fool.

The sun had risen behind Cock Hill when Dr. Wrench and Caroline came out of the cottage together. Widgeon was waiting for them, he had a large wooden box in his arms. Caroline was quite shocked at Widgeon's appearance. His hair was wilder than ever, his face was as white as a sheet and there were dark circles beneath his eyes. Perhaps Dr. Wrench was shocked, too, for he patted Widgeon on the shoulder.

"They'll be all right, Widgeon," said Dr. Wrench.

"Thank you, sir," said Widgeon gravely. "Thank you for coming an' — an' everything. I don't rightly know 'ow to thank you — all you've done an' us not your patients, even!" He hesitated and then added, "P'raps you'd take a dozen pots of 'oney, Doctor. I'll put it in your car. It's nice this year — clover an' beans — I got a prize for it at Chevis Green Flower Show."

"That's a kind thought, Widgeon," replied Dr. Wrench cheerfully. "Yes, I'd like a few pots of honey. Give me three pots — a dozen is far too many."

Widgeon laughed shakily. "That's funny, that is," he declared. "You think twelve pots of 'oney is too much — too much for coming 'ere an' saving Sue? I'd thought I should be giving you the bees — the cow, the cottage, everything I've got — Sue's worth it all an' more. Sue's everything. I'd live without my meat an' drink much easier than I could live without my little Sue. I'd give you my right 'and . . ."

"You keep your right hand to work for Sue and your little daughter," Dr. Wrench told him.

"Yes," agreed Widgeon, looking at it in a dazed way. "Yes, Doctor, that's what it's for."

Dr. Wrench followed Caroline down the path. "He's a good fellow," said Dr. Wrench. "It's curious how one gets the swing of blank verse when these country people are deeply affected. I've noticed it before. The townsman has lost it, but it still lingers in country places — Shakespeare's English . . ."

Caroline made no answer; she was struggling with tears, which was quite ridiculous because everything was all right and there was nothing to cry about.

20

HARRIET'S car was a novelty to the Dering family. There was not enough petrol to go for long runs, but there was a little in the tank, and one fine Saturday afternoon Harriet offered to take her relatives for a picnic to Farling Woods. The girls accepted with delight but Caroline refused, saying she had not yet written her weekly letter to James and it must be posted that evening. She saw them off with all the paraphernalia necessary — with coats and rugs and sandwiches and thermos flasks — and then she went back into the house and sat down at her desk.

As usual Caroline had a lot to tell James, but it was quiet and peaceful and there were no interruptions (except from Comfort who looked in to say that this seemed a good opportunity to polish the hall floor) so the letter got written quite quickly and Caroline was just addressing the envelope to the base at Kuala Lumpur when the telephone-bell rang.

She picked up the receiver and said, "Hallo!"

"Is that Mrs. Dering?" inquired a man's voice — rather a deep voice and somehow vaguely familiar.

"Yes, Mrs. Dering speaking," said Caroline.

"Mother!" exclaimed the voice. "Mother, this is James!"

Caroline was speechless.

"Are you there?" asked the voice anxiously. "This is James. I'm in London. I flew home, I didn't tell you I was flying home because I knew you'd worry yourself frantic. I've arrived safe and sound."

"James!" said Caroline faintly.

"Yes," said the voice. "Yes, James. I'm here in London. I'm taking the next train to Wandlebury. I get to Wandlebury — wait a minute — yes, I get to Wandlebury at five-ten. Can you meet me or shall I just find my way over to Ashbridge? I suppose there's a bus or something."

"I'll meet you," said Caroline.

"Are you all right?" asked the voice in urgent tones. "I mean, you sound awfully far away — "

"I'm perfectly all right. I'll meet you — "

"Not if it's a bother," the voice adjured her.

The line went dead. Caroline listened for a few moments, but nothing happened, so she laid down the receiver. Her hand trembled and she had some difficulty in fitting it on to its stand.

"I heard!" exclaimed Comfort, appearing at the door. "I couldn't help hearing! It's Mr. James! Oh, isn't it lovely!"

"Yes," agreed Caroline in a dazed voice. "I suppose it's *true*. It wouldn't be a — a joke or anything."

"A joke! Goodness no! It was Mr. James's voice, wasn't it!"

"Yes," said Caroline. "It seemed to be. At least — "

"Of course it was," declared Comfort. "It was him, all right."

"I must think," said Caroline, trying to rouse herself and take a grip of the situation. "He's arriving at Wandlebury at five-ten, so I must get the four o'clock bus — "

"No, a taxi," said Comfort firmly. "Then you'll have it to come back in — see? It's much the best. I'll ring up Mr. Black and tell him to bring his big car. You'll need the big car for the luggage. You go and change, Mrs. Dering. You'll put on your blue tweed and the little hat with the feather, won't you?"

"What about food — "

"I'll see to it," Comfort assured her. "I'll stay and do the supper."

Caroline was absolutely dazed. She had been writing to James in Malaya and now he was here — here in London — she could not believe it. She changed and drank a cup of tea and by that time the taxi was standing at the gate.

Comfort saw her into the taxi. "Have you got your bag?" asked Comfort.

"No, I must have left it — "

"I'll find it," Comfort assured her.

Comfort waddled back to the house, found the bag lying on the kitchen table and returned with it. "There," she said handing it in at the window. "There it is. You'll be all right, won't you, Mrs. Dering?"

"Yes, of course," agreed Caroline.

The taxi was about to drive off when Caroline leaned forward. "Comfort," she

aid, "I don't know what on earth I should
do without you."

Comfort watched the car drive off and
then went back to the kitchen; she stood
quite still for a few moments with tears
trickling down her cheeks . . . it was like
one of her imaginary stories, very nearly,
but it was true. She hadn't imagined it.

"Fat old fool!" said Comfort mopping
her eyes. "Standing here snivelling!"

There was a rabbit in the larder, so she
would make a stew with thick brown
gravy; she would open a bottle of blackberries and make a tart . . . but first she
had better look out the sheets.

The London train was late. Caroline
walked up and down the platform and
waited for it. The dazed feeling had
passed off and she was keyed up to the
most frightful pitch of excitement. James
was coming, it was incredible but true.
She would see him in a few minutes, her
very own James (the fat little baby that
she had held in her arms, that she had
bathed and dressed and fed; the little boy
who had run to her with scraped knees and
cut fingers; the big beautiful son who had
gone away from her three long years ago

. . . her own James). He was coming now he would be here any minute, he was safe and sound.

But perhaps he wouldn't come, thought Caroline, pausing in her walk. He might have missed the train . . . or there might have been an accident. James had survived the most appalling dangers, he had hunted Terrorists in the jungle and flown home thousands of miles across the sea but there might have been an accident on the way down from London . . . perhaps that was why the train was late. Caroline's imagination took charge in its usual commanding manner and began to torment her with visions of the train overturned, the carriages lying upon their sides and enveloped in flames and James trapped in the debris, unable to move. She was so appalled by these visions that she tackled the station-master.

"You don't think there's been an accident?" she inquired.

"An accident! No, no, the train's often late these days. We don't go in for accidents on this line," he added jovially.

Caroline was slightly pacified. "I suppose they would let you know — " she began.

"Here she is! Safe as the Bank of England!" exclaimed the station-master and hurried away.

Here she was chuffing importantly as she slid into the station. Caroline's eyes sought feverishly for James as the windows flickered past. There he was . . . no, that wasn't James. People leaped on to the platform, dragging out suit-cases, slamming doors, shouldering their way to the barrier. She saw a young officer in battle-dress with a smooth, brown head and rushed after him . . . but it wasn't James. Tears pricked her eyes; he had missed the train; he hadn't come.

Then somebody caught hold of her (a great, strong, broad-shouldered man with a brown face) and cried, "Mother, here I am!"

"Oh!" she exclaimed. "Oh, James!"

She was being hugged to death almost. She was being kissed. "Gosh!" he was saying. "Gosh, how small you are! A tiny mother! You've shrunk or something."

James had not shrunk. She was amazed at the size of him. He had gone from her a tall, slim boy with a pink-and-white complexion, he had come back a big man with a brown face and a small fair moustache . . . but his deep-blue eyes, which were so like her own, were James's eyes. Her own James was looking at her out of them.

"Oh, James!" she cried, clinging to him. "It's really you."

"Of course it's me," he declared, laughing. "Who did you think it was? Are you in the habit of hugging strange men in railway stations?"

He had no luggage with him except a kit-bag. "It's all coming by boat," he explained in the deep voice which was like James's voice and yet was slightly different. "I couldn't bring it with me on the plane. We'll get a move on, shall we? Do we go by bus or what?"

"I've got Black's taxi," Caroline told him.

"I wondered if you'd know me," said James as he took her arm and steered her through the crowd.

"Of course, I'd have known you. I didn't *see* you," Caroline declared . . . but would she have known him? If she had met him in the street would she have stopped him and said, *"You're James?"*

Could she have picked him out from twenty young men and said confidently, *"That's my son?"* Surely her heart would have told her. But it wasn't right, thought Caroline confusedly. There was something wrong with a world in which mothers were parted from their sons for years and years; for so long that when the sons came back their own mothers found them almost unrecognisable.

"I'm sorry I gave you a shock," James was saying. "You did get a shock when I phoned, didn't you? I thought you sounded a bit bowled over. The fact was I couldn't make up my mind what to do: whether to cable that I was coming — but then you'd have panicked, wouldn't you? I mean you'd have had one of your 'things' and imagined the plane falling into the sea and me swimming about in the water. You would, wouldn't you?"

"I might," admitted Caroline with a shaky laugh.

"And then I thought: shall I just roll up at the cottage without saying a word? But that seemed a bit too dramatic. Gosh, here's Black!" cried James. "How are you, Black? You haven't changed much."

"You've changed a good deal, Mr James," said Black, looking at him in amazement.

"Yes," agreed James. "Yes, I believe I have. Everybody seems to think so."

They sat side by side in the taxi. James had taken her hand and was holding it in a firm clasp. "You can't believe it, can you?" he said. "I feel exactly the same. It's incredible that I should be here — in Wandlebury. I didn't know I was coming until the night before I started. A fellow got ill — he was going home in the plane and I managed to wangle his seat. I packed all night; it was a rush I can tell you. Ten days ago I was thinking vaguely that I'd be coming home next Spring — and here I am. Here I am and here you are," said James, giving her hand a little squeeze.

"It's marvellous," Caroline told him. "I've been terrified all the time — every moment."

"Everything is just the same," said James. "Even Black's ears. I remember him taking us to parties and his ears always fascinated me; I've never seen any one with such enormous ears. Goodness!" he exclaimed leaning forward and craning his head out of the window. "There's the dear old Apollo and Boot! They've painted the woodwork brown. The cottage isn't altered, is it?"

"No, it's just the same."

"Chrysanthemums in the front garden?"

"Yes."

"Good," said James, nodding. "I was thinking of it coming over in the plane. I thought, it's too late for hollyhocks but the chrysanthemums will be at their best. It's too late for blackberries, I suppose."

"Yes, I'm afraid so."

"I thought of you on my birthday. You *did* go up to the gravel-pit on my birthday?"

"Yes," said Caroline.

"You didn't think of me when you were picking them, of course."

"Of course not," said Caroline smiling. "Why should I think of you?"

"Golly, there's a cow! There's a nice fat cow," said James with intense satisfaction. "It's eating nice green grass. How's Comfort?"

Caroline laughed.

"She hasn't got thin or anything?" inquired James anxiously.

Caroline was able to reassure him.

"Are you feeling all right?" he asked suddenly. "You seem a bit — I mean you sound rather — but you're all right, aren' you?"

"A little giddy . . . with happiness," she told him.

He squeezed her hand. "Chinny," he said. He had called her Chinny when he was chin high, when his head had jus fitted beneath her chin. Now she could fi in under his, thought Caroline.

"Oh, James, I don't want to wake up," she said shakily.

21

VITTORIA COTTAGE had been a
houseful of women for years but
with the advent of James the
atmosphere changed completely. The hall
wore a different aspect; James's cap was
usually lying upon the chest; his mackin-
tosh and overcoat hung on the pegs. His
bedroom door stood open; there were
large sponges in the bathroom — and
shaving tackle. The house resounded to
his cheerful whistling. Caroline ceased
to be bored with food, for it was worth
while thinking about food and planning
it when James was there to enjoy meals.

It was delightful to have James at home;
Caroline could scarcely take her eyes off
him. Her knitting would lie idly in her
lap and she would look at him sitting back
in the big chair reading the paper, or a
book. His light-brown, glossy head lay
against the cushion and his long legs were
stretched out towards the fire, and his
feet were half in and half out of his red

morocco-leather slippers. Sometimes he would feel her eyes upon him and would look up and smile.

He was happy and comfortable — that was the joy. Caroline knew he had a soft bed with a hot-water bottle in it, so when she got into her own bed there was no need to wonder where James was, and what sort of night he was having (perhaps sleeping on the ground in the damp jungle with mosquitoes buzzing round and terrorists lurking in the bushes) and there was no need, when she took up her knife and fork, to wonder if James had anything to eat.

There were many things to discuss. Caroline found she could talk things over with James; she was surprised at his maturity and his breadth of outlook. It was a new sensation and a very pleasant one to find someone who could advise her sensibly, who was deeply interested in all that concerned her. They talked about Leda's engagement and the failure of *Eve's Dilemma* and the problem of the hens.

"I wouldn't make an illicit pact with Widgeon if I were you," said James after due deliberation. "It's tempting, I admit, but you'd worry about it — I know what you are — and it isn't worth worrying about. I should sell them and just keep twenty-four for your own use. Then you'll have no bother at all. If you're feeling generous-minded you could give the Widgeons a few for Christmas, couldn't you?"

"Could I?" asked Caroline, with a worried frown. "I mean that wouldn't be against the Law?"

"Against the Law! They're your hens, aren't they?"

Caroline had begun to think they were not.

"Of course you can," James said. "Nobody can possibly object. That's what I should do, Mother."

"And that's what I *shall* do," declared Caroline smiling at him. She could lean on James.

James had problems of his own, or more correctly one problem and, unlike Leda, he wanted Caroline's advice. He had decided to leave the Army and the question was, what should he do? One of his fellow officers had offered him a business partnership, but it meant putting money into the business; another friend was the son of a well-known publisher and James had been offered a post in the firm. Neither job appealed to James, he was not sure what *did* appeal to him — except farming, of course.

"Well, why not farming?" asked Caroline. "There's Uncle Jock, you know."

"Uncle Jock! D'you mean he would have me? Would he teach me — show me the ropes?"

Caroline said she was sure of it. She did not tell James that Jock Johnstone had spoken of making James his heir, for Jock might have changed his mind.

"That would be wonderful," declared James. "I'd like that better than anything. I like Mureth better than any place on earth — it seems to fit me if you know what I mean. I think it's because you're Scots and I'm like you. There's only one snag," said James . . . and there he stopped rather suddenly.

Caroline waited for the one snag to be uncovered, but James did not uncover it.

"Well, think it over," she advised. "There's no hurry and you need a rest."

He certainly needed a rest, for he was too thin and, beneath the brown tan, he was much too pale. He had had malaria rather badly — so he said — and that was the real reason why he had been able to wangle the seat in the plane all of a sudden at the last moment.

James was quite as happy to be at home as Caroline was to have him. It was delightful to be absolutely free — free to do anything he liked or to do nothing. For several days he did nothing except sleep and eat and talk to his relations, and all Bobbie's persuasions could not move him to do anything else. Bobbie wanted to take him to the village and show him off, she wanted him to bicycle over to the Meldrums or to go to Wandlebury and see a picture, but James only smiled and shook his head. He had dreamed of his home for three years and now he was here he wanted to stay in it.

"I shall make my *début* at Rhoda's Birthday Party," said James with absurd gravity. "I shall burst upon Ashbridge in all my glory. It would spoil the effect if I were seen bicycling through the village."

"And what are you going to wear?" inquired Bobbie.

"Wouldn't you like to know!" retorted James.

He and Caroline had already debated the matter of what James was to wear and they had discovered that his father's evening clothes, which had been carefully put away, fitted him not too badly.

The other members of the family were much exercised upon the subject of garments for the party at Ash House, indeed a great many female inhabitants of Ashbridge were so exercised, for this was a Social Event of the first magnitude. Those who could not afford coupons or cash for new frocks had a busy time altering old ones, letting down hems and taking in bodices and ironing out frills and furbelows. Leda had a new pink frock for the occasion, it had a long, full skirt and a tight-fitting corsage and little puff sleeves; Bobbie's blue silk had been let out at every seam and let down with strips of contrasting ribbon. It was a work of art when it was finished and even Harriet said it was charming. Caroline had been too busy with Bobbie's dress to bother about her own; she resurrected a black velvet gown which was old enough to have the New Look. Comfort seized it and steamed it carefully and when Caroline put it on and put on the family diamonds, which had been reposing in the safe for the last ten years, she decided she would do. It was Harriet, of course, who shone most brightly. Harriet wore a stiff silk dress of broad sugar-stick stripes, it was long and very full-skirted — almost like a crinoline. She had bare shoulders and arms and a sugar-stick bow in her hair. When James saw her he told her she looked good enough to eat.

22

RHODA had determined that this should be a "pre-war party" by which she meant that it was to be in the grand manner with a "proper dinner" and dancing to follow. The dinner started with soup, went on to game (pheasants shot by the host and carefully preserved for the occasion) and finished with a huge plum-pudding — hardly a pre-war plum-pudding owing to shortage of fruit, but quite a respectable substitute. Sir Michael produced some good hock and there were apples and pears and nuts in plenty.

The long mahogany table was dark and shining; there were candles in shining silver candelabra and shining silver dishes and bowls of roses and glittering glass. How many dinner-parties had this table seen! Dinner-parties of twenty or thirty people with seven or eight courses and a different wine for each course! Caroline thought of this as she took her place; she and Arnold had often dined here. Alice Ware — who loved entertaining — had sat at the end of the table where Rhoda was sitting now. Was Sir Michael remembering, Caroline wondered, and then she caught his eye and knew that he was. She shared the memory with him; nobody else shared it . . . but perhaps this was as well for memories of the past are apt to cloud the gaiety of the present.

It was a gay party. All the more so because parties were rare events nowadays, and to most of those present the knowledge that they were "all dressed up" and looking their very best was slightly intoxicating. When you are accustomed to going about in old tweeds and a darned pullover it is a pleasant change to be arrayed like the lilies of the field. Anne Severn looked sweet, Caroline decided. She was wearing a grey silk frock with pink roses at her waist. Mrs. Severn had once had a grey silk dress, Caroline remembered, but if this were indeed the same garment it was a masterpiece of transformation. Mrs. Severn was an expert dressmaker of course. Rhoda was wearing a brown picture-frock, she looked lovely with her pure-gold hair framing her face like a halo.

The men of the party had made an effort too. Sir Michael had decreed dinner-jackets (he was aware that several of his male guests possessed no tails) and his male guests had produced the goods, all except an Art-School friend of Rhoda's who was in a brown velvet coat and a flowing yellow tie. This gentleman had been introduced as "Bubbles" and appeared to have no other name. Mr. Shepperton was here, so too was Alister Smart, the doctor's son, who had just been demobbed and intended to take up medicine and follow in his father's footsteps. Caroline counted the party and found there were twelve.

Leda and Derek were sitting next to one another, but they did not seem to be talking much; Harriet was talking to Mr. Shepperton and ignoring her host who was on her other side. James was engrossed in Rhoda, his head was turned towards her and he was leaning forward and forgetting to eat. They had always been friends, those two, thought Caroline; they had the same adventurous spirit, the same happy outlook upon life. Perhaps Rhoda was the "snag" . . . and if so it was rather a big snag, for one could not imagine Rhoda settling down at Mureth as a farmer's wife.

Bobbie was enjoying herself. She was sitting beside Alister, listening to what he was saying and nodding to show that she was taking it all in. Suddenly there was a pause in the general conversation and Bobbie's voice rang out:

"Uttering!" cried Bobbie. "Alister, how extraordinary! I never knew people were put in prison for using bad language."

The whole table rocked with laughter.

"What's the joke?" demanded Bobbie. "Alister knows a man who was given five years' imprisonment for uttering!"

"Alister has some funny friends," declared Derek.

"But what did he say? That's what I want to know."

Bubbles leaned forward. "He said," began Bubbles solemnly. "He said . . . no, I can't tell you what he said. You see I might be given five years' imprisonment if I said it."

When dessert was over Rhoda signalled

to Harriet, who was the guest of honour, and the ladies withdrew.

"You're going to wash up, I suppose," said Derek.

"Not on your life," declared Rhoda. "This is a 'pre-war party' and we're going to sit in the drawing-room and pull our friends to pieces while you finish Dad's port. Don't be too long about it because we want to dance."

The port was circulated. It was extremely good port for Sir Michael had an extensive cellar and had always kept it well stocked.

"You must have had an uncomfortable time, James," said Sir Michael. "I want to hear about it some time. Bandits must be almost worse to tackle than civilised troops."

"Yes, sir," agreed James, "but of course I've never had any experience of warfare against civilised troops, only of guerrilla fighting against these Communist Terrorists. They roam about the country holding up cars and attacking isolated bungalows; you never know where you are with them. Some of the bands were trained during the Jap War, of course. Personally I think things will settle down if we can get more food into the country. The shortage of rice is very serious."

"Oh, you were in Malaya!" exclaimed Bubbles. "I was there at the very beginning when the Japs came swarming down the peninsula. I only escaped from Singapore by the skin of my teeth."

They all began to talk of where they had been: Sir Michael had spent most of the war in the Mediterranean, Alister had been at Alamein, Derek had been at the crossing of the Rhine.

"It's interesting, isn't it?" said Alister. "I mean here we are, all sitting round this table, and — and I mean — "

"We've seen a bit of the world between us," his host agreed smiling.

Derek leant forward. "Yes," he said. "We've all pulled our weight except Mr. Shepperton; he doesn't seem very keen to tell us what he did in the Big War."

"I was a spy," said Robert Shepperton quietly.

There was a short but somewhat embarrassed silence.

"Brave fellows, spies," Sir Michael said.

"I'm with you, sir," declared James. "It must be worse than jungle-fighting."

"Rather like jungle-fighting," said Robert Shepperton, smiling.

James nodded. "I see what you mean. People all round you — never knowing from what direction the danger will come."

"That's it," Bubbles put in. "That's jungle fighting. I used to long for a nice solid wall to put my back against; I used to wish my head would turn round and round on a swivel."

"Invisible enemies," said Robert, turning his glass so that the light was caught and coloured by the ruby wine. "My enemies were not exactly invisible but I often longed for a wall at my back."

"You must tell me about it, Shepperton," said Sir Michael. "You must come some evening when I'm alone . . . meanwhile we'll join the ladies, shall we? Rhoda wants to dance."

James would have liked to hear about some of Mr. Shepperton's adventures here and now, but there was no evading the Admiral's orders, so he rose and opened the door — he was nearest to it. Mr. Shepperton went out followed by

Alister and Bubbles; Sir Michael and Derek had stayed behind to snuff out the candles.

"Derek," Sir Michael was saying. "Derek," I should like to remind you of something which you seem to have forgotten, rudeness to a guest is inexcusable."

"I wasn't rude," muttered Derek.

"You were impertinent, which is worse . . ."

At this point James deserted his post at the door and hastened after the others; he had no wish to hear any more.

The drawing-room was ready for dancing; the furniture had been moved to one end and the floor polished. Several other guests had arrived and were standing about, chatting to one another. James looked round eagerly and, seeing Rhoda at the radiogram, he made a bee-line across the room towards her.

"Me first," said James.

"You first?" she asked, smiling at him. "Why should you be first, I wonder."

"Because of all sorts of things," he replied. "Because I haven't seen you for three whole years and because your hair is golder than ever — that's two of them."

She turned on the music and slid into his arms.

Robert Shepperton sat down beside Caroline. "I won't ask you to dance this," he said. "I'm not *au fait* with modern dances, but perhaps you'll let me have a waltz?"

"I should like that," she replied.

They were silent for a few minutes watching the dancers. Leda and Derek were dancing together, Bubbles and Anne, James and Rhoda. Alister had been dashing and had secured as his partner the magnificent Miss Fane, but he was not a star performer and was finding her a little too much for him. Sir Michael had asked Mrs. Meldrum to take the floor (he had felt bound to do so, for the Meldrums had not been asked to dinner and therefore were on his conscience) and, Mrs. Meldrum having accepted, he was pushing her round manfully.

The pattern changed with the next dance and changed again, Caroline danced with Robert and with Sir Michael and then with James. She sat out several times. She talked to Mrs. Meldrum about the Women's Institute and tried not to disagree with her, and she listened to Mr. Meldrum talking about fishing. She noticed that James was dancing with Rhoda as often as he could, and she noticed Robert and Harriet dancing together and then sitting out together on the big sofa. They were talking earnestly. It was obvious that they found one another extremely interesting. Robert and Harriet, thought Caroline, looking at them. She ought to be pleased to see them getting on so well (she liked them both enormously so she ought to be pleased if they liked each other) but somehow she was not very pleased . . . there was an odd sort of pain in her heart . . . there was a queer sort of chill . . . as if two people had drawn up their chairs to the fire and left her out. But that's selfish, Caroline told herself as she nodded at Mr. Meldrum. That's absolutely horrible of me. Of course I'm glad . . . and she tried to forget about Robert and Harriet sitting together on the sofa and listen to Mr. Meldrum properly with both ears instead of only one. But, instead of listening properly, she began to wonder why it was that people like Mr. Meldrum could never see what frightful bores they were. I should *know* if I were boring someone to death, thought Caroline. James would know, so would Harriet and Robert; Rhoda would know but not Derek. That's interesting. I believe I've got something there. This was one of James's expressions and Caroline smiled at the thought of how aptly it applied to the case.

"Yes, it was rather amusing, wasn't it?" Mr. Meldrum said.

It was true that Harriet had found Robert Shepperton interesting, they had much in common for they were both refugees from the big bad world. They both knew London well and not only London. Harriet had travelled widely before the war and it appeared that Mr. Shepperton had travelled widely too. She got on with him so well that she could talk to him freely.

"Yes, it was a flop," she told him. "It was a poor play and we all knew it, so we couldn't put it across. An audience is a strange thing; it's a *whole*, you know. It isn't just a conglomeration of individual people. The mere fact of sitting in the dark, shoulder to shoulder, seems to have a magical effect. An audience judges as

244

one . . . and has a better judgment than the individuals who make it up."

"A mob is one unit," said Robert Shepperton thoughtfully. "But a mob has less judgment than its individual members."

She nodded. "There was one exception," she said with a humorous lift of her brows. "There was one person who liked *Eve's Dilemma*. Caroline liked it. She would like anything if I happened to be in it."

"I'm sure she would," he agreed, smiling.

"She's a wonderful person," continued Harriet earnestly. "I've always admired Caroline. She had the most awful life with Arnold and she bore it with the most heavenly patience. Arnold thought himself ill-used by Fate. He considered himself a martyr and let everybody know it. Sometimes he was humble and declared that it was all his own fault, but usually it was other people's fault, the fault of the World which had never appreciated him at his true worth. His voice used to drive me mad, it was a nagger's voice with a high-pitched drone — a sort of whine like a Moslem beggar — it was sympathy Arnold begged for. Perhaps if he hadn't begged for it so continually one might have given it to him. He was terribly gloomy — though sometimes, if he were predicting frightful catastrophes, he would smile and his eyes would gleam with pleasure and excitement. It was the only time he really enjoyed himself."

"He sounds insane!"

"No, I think he was just spoilt — and gloomy. Some people enjoy predicting disasters. I believe Jeremiah did."

Robert laughed. Miss Fane amused him.

"Don't laugh," said Harriet. "It isn't funny — not really — not when you have to listen to a Jeremiah, day in and day out. He almost succeeded in breaking Caroline. I think he would have broke her if he had lived a year or two longer. I wanted to kill him. Honestly," said Harriet, turning her head and looking at her companion with perfect gravity. "Honestly, I wanted to kill Arnold."

"I wouldn't have blamed you," he returned.

"No, you wouldn't have blamed me if

you had known him. You'd have helped. We might have done it together," said Harriet with the ghost of a smile.

"The perfect crime."

"Of course. It would have been a success, I feel sure. Fortunately it wasn't necessary. He killed himself. I don't mean he took his own life," said Harriet hastily. "I just mean that his nerves became affected and he got some strange nervous disorder which eventually affected the muscles of his heart. Caroline nursed him night and day. He wouldn't let her out of his sight. Caroline must be there to give him his medicine, to feed him, to hold his hand while he slept . . . Did I tell you he had no consideration for Caroline's health or comfort?"

"You implied it, Miss Fane."

"Harriet, please," she said with a confiding glance. "All my friends call me Harriet and I've been wanting to call you Robert for the last half hour."

Robert nodded. "It's a bargain, Harriet," he said.

"Now," said Harriet, changing the subject. "Now tell me about Leda and Derek. You've been here all the time and

I haven't. Caroline isn't very happy about it, I'm afraid."

He did not pretend to misunderstand but after a moment's hesitation he said, " 'Good faith, this same young, sober-blooded boy doth not love me, and a man cannot make him laugh.' "

"You're clever, aren't you?" said Harriet, looking at him. "That just fits Derek. Derek is sober-blooded, but unfortunately he's weak, too. It's a bad mixture. Poor Leda, what was she thinking about to fall in love with him!"

Their eyes strayed across the room to the young man in question. He was talking with animation to Joan Meldrum while Leda stood by, listening with a fixed smile.

"Go and dance with her, Robert," said Harriet urgently. "Please, do."

He rose at once and did as he was told.

It was the first time, but by no means the last, that Robert obeyed the orders of Harriet.

23

ROBERT was now quite at home with the inhabitants of Vittoria Cottage; with all except Leda. Robert was very intuitive, his life had made him so, and he could feel a definite enmity in Leda. The strange secretive girl distrusted him, perhaps she was jealous of him . . . or perhaps the whole trouble arose from his clash with Derek that very first afternoon. Leda was the type of person who will nurse a small grudge for months until it grows into a lusty hatred.

Robert was thinking of this, and regretting it, when he called at Vittoria Cottage the afternoon after the dance to see how everyone was feeling. He found James sweeping up the leaves under the direction of his aunt.

"Look at him, Robert!" cried Harriet. "He may know how to fight bandits but he doesn't know how to sweep leaves."

"What's wrong?" asked James, grinning.

"You're sweeping against the wind. Sweep *with* the wind, James."

James turned, laughing, and swept the leaves in her direction so that they rose in a cloud and swirled about her like coloured snowflakes.

"Lovely!" cried Harriet, pirouetting and holding out her hands to catch them as they fell. "Lovely, lovely leaves . . . happy months!"

Robert joined in the fun — for Harriet's spirits were infectious — he laughed like a boy and pelted her with leaves.

It was a gay scene, thought Caroline as she looked out of the window — it was like a scene in a play, with Harriet in the leading part — and once again Caroline experienced that odd feeling of being left out in the cold. But it was ridiculous, of course. She was fond of them all, James and Harriet and Robert, she wanted them to be happy . . . she wanted Robert to be happy. He had been through so much. When he first came to Ashbridge he had been a sick man, sick with misery; gradually she had seen him recover, she had seen his shoulders straighten and a brightness come to his eyes. She had helped — she knew that — and she had felt a warm glow of happiness to know it. Caroline had given him sympathy and friendship, her heart had gone out to him . . . but now it seemed that Harriet could do even more for Robert, Harriet could make him laugh. He had laughed like a boy.

It was tea-time now and the three came in, somewhat breathless from their exertions.

"It's hard work sweeping leaves," declared Harriet, sinking into a chair.

"Sweeping leaves!" exclaimed James. "The leaves are scattered to the four winds thanks to the hard work you put in. I shall have to start all over again, that's what it comes to."

Harriet and James were tremendous friends and enjoyed teasing one another, they continued to argue about the leaves while they ate their tea and the argument occasioned a good deal of laughter. Robert sat and listened and sometimes joined in . . . it was easy to see that Harriet amused him.

The girls had gone over to the Meldrums, so, when they had finished tea, Caroline rose and began to clear the table.

"Let me do that," Robert said. "I haven'
done any work; I didn't even help with the
leaves." He rose as he spoke and took the
dishes from Caroline, piling them neatly.
sweeping the crumbs on to a plate.

"You should take him as your butler,
Caroline," Harriet declared. "If you don't
I will. He's fully qualified for the post."

Robert did not smile. "Yes," he said.
"I'm fully qualified. I was a waiter for
years. It isn't the sort of thing one forgets."

They had been talking lightly, having
fun together, but they realised that this
was serious. Caroline and Harriet were
struck dumb with amazement. James was
less surprised.

"Was that when you were . . ." began
James in doubtful tones.

"When I was a spy," nodded Robert.

They were all looking at him, they were
waiting for more, and Robert realised that
he must tell them his story. He had felt
for some time that the story would have to
be told but he had shrunk from the telling
of it. He had not spoken of it before,
except officially, and that was quite different of course.

These people were his friends, they

wanted a personal story; they wanted to know what he had done and thought and felt. If he had had any doubts about their interest the doubts were soon dispelled. They listened spellbound.

Robert began a little diffidently for it was not easy to go back and remember things which he had deliberately forgotten, but after a few minutes he got into his stride . . . soon he was remembering everything almost too clearly. He was remembering the big luxurious hotel in Berlin. The work was hard and extremely tiring, waiting at table, carrying trays, running to fetch the different dishes demanded by the diners . . . or waiting at parties given by German officers in the private rooms behind the big dining-hall . . . and always listening to the conversation, listening, weighing, noting it in his mind. Sometimes weeks passed and there was nothing worth sending through the complicated system which had been arranged for him, and for others of his kind, to transmit information to Headquarters . . . and Robert would despair, he would feel that all this misery was useless, he was bearing this terrible burden and doing his country no service, it would be better if he could do his part in the battle with a gun in his hand like other men. Then when he was least expecting it he would hear something — a few words, perhaps, passed casually from one friend to another — and he would realise what these few words portended. Yes, it was worth passing on. He would go out dressed in his shoddy suit, and sit at a certain table in a certain restaurant reading a certain book until somebody came and sat down beside him. Pass-words would be exchanged — innocent-sounding remarks about the weather — and a tiny roll of paper would be passed from hand to hand. Then Robert would rise and pay his bill and go. He was always reluctant to go, he would have liked to sit there quietly without speaking for a long time, for it was the only opportunity he had of seeing a friend (if you could call this complete stranger a friend) it was the only communication he had with his own people.

It was no use playing the part of a waiter, he had to live the part. He was not Robert Shepperton, he was Fritz Schneider. He became friends with the other waiters, sharing their jokes, their troubles,

heir hopes and their fears. He had a
efinite entity which had been provided
or him by the department which he
erved. Fritz Schneider was a definite
erson who had been taken prisoner in a
aid and had afterwards died of wounds,
e had lived in Imst, a little town in
Bavaria, his identity had been borrowed
o clothe a British spy.

There were attics in the big luxurious
hotel, tiny rooms high up beneath the
roof, and one of these was allotted to
Fritz Schneider. It was cold in winter, so
deadly cold that he put on all the clothes
he possessed before creeping into bed;
summer it was so hot that he was almost
stifled. The room contained a hard lumpy
bed, a cane chair, a broken mirror (in
which every morning he saw his gaunt
face) and a few hooks on the wall where his
miserable clothes hung. At night he could
hear planes flying overhead and knew that
they had come to destroy the city in which
he was living. If he had wanted he could
have gone down to the shelter when the
bombs began to fall but he never did. He
stayed where he was and listened to the
noise of the engines. There were men

up there and they were his friends, he welcomed them, he greeted them. "Good luck to you," he told them. He did not believe he would be killed by a British bomb — it just wasn't possible — and he was right of course. Bombs fell all round but not upon him. He happened to be out when a bomb hit the hotel. This did not surprise him in the least.

His life was monotonous for the most part but not all the time; he had some pretty narrow escapes. On one occasion he was in the room of a German officer looking for some papers and especially for one paper — a map of Stuttgart — which he was sure the officer possessed. The officer had gone out (and Robert seized his opportunity) but unfortunately he returned sooner than he was expected. Robert hid behind the door and knocked him out with one well-directed blow behind the ear; he went down like a log and never knew what had hit him. There was a tremendous row over the incident, several innocent people were suspected but not the guilty one. Fritz was so quiet and well-behaved, nobody suspected Fritz. It was a nine days' wonder and then some other wonder took its place and the incident was forgotten. He had adventures in which women were involved. German women did not interest him but he found they were interested in him and resented it when their offers of friendship were ignored. This sometimes caused trouble with the other servants.

One day a young officer came into the hotel; he was from Imst, which was Fritz Schneider's home, and on hearing that his waiter was a fellow-townsman he spoke to him of the little town and of the people. He was very young and somewhat home-sick. Robert had been given a good deal of information about Imst; he pretended to be shy and stupid and somehow he managed to play his part, but his hands were wet and he was trembling in every limb when at last he was allowed to go. The sequel to this conversation was a letter from a girl in Imst. She wrote with joyful excitement saying that she had seen the officer and he had told her about Fritz and given her his address. They had all thought him dead. Why had he not written? She had a little son, now — it was Fritz's son of course — a little boy of three years old with fair hair and blue eyes. "You will love him, Fritz," and she pleaded with him to get leave and come home and marry her "so that little Fritz will have a proper father". This letter distressed Robert terribly, it weighed upon his mind like a stone. He wanted to write to the girl and tell her Fritz was dead, that he had died fighting bravely for his fatherland, but this he could not do. He tried to think of something he could do for the girl, but he could think of nothing.

Homesickness was one of Robert's ailments. It was the unfriendliness of the land that distressed him. He longed for his own country, for the land where his forebears had walked. A man's own land breathes a silent sympathy, it soothes and comforts him . . . in this strange unfriendly land he felt utterly forsaken. Birth and death are solitary but no more solitary than the life of a spy in an enemy camp; he can have no friend, no companionship, he is never off duty; there is no moment when he can safely relax, there is no soul with whom he can share an idea. Self-control must be perfect and it must be control not only of expression but of feelings as well (when Robert heard of British and American victories he must control his feeling of satisfaction. He must be apprehensive and dismayed when the Allied Armies advanced). Spiritual solitude in a crowd is more wretched than the solitude of Robinson Crusoe upon his desert island.

Life is a series of near misses, the sword passes and the victim goes on blithely, unaware of the danger which has passed him by . . . but Robert developed a sixth sense and knew when danger threatened, he could feel the wind of the passing sword. He had hoped to be relieved when the Russians occupied the sector of Berlin in which he lived, but no word came to him from Headquarters so he stayed on. Everything was disorganised, of course, the muddle and confusion was beyond belief but the hotel carried on and Robert continued to serve meals as usual . . . and then suddenly the blow fell; Robert was accused of theft and thrown into prison.

He passed over this lightly, for even now he could not bear to think of it (it was beyond all limits of endurance). Even now he sometimes awoke in the middle of the night and imagined himself in that dim cell with the stone walls and the grated window, and he would have to get up and walk about to calm his nerves and to control the trembling of his limbs. What alarmed him most was the fact that the accusation was a trumped-up charge with no shadow of truth behind it — and this meant they had something else against him, he didn't know what. He was not questioned nor had he any trial, he was simply put in prison and kept there for months . . . and then one day the prison door was opened and he was told to go. No explanation was given, Robert never knew the real reason for his imprisonment nor the reason for his sudden and un-expected release. It remained a mystery.

The shock of his release was almost too much for him, he could hardly walk. He waited until dark and made his way to the British sector of the city and fainted in a sentry's arms. After that he remembered no more until he awoke in hospital and the nurse told him he had been ill for weeks.

Robert told them all this and more. Once he had started he found it easier than he had expected and it was a relief to get it off his chest. They listened intently and without remark; Caroline sat gazing at the fire, she did not move, she did not look at him. At last he came to the end of his story and there was silence.

James was the first to speak. "How frightful!" he said in a low voice. "I couldn't have stood it. Few people could have come through it alive — and sane."

"I don't think I was very sane when I came to Ashbridge," Robert replied.

"What made you come here?" asked Harriet.

"It was pure chance," he told her. "I was standing looking at the ruins of Chelsea Old Church when a girl came up and spoke to me. She was the first person in London who seemed to care what became of me, and I was grateful to her. I told her a little of what I was feeling and she listened — I felt her sympathy. "You must go away," she said. "Go anywhere. Go to Ashbridge. It's quiet enough there! The girl was Rhoda Ware."

"Rhoda!" exclaimed James in amazement.

He nodded. "Yes, Rhoda. Of course I

didn't know it was Rhoda until I saw her last night. I remembered her at once, there couldn't be two people in the world with hair like that, and surprisingly enough she remembered me. She was astonished to find I had taken her advice and come to Ashbridge; she seemed quite shocked. I had taken her casual words seriously and acted upon them. 'But I might have said anything,' she told me, 'I might have said go to Timbuctoo. Would you have gone?' "

"How like Rhoda!" said James, smiling. They all smiled, it was a relief to smile.

24

PETER PODBURY was the son of Silas, the ironmonger at Ashbridge, he was nine years old and he held the distinction of being the only only-child in the Podbury connection. Silas had to endure a good deal of chaff on the subject of his family but it worried him not at all; he usually replied to it by saying that one was enough — when that one was Peter — and that more than one Peter would have driven him and Lily stark, staring mad. Peter was angelic in appearance; he had fair curly hair a wide, innocent forehead and large blue eyes; and when he sat in the choir attired in a large Eton collar and a snowy white surplice he looked too good to live . . . but beneath that snowy surplice there beat a heart full of mischief and behind that wide, white forehead dwelt a brain that was forever plotting devilries.

Peter was popular with his contemporaries for he was amusing and his imagination was fertile. There was never a dull moment in Peter's company. It was Peter who led a band armed with catapults to an empty house and instructed it by example and precept to break a number of windows; it was Peter who baited the bull at Betterlands Farm, who found a board saying ROAD CLOSED and diverted the traffic in the High Street; it was Peter who haunted the building site and set booby traps for the workmen, and it was most certainly Peter who climbed on to the roof of the village hall and put back the hands of the clock.

This last exploit, undertaken in company with his faithful crony, Ted Mumper, was the most amusing in Peter's estimation, for the bus to Wandlebury went by the village clock and was twenty minutes late in starting — and therefore twenty minutes late in arriving at its destination. Passengers who had important appointments in Wandlebury were annoyed to find themselves belated, and passengers who had intended to catch the London train were even more annoyed to arrive at Wandlebury station in time to see the train disappearing rapidly in the distance.

Silas Podbury was an old-fashioned

parent and used the strap freely. Lily Podbury had modern ideas about bringing up her child; she bought books on child psychology and tried out the methods recommended, but neither the strap nor the psychology had any effect upon Peter. He was incorrigible. It was not that Peter intended to be naughty — far from it — but when an idea came into his head he could not resist putting it into practice. It was such fun to watch the traffic turn into a back street and become hopelessly entangled. (When you knew that you, yourself, had accomplished this diverting mess it was absolutely enchanting.) It was such fun to watch the bus standing idle and to know that it should have been well on its way to Wandlebury by this time — and would have been but for you. It was such fun to aim a stone at a window and to hear the satisfactory crack which meant a direct hit had been registered . . . and to see the splinters flying in all directions. It was such fun to hear the work-men swearing when a pail of water tipped on to their heads. Was it Peter's fault that he was visited by so many marvellous ideas — ideas of such a varied nature ?

Caroline had promised Anne Severn to help with the Christmas carols, so she walked over to church on Saturday morning. The choir practice had begun when she got there so she sat down in a front pew and watched and listened. Peter did not look quite so angelic as usual without his surplice, but his voice was lovely; he was singing a verse of *The Holly and the Ivy* as a solo . . . his singing reminded Caroline of a bird. When she shut her eyes she could see a thrush upon a spray of hawthorn. It was spring and the sun was shining in a clear blue sky.

Several other people had come for the practice: the Meldrums and Robert Shepperton and Violet Podbury, who was in the telephone exchange.

When Robert saw Caroline he came across the aisle and sat down beside her. "What a lovely voice that boy has got!" he whispered.

Caroline nodded. "He looks so beautiful, too," she said. "But as a matter of fact he's an imp of mischief. People say he's the worst boy in Ashbridge — but you can't help liking him, somehow."

"I'd like to talk to him," said Robert thoughtfully.

Caroline had not seen Robert since Wednesday, when he had told them the story of his experiences in Berlin, and she felt a little awkward with him. She had been thinking about him constantly, thinking of all he had endured: the loneliness, the danger, the discomfort. The story had moved her so deeply that she could hardly bear it . . . now, here he was, sitting beside her and smiling at her as if nothing had happened. She realised that it was foolish to feel like this for it was all past and Robert had come through it without harm.

"Robert," she said, looking up at him. "I couldn't say anything on Wednesday. I wanted to say so much."

He was still smiling as he turned his head towards her, but his smile was different. "I could feel your sympathy — " he began.

At that moment Mrs. Meldrum approached. "I don't know what you think," said Mrs. Meldrum in a low voice, "but I think it's absurd to have *The Holly and the Ivy*. It's so hackneyed. We should have something fresh."

"But people like the old carols best," objected Caroline. "And Peter sings it so beautifully — "

"Peter shouldn't be in the choir at all," declared Mrs. Meldrum.

"How can you say that?" Caroline returned. "It's good for him to sing and it's good for us to listen . . . who are we to say Peter shouldn't sing in the choir!"

Anne had followed Mrs. Meldrum; she was amused at the exchange, for it was a well-known joke in Ashbridge that the two ladies always took opposite views. Anne agreed with Mrs. Dering; she intended to have *The Holly and the Ivy*, and she knew that neither her father nor Mr. Forbes would dream of turning Peter out of the choir (her father because he was of the opinion put forward by Mrs. Dering, and Mr. Forbes because Peter was his best treble), but Anne was the vicar's daughter and had learned to hold her peace. So, instead of airing her own ideas, Anne smiled and asked if Mrs. Dering and Mrs. Meldrum were ready for the next carol in which they had promised to take part.

" 'Unto us a boy is born,' " said Anne persuasively. "It's a lovely carol, isn't it?"

"Lovely," agreed Mrs. Meldrum. "And so appropriate . . . I mean the little prince, of course."

"Oh!" exclaimed Caroline. "Oh, but really — " and then she stopped, for Anne had caught her hand and was squeezing it gently. The gentle squeeze said a good deal. *Don't*, it said. *Just leave it. The woman doesn't mean any harm — she's a fool, that's all — and nothing we can say will do any good.* So Caroline swallowed the things she had meant to say and opened her book of carols without more ado.

It was raining when they came out of church. Those who had brought umbrellas unfurled them and hastened away, but Caroline was umbrella-less, so she sat down in the porch hoping that the shower would soon be over. She was joined by Robert, who sat down on the opposite seat.

"I think it will be over soon," said Caroline, looking out at the slanting spears of rain.

"Not too soon, I hope," replied Robert. "As a matter of fact I want to talk to you about something, Caroline."

At this moment the church door opened and Peter Podbury and his friend Ted

Mumper appeared. They lingered in the porch.

"You aren't frightened of a little rain, are you?" inquired Robert.

"Not us," replied Ted. "We're just waiting for — for something."

"You sang beautifully, Peter," said Caroline.

"Yes," agreed Peter, who had no false pride about him. "Yes, it was pretty good, wasn't it? I like carols — they give you a nice feeling inside," and he began to sing softly:

"The holly and the ivy, when they are both
    full grown,
"Of all the trees that are in the wood, the
    holly bears the crown.
"The rising of the sun and the running of
    the deer,
"The playing of the merry organ, sweet
    singing of the choir."

The others joined in. Robert had a very pleasant soft baritone. It was really a delightful rendering of the quaint old lay.

Mr. Spawl, the verger, came out just as they were finishing. He locked the church door with a large key. "That was nice," he said. "You ought to be in the choir, Mr. Shepperton. I suppose you're waiting for the rain to go off, Mrs. Dering. What are you boys waiting for?"

"For the rain to go off, Mr. Spawl," replied Peter, looking up at him with large blue, innocent eyes.

Mr. Spawl stared at him suspiciously. "Waiting for the rain to go off?" he said in doubtful tones. "You've got your waterproofs — "

"There isn't no harm in sheltering, is there, Mr. Spawl?"

"Well . . . no pranks, Peter," said Mr. Spawl, and with that he hurried away down the path.

The boys giggled.

Caroline felt pretty sure they were up to something. "What *are* you waiting for — really and truly?" she inquired.

"For Mr. Spawl to go off," said Ted, grinning mischievously. "The rain don't bother us, but he does. He's a silly old geezer."

"What are you going to do?"

"It's nothing wrong," Peter assured her. "Old Spawl wouldn't like it, but that don't mean it's wrong. Old Spawl thinks the churchyard belongs to him — but it don't."

"It belongs to Peter," added Ted.

"The churchyard belongs to Peter?" asked Caroline in surprise.

" 'Cos why?" said Peter. " 'Cos there's hundreds of Podburys here — an' if that don't mean it belongs to the Podburys, what does?"

"So the churchyard belongs to you," said Robert with a thoughtful smile. "I don't know whether the law would agree with that, but it certainly seems to give you a claim. What do you intend to do with your property, Peter?"

The boys looked at one another. " 'Tisn't wrong," declared Peter. He took a piece of cord and some large wooden pegs out of his pocket as he spoke.

"Rabbit-snares," nodded Robert. "Yes, it's quite a neat little poacher's trick. I used to set them when I was a boy."

" 'Tisn't wrong," repeated Peter with some anxiety.

"No, I don't think your ancestors would object. They probably knew a good deal about these toys. Let me see — how does it go?"

Caroline was less easy in her mind. Peter's ancestors might not object, but she felt sure Mr. Spawl would be shocked at the idea of a rabbit-snare in the church-yard . . . and Mr. Spawl was the custodian, he was alive and active, whereas Peter's ancestors were not. She tried to explain her views to her companions but they were deaf to her words. She was one against three — one female against three males imbued with the instinct for hunting and killing, an instinct which has survived since prehistoric ages when man went forth from his cave armed with flint arrows to hunt the mammoth in forests and swamps. Caroline might have saved her breath and, being a sensible woman, she soon realised this fact and ceased to interfere.

The boys had discovered a rabbit-run between two gravestones (*Podbury grave-stones*, said Peter, who obviously was of the opinion that this gave him a legal right to set his traps there) and they had seen several rabbits using the run. They explained to Mr. Shepperton that they wanted to catch two if possible, one for Peter's family dinner and one for Ted's. Mr. Shepperton took the cord and the pegs and showed them how the noose should be made and the distance from the ground at which the noose must be suspended to catch the rabbit's head. The boys leaned against him — one each side — and absorbed his instruction avidly.

Caroline felt it was the wrong place for instruction of this nature, but in spite of her misgivings she was enchanted at the sight of Robert manipulating the cord and the pegs, and of the boys leaning upon him so confidingly. Robert had always seemed so mature — so much a man of the world — this was a new side of Robert and a side which seemed to Caroline very endearing. She thought of Philip and decided that Philip had chosen wrongly when he had given up this father and attached himself to another . . . Mr. Honeyman might be everything that was good and kind and generous, but Robert was an ideal father for a boy.

It was still raining but there was a brightness in the sky and the slanting spears of silver rain were full of rainbow colours. It would be fine in another ten minutes and Caroline would get home dry. Meanwhile the boys, having absorbed all the information possible upon the subject of rabbit-snares, had begun to chat about other matters. They had accepted Mr. Shepperton as a friend so their conversaton was uninhibited and amusing.

"It was a lovely pick-cher," Peter was saying. "Me an' Ted went over to Wandlebury an' saw it You'd like it, Mr. Shepperton — wouldn't he, Ted? It was about a chap what had a father an' a mother, an' there was another chap, an' he poisoned the chap's father — see? Nobody knowed about it. He did it quiet-like. Then, what does he do but marry the chap's mother straight off. Well, the chap doesn't like this much, an' he begins to get a bit suspicious, an' then he goes out in a fog an' he meets a funny old geezer what tells him his father was murdered — spills the beans good and proper. So then the chap gets in a wax an' goes after his mother an' nearly shakes the life out of her . . . an' then he finds an old chap listening behind the curtain so he lays him out . . . he's gone a bit queer in the head, see?"

"You've forgotten the bit when he has a row with his girl," put in Ted.

"Crumbs, so I have! This chap has a

row with his girl an' he knocks her down an' leaves her lying on the stairs, howling," said Peter with relish.

"What a dreadful film!" Caroline exclaimed. "It's positively wicked to make films like that!"

"It's great," declared Peter. "You'd like it, Mrs. Dering. Honestly you would. It gets more exciting and more exciting all the time. The next thing is the chap goes for a cruise an', while he's away, his girl goes off her chump an' throws herself in the river an' drowns herself — see? So then they have to dig a grave for her. Lots of people have been buried there before — just like Ashbridge churchyard — an' they digs up a whole lot of bones. Then they gets busy burying the girl, an' 'alfway through the service Hamlet arrives home — "

"Hamlet!" cried Caroline in amazement.

"That's the chap's name — see?" explained Peter.

Peter could never understand why his audience, which had been listening so intently to his story, suddenly burst out laughing . . . and laughed and laughed and laughed. He was very anxious to continue, for — as he had so truly said — the story became more and more exciting as it went on; but the laughter spoilt everything, and when at last Mrs. Dering and Mr. Shepperton managed to control themselves and were blowing their noses and wiping their eyes, the rain had stopped and it was nearly time for dinner.

"I dunno," said Peter in perplexed tones as he and Ted watched the audience walk down the path together.

"It's a funny name — *Hamlet*," suggested Ted.

"Not as funny as all that," objected Peter.

25

"WE ought to have a party," said Leda. "We haven't had a party for years — not since we were children."

Caroline was dubious. "What sort of a party?" she inquired.

"Not a dinner, of course," replied Leda.

"No indeed!" cried her mother in horrified tones.

"An evening party," said Harriet. "We could have hock-cup and cake and little biscuits. What about that?"

Caroline said that was more like it, she had just received an American parcel full of dried fruit and fat and crystallised cherries, so a large cake and some little biscuits were not beyond her powers.

"I'll ask Mr. Herbert about hock, or something," said James. "You can leave the drink to me."

"Let's have it soon," said Leda. "Let's have it next week — it's horrid waiting for things. I'll ring up Derek and see what day he could come."

"That's very short notice," objected Caroline. "Why not wait till after Christmas?"

"Nonsense," exclaimed Harriet. "You never send out long invitations nowadays. I'm often asked to parties the same day — and they aren't fiddler's invitations. We'll make out a list and the girls can ring up everybody and tick them off, it's much the easiest way."

Caroline protested feebly but was overruled, for if Miss Harriet Fane didn't know what was what, who did?

The list was not difficult to make; it was the sort of party to which everybody they knew could be invited (everybody within ten miles, for you could not expect people to come farther with petrol so scarce and precious). There were thirty names on Leda's list and Caroline added a few more.

"Not enough," Harriet said. "The room will be bare and the party will be a flop. We can count on about half the people accepting, so — "

"Half the people!" Caroline cried. "You may know all about London but you don't know the first thing about Ashbridge.

If we ask thirty people we may expect at least thirty-five. People ring up and say 'I'd love to come, may I bring Aunt Susan? She loves parties.' Or else 'My niece will be here for the Christmas holidays, do you mind if I bring her along?' Thirty-five people will be enough. We can open the double doors between the drawing-room and the dining-room."

"We can act a play!" cried Bobbie. "Here's Aunt Harrie! It would be a frightful waste not to act a play."

"Not unless I can be an animal," said the famous Miss Fane firmly. "I don't mind acting with you if I can be an animal . . . we might do Goldilocks and the Three Bears or Beauty and the Beast — "

"Or St. George and the Dragon," suggested Caroline sarcastically. "I should love to see you and James as St. George and the Dragon."

"We might and all," said Harriet thoughtfully. "A Morality Play . . . yes, it's quite an idea."

Harriet was intrigued with the idea of a Morality Play — it would be amusing and it could be quite informal — and after some persuasion, James said he was willing to play the part of St. George if he didn't have to speak.

"If you don't have to speak!" exclaimed his aunt in surprise.

"I can't stand up and spout in front of all those people," said James firmly. "I'll do it if I don't have to speak."

This pronouncement might have discouraged a woman with less initiative and resource, but it did not discourage Miss Fane. She decided that it must be a Mumming Play and she would have a spokesman to speak the lines and explain the action. Her choice for this rôle fell on Robert Shepperton. Robert needed even more persuasion than James, but at last gave in and said he would be the spokesman if he need not appear upon the stage. Harriet pinned him down at once, he could remain hidden behind the curtain. She was thus possessed of a cast, one of whom refused to be heard and the other refused to be seen, but she was still quite undaunted. She was undaunted by the fact that she was author, producer, wardrobe-mistress and one of the chief actors; nothing could daunt Miss Fane . . . except silence and burglars.

The production necessitated a great deal of rehearsal, which meant that Robert was to be found at Vittoria Cottage pretty frequently and for long periods, and the cast of three shut itself up in the drawing-room. From the beginning the producer found her cast obstreperous, Robert and James had their own ideas about the production and aired them without fear or favour.

"Those doggerel rhymes of yours are frightful, Aunt Harriet," said James. "A Mumming Play should be written in Spenserian English."

It was the outraged author who replied, "Write it yourself, then," but nobody was more surprised than she when James sat down and re-wrote it and presented her with something a good deal better than her own crude effort (she acknowledged at once that James had out-done her, for there was nothing small or petty about Harriet). Robert was surprised, too. He realised that James had managed to catch the true atmosphere of the Mumming Play — his lines had the authentic touch, Robert thought.

Harriet had not intended that the play

should be a secret from the other inhabitants of Vittoria Cottage, but the interruptions nearly drove her mad. Caroline looked in to see if there was anything they wanted; Bobbie looked in and giggled uncontrollably; Leda looked in and offered useless advice; Comfort came in to make up the fire and lingered to chat. The cast was difficult enough to control without the complication of fond admirers and half-baked critics, and at last the producer lost patience and locked the door.

"I'm sorry," said the producer, "but if we don't get a little peace we can't possibly be ready by Wednesday."

So the Mumming Play was nourished in secret, and in secret it took form and grew to maturity. A great deal of talk and laughter came from behind the locked door and occasionally shrieks of agony — which might be supposed to emanate from a wounded dragon. It was obvious that Harriet and James and Robert were having a good time.

Caroline was glad to hear them enjoying themselves . . . or at least she tried very hard to be glad. It was ridiculous to feel shut out. They were rehearsing the play and, as she was not taking part in the play, they did not need her. She told herself this several times a day, she besought herself not to be silly. Robert had liked her . . . he still liked her, but he liked Harriet better. How natural that was! Harriet was younger than herself, younger, gayer and prettier, naturally Robert liked Harriet, any one would . . . and of course Harriet liked Robert; that, too, was natural.

There was no doubt about it in Caroline's mind. She had seen, at the Wares' party, that Robert and Harriet had liked one another immensely, and her surmise had been confirmed when she had watched them playing with the leaves. Robert was still friendly and kind towards her — he had been delightfully friendly the day they had gone to the carol practice — but with Harriet he was on a different footing altogether.

James noticed it, too, and teased his aunt gently about her boy-friend. "Gooseberry is my middle name," said James, heaving a sigh.

"Donkey is your middle name," retorted his aunt, blushing to the roots of her hair.

It was not until now, when she saw that she had lost Robert, that Caroline discovered how much he meant to her . . . she looked back and tried to determine exactly when her friendship for him had grown into love. It was a useless occupation, of course, and quite fruitless, for now it seemed to Caroline that she had always loved him. Perhaps the seed had been sown all those years ago at Elsinore and had lain dormant in her heart. She loved him in all sorts of different ways: she admired his character and enjoyed his humour, she felt an immense tenderness towards him and her heart beat faster when he was there. These feelings were so strong that they were difficult to disguise, and it was only by damping herself down that she could bear to be in the same room with him.

Fortunately Caroline had learnt the lesson of renunciation; her life had taught her how to withdraw gracefully inside herself and how to bear disappointment and heartache with a smiling face, so instead of brooding upon her troubles she tried to banish them. She set to work and made a cake for the party. It was to be a magnificent cake, large and rich, full of eggs and fruit — an absolute pre-war cake. Comfort stood at her elbow, watching eagerly, helping to beat the mixture, breathing heavily with her exertions and chatting the while.

"They're having fun, aren't they?" Comfort said. "It's nice, isn't it. It's nice for Mr. James to have a bit of fun after all those years in Malaya. I like that Mr. Shepperton, he's nice, isn't he? When he looks at you he *really* looks at you — with his eyes smiling — as if he really sees you. It sounds silly-like, but lots of people don't. Lots of people look at you as if you were a chair or something — but he doesn't. It's almost as if he knew all about you," said Comfort thoughtfully. "Not that he *could* know, of course — him being a real gentleman as anybody can see — I mean he couldn't know what it's like to be poor and fat and have troubles, could he, Mrs. Dering? But it seems as if he did."

"Yes, I know what you mean," said Caroline.

Comfort was aware that something was worrying Mrs. Dering. It was that Miss Leda, she supposed. She wanted to do something for Mrs. Dering, to cheer her up and make her feel better — but what could she do?

"It's nice having the house full of people, isn't it?" continued Comfort with determined cheerfulness. "Beryl was saying to me the other day, 'You must be having a time of it,' she says. 'All those people in the house,' she says. 'I wonder you stand it — I wouldn't.' But Beryl's lazy, that's what's the matter with *her*. I like the house full. It's cheery. Mr. James — well, he *is* a caution, isn't he? And Miss Fane is nice. I like Miss Fane . . . the things she says! She doesn't 'arf make me laugh. You'd never think she was a wonderful actress, would you?"

"No, you wouldn't, would you?" Caroline agreed.

"It'll be nice on Wednesday night," Comfort continued. "I like parties. I like a bit of excitement. Mother wondered if you'd like her to come and help; she looks nice in her black dress and I could lend her an apron. She'd be nicer than me for handing round trays and that, wouldn't she?"

"Nobody could be nicer than you," said Caroline in a shaky voice. She turned from the table and stood looking out of the window.

Comfort was aghast. Something frightful was the matter — and what could she do? What *could* she do to help?

"I'll have that treatment," said Comfort, playing her last card.

"You'll . . . what did you say?" asked Caroline in surprise.

"I'll take that stuff," said Comfort. "That celluloid or whatever it's called . . . the stuff to make me thin. I will, really, I'll go and see doctor tomorrow."

"But, Comfort — "

"You'd like me to, wouldn't you, Mrs. Dering?"

"Comfort . . ." began Caroline, and then she stopped. What on earth was she to say?

Comfort had intended to cheer up Mrs. Dering and take her mind off her trouble (whatever it was), and, although she might not have accomplished her first object, she most certainly had accomplished her second. She had given Mrs. Dering a problem which required careful thought, and Mrs. Dering immediately banished her own problem and gave her mind to the problem of Comfort. She turned round and leant against the dresser and looked at Comfort earnestly.

"Do you really want to have the treatment?" she asked.

"Yes," nodded Comfort.

"I don't want you to have it if you're frightened."

"I'm not frightened," said Comfort boldly. "I'll see about it tomorrow. You'd like me to be thin, wouldn't you, Mrs. Dering?"

"You won't be *thin*," said Caroline hastily.

"Well — thinner," amended Comfort. "You'd like that."

"I don't mind," said Caroline, choosing her words carefully. "I don't mind a bit, Comfort. I like you as you are and I should like you just the same if you were thinner. It's for your own sake I should like you to be thinner — not for mine."

She had put it as plainly as she knew how, but she had little hope that Comfort would understand — and Comfort didn't.

"But you'd like it," Comfort said.

Caroline sighed. The responsibility was hers and whatever she said or did she could not escape it. "Why not wait?" she suggested. "Ask your mother — "

"I know what she'd say — just the same as she said before — and it isn't a bit of use waiting. I want to be thin soon."

"Really?" asked Caroline. "Are you quite sure?"

Comfort nodded. "You'd like it," she said.

The responsibility was firmly fixed. "Yes," said Caroline, making up her mind and at the same time deciding that, if it were to be, there must be nothing half-hearted about it. "Yes, I should like it. I'll come with you to Dr. Smart and we'll find out all about the treatment and fix it up. Meantime I think it would be better not to tell any one — not even your mother."

"Not tell mother?" asked Comfort in surprise.

"Not tell any one," said Caroline (for the responsibility was hers and she was taking the risk, and the risk would be greatly increased if Mrs. Podbury knew what was going on and worried Comfort by prodding and poking at her and asking if she were beginning to feel "queer")

"Not tell any one at all," repeated Caroline firmly. "It will be a secret between you and me."

So saying, Caroline took up her spoon and began to beat her cake mixture with energy and determination . . . and, to Comfort's joy, she looked quite cheerful.

The day of the party arrived. It was a busy day for everybody. Caroline was polishing furniture, Bobbie was polishing glass, Harriet and James had undertaken the all-important task of mixing the "cup", and as this necessitated a good deal of tasting they became quite merry over it. The telephone had been ringing all morning (some of the guests had found they could not come after all, and others were anxious to bring someone else with them), so it surprised nobody when it rang again, and James had no qualms as he lifted the receiver.

"It's Oxford," said James. "Where's Leda? Somebody tell Leda it's Oxford."

"Leda has gone out," said Bobbie. "You had better take a message, James. I hope it isn't to say Derek can't come; she'll be in an awful rage."

The same idea had occurred to Caroline and she listened anxiously while James took the message, for although only one side of a telephone conversation is audible to eavesdroppers, it is often possible to guess its trend.

"Yes," said James. "Yes, I'm James Dering. Can I take a message? . . . Good heavens!" cried James. "How did it happen? . . . Gosh, what bad luck! . . . Yes, I see . . . yes, is he getting on all right? . . . yes, it was . . . no, of course not . . . yes, tell him we're all very sorry indeed. . . ."

"Derek has broken his leg," said James as he laid down the receiver. "That was a Miss Bright. Derek was staying at the Brights' house for the night, and this morning he fell down the stairs and broke his leg. The doctor set it and says it will be all right, but he's not to be moved. Miss Bright phoned to let us know he couldn't come to the party."

Everybody exclaimed at once and continued to exclaim and to ask James questions which he could not answer. They were still discussing the matter and regretting poor Derek's misfortune when Leda returned. Leda was horror-stricken at the news, she wanted to ring up the Brights and ask for further information, she wanted to start off to Oxford at once, she wanted to put off the party.

"Don't be an ass, Leda," said James with brotherly candour. "Derek will be all right; the girl said so. A broken leg is nothing; it simply means he'll be in bed for a few weeks, that's all. He wouldn't thank you for making a fuss. I expect he feels an awful fool — anybody would. Fancy falling down the stairs!" said James, chuckling heartlessly. "*Falling down the stairs!* As for putting off the party that's impossible and absurd. It's far too late to put off the party . . . and why should we anyhow? You'd think the fellow had broken his neck!"

Leda listened to James — he was the only person who could make her listen. "Yes," said Leda quite meekly. "Yes — well — perhaps he wouldn't like a fuss. You're sure they said he was getting on all right, I suppose?"

"I've told you," said James. "I can't tell you any more. We can ring up tomorrow if you want to."

26

VITTORIA COTTAGE looked very gay in its gala attire. The drawing-room had been arranged to make more space for the guests, the folding doors were open, there were flowers everywhere. Caroline made up the fire carefully and had a last look round to see that everything was as it should be. She moved a chair slightly and rearranged a bowl of white chrysanthemums and then went slowly upstairs to dress. It was so long since she had given a party that she was nervous — she felt quite shivery with nerves — and the fact that she was upset about other matters added to her unease.

Like Martha, she was anxious about many things. First and foremost there was her own private and secret trouble and the necessity for keeping it a secret, the necessity for hiding it behind a smiling face so that nobody should guess she was unhappy. Then there was the responsibility of Comfort's treatment. Comfort was taking the treatment for her sake — she knew that, of course — and therefore it was up to her to see that it was properly carried out. Caroline had undertaken to measure out the medicine and give it to Comfort at the proper hours; a most necessary precaution; for Comfort, though a perfect dear, was also a perfect fool and was quite capable of forgetting the medicine for a whole day and then taking a double dose to make up for lost time. Comfort had now been taking the medicine for three days and so far she was no thinner; this did not surprise Caroline, who had not expected a miracle to occur, but it surprised and disappointed Comfort, who had. Comfort measured herself all over several times a day with a tape-measure which she had bought for the purpose, and several times a day she reported the lack of progress to her mistress. It had been funny at first, but now it had ceased to be funny and had become annoying and slightly alarming. Was this the first symptom of "queerness"? What would happen if the thyroid did not have the desired effect? Then there was Derek's accident, Caroline was worried about that. It was not a serious accident, of course, and, as James had said, it would simply mean bed for several weeks until his leg mended; but somehow or other Caroline was worried about it. Derek's accident seemed just about the last straw.

Caroline thought of these things while she was dressing and then she caught sight of her troubled face in the mirror. (What an unhostess-like face! It was enough to frighten away any guest!) and she decided that for tonight at least she must banish care. If she could not enjoy herself she must pretend to do so; she must do her utmost to make the party a success. She decided that she was an actress, dressing for her part in a First Night Performance. This idea helped a good deal, though, of course, the analogy was not strictly correct: the actress had an advantage over Caroline for she knew her part, knew the words she would say when she stepped on to the stage and, even more important, she knew what the other actors in the drama would reply. Caroline's part was unknown and therefore much more difficult and alarming . . . but I look quite nice, she thought, as she took a last glance in the mirror. This time the reflection was reassuring. She was wearing the same black velvet gown which she had worn at the Ash House party — she had nothing else to wear — but she had pinned some red velvet roses on her corsage. Her cheeks were slightly rouged and her eyes were sparkling.

"Not bad at all," said Caroline, nodding at her reflection and with that she tilted her head courageously and went downstairs.

Robert had just arrived. He was in the hall. He came forward quickly and met her at the bottom of the stairs and took her hand.

"Are we saying how do you do?" asked Caroline with a little smile.

"That's hardly necessary, is it?" returned Robert. "It wasn't that, it was just . . ." he paused. How could he say that as she came downstairs it had seemed to him that a light shone in her face, that he had taken her hand impulsively, that he had not been able to help taking her hand. Perhaps he might have found the right words if there had been time, but the house was full of bustle . . . Mrs.

Podbury came out of the pantry with a tray of glasses.

"What is it?" asked Caroline, smiling and withdrawing her hand.

"Nothing," he replied. "At least — nothing I can say now."

"Nothing wrong?" she asked in sudden anxiety.

"No, nothing."

The little incident was over (it was a mere nothing, a whole series of nothings). Bobbie came running downstairs, James came out of the dining-room, and a moment later the bell rang and the first guests had arrived.

As is usual with parties, the dullest guests arrived first. The Meldrums, the Burnards and the Whitelaws. The Burnards and the Meldrums were not on speaking terms, Mrs. Burnard having quarrelled irreconcilably with Mrs. Meldrum over the Hallowe'en Party at the Girl Guides' hut. Caroline knew about this, of course, for she had heard the whole story from each of the combatants in turn, but she had thought that with thirty-odd guests the fact that two of them were not on speaking terms would not matter . . . and t would not have mattered if one or other or both of the ladies had been late in arriving. Who could have foreseen that both would arrive early, thought Caroline as she saw her guests glare at each other like strange cats and gravitate to opposite sides of the large empty room.

The Whitelaws (a young married couple who had just come to live in the district) knew nobody, of course. Caroline had asked them because she thought it would be nice for them to meet some of their new neighbours . . . but apparently the Whitelaws thought otherwise. They stood together in the middle of the room and nothing would move them, they answered their hostess's inquiries as to their health and well-being in as few words as possible, they refused to be drawn into conversation about the weather, they were practically dumb on the subject of their garden. Perhaps they were shy, thought Caroline, giving them the benefit of the doubt.

Caroline prayed for more guests to arrive quickly. She began to wonder if more guests would come. How awful if everybody except the Meldrums, the Burnards and the Whitelaws had decided that they couldn't be bothered to go to the party at Vittoria Cottage! She could almost hear them discussing it. "We shall be more comfortable at home," they would say. "It doesn't matter, does it? No need to let them know we aren't going. There'll be such a crowd, the Derings won't notice if we don't turn up." Others would suddenly be afflicted with toothache or would discover that the car wouldn't start. It was one of Caroline's flights of fancy — one of her "things" and a very uncomfortable one.

She was beginning to feel quite desperate when the door opened and dozens of people poured into the room; and the room, which had seemed so large and bare and empty, was suddenly full of a chattering throng. The Whitelaws, the Meldrums and the Burnards were swallowed up and engulfed in the flood; their hostess abandoned them to their fate and saw them no more. Everybody knew everybody — or very nearly — and they were all delighted to meet . . . and soon every guest had a glass in one hand and a piece of cake in the other, and the party had begun to roll along as merrily as any hostess could desire. It was like a wedding, thought

Caroline (as she went from one friend to another, smiling and chatting and asking after sons and daughters who were absent from the rout), it was like a wedding without the principal actors; there was wine and cake and flowers, but no bride and bridegroom to receive congratulations and no bridesmaids in pretty frocks to be admired. Perhaps it had been a mistake to have this kind of party *now*, for if Leda and Derek were to be married next year the party would have to be repeated — and repeated in exactly the same form.

Derek's absence was noted, of course — especially when Sir Michael and Rhoda arrived without him — and soon everybody in the room knew what had happened and regrets were being expressed on every side. "Poor Derek!" people said, or "Poor Leda, what bad luck!" or "Have you heard about Derek's accident? Yes, *isn't* it unfortunate?"

Harriet, like a good stage manager, gave her audience plenty of time to settle down before beginning her entertainment. The Mumming Play was not the only item on the programme; Anne was to sing; the Meldrum girls had offered to perform a duologue from *Pride and Prejudice*, Elizabeth Bennet's interview with Lady Catherine de Bourgh. Joan was Elizabeth, of course. That was enough, decided Harriet; she was fully aware that it is better to give people too little rather than too much.

Leda's song was cut, she did not feel like singing, but the rest of the entertainment went well. Harriet thought poorly of the duologue — naturally she could have done it better. The girls were sticks, thought Harriet; Margaret was shy and far from word perfect, and Joan was full of ridiculous airs and graces (which Elizabeth Bennet most certainly was not). Fortunately the audience was not as critical as Miss Fane (the audience was of the opinion that it was *so* clever of Joan and Margaret to act like that) and the applause was satisfactory if not prolonged.

The Mumming Play was last on the programme, and the audience, having heard a good deal about it, was keyed up to the proper stage of anticipation. There was complete silence when Bobbie drew back the curtains and disclosed the scene. It had not been possible to prepare scenery in the short time at their disposal, but the "stage" was dimly lighted and there were plants in pots to give the illusion of a forest grove . . . and in the centre lay a large green dragon with a huge hideous head and glowing eyes. A gasp went up from the audience — and Caroline did not wonder for it was a most alarming sight. Caroline was aware that the dragon's head was fashioned from green gauze and hat wire, and its glowing eyes were pieces of glass from an old pair of spectacles with an electric torch behind them, but even this knowledge could not destroy the illusion and even she was horrified at the dragon's appearance.

The dragon writhed about for a few moments, showing its paces, and then the Hidden Voice began to speak:

"Here in this bosky thicket is the haunt
  Of a foul dragon, strong and fierce and
    gaunt.
The bones of many a victim lie around
Strewn far and wide upon the trampled
    ground.
Behold the monster! Mark his glowing
    eyes —

The very mountains tremble when he
    sighs —
Sharp are his talons, fiery is his breath;
He fears nor man nor beast, he fears not
    death.
The land he ravages — north, south, west,
    east —
He is the very devil of a beast.
Brave lads and gentle maidens are his
    prey;
All England cowers 'neath his dreadful
    sway.
Many, to end his horrid life, have tried,
None have been strong enough to break
    his pride.

"But lo, a paladin comes out to fight;
His shield is stainless and his sword is
    bright.
In silver chain, from head to foot, he's
    mailed —
Will *he* succeed where other men have
    failed?
See him stride forth and mark his doughty
    mien!
Never such noble champion was seen.
'What ho!' he calls. 'Avaunt thou Beast of
    Night!

'St. George for England! God Defend the Right!' "

St. George was a truly magnificent figure. There he stood, mailed from top to toe in silver cardboard armour, while the Hidden Voice enumerated his exploits and extolled his virtues. The dragon, meanwhile, became more and more enraged, snarling and growling and flashing its eyes; then, all of a sudden, it reared its ugly head and snapped ferociously at its challenger . . . the fight was on.

At first the combatants seemed evenly matched. St. George was more mobile, of course. He rushed about with tireless energy and dauntless courage, stabbing the dragon repeatedly from different angles, while the dragon writhed and roared and managed to deliver some shrewd blows with its terrible claws in return . . . but St. George's silver armour saved him from harm and, if he retired for a moment, it was only to clear his arm for a mightier thrust. Presently the dragon lost heart, its attacks had less pertinacity, its roars were less furious, more despairing . . . and, seeing this, St. George redoubled his efforts. He leapt upon it and plunged his sword into its black heart. Now the dragon was dying — there was not a doubt of that — it was dying in agonies, rolling upon the ground and groaning and shrieking like a lost soul. (Its death throes were so realistic that Caroline began to be alarmed and to wonder whether James, by mistake, had pierced his aunt in some vital portion of her anatomy, and she looked round anxiously to see if Dr. Smart were still there, over near the fire, where she had been talking to him a few minutes since.)

There was a storm of applause when the fight ended and St. George stood erect with his sword outstretched and his foot firmly planted upon the dragon's head.

"Again!" cried somebody. "Do it again Encore!"

"Encore! Encore!" cried everybody clapping like mad.

But the dragon had had enough. "No thank you," said the dragon, rising to its feet amongst folds of green cloth (which looked to Caroline extraordinarily like her spare-room curtains). "Not again," said the dragon firmly. "It's very nice of you to be so appreciative, but once is enough

James — I mean St. George — got a little carried away. An audience sometimes has that effect upon an amateur . . ." The remainder of the dragon's speech was drowned in roars of laughter and in loud calls for the author, the producer and the actors.

The Derings had expected their guests to depart when the dramatic entertainment was over, but nobody made any move to go until long after midnight, and it was nearly two o'clock before the last guest said good-bye.

"It was a howling success," declared Harriet, sinking into a chair. "It was simply terrific . . . and I'm absolutely exhausted."

"We may as well finish up the drink," said James.

They finished it, sitting amongst the *débris* of the party, talking about all that had happened.

27

CHRISTMAS DAY was damp and muggy, as it so often is, but, although the weather was not of the snow and robin variety, the scene inside Vittoria Cottage was as Christmassy as could be. The presents were opened after breakfast and soon the drawing-room was in fine confusion with gifts upon every chair and the floor covered with boxes and papers of every size and hue. Harriet was always generous, and this year she had fairly let herself go. Her presents included cardigans and silk stockings and pullovers . . . it was a wonder how she managed to spin out her coupons to cover all her gifts. Bobbie was certain that the thing was quite impossible and charged her aunt with having a secret source from which she was able to procure an inexhaustible supply of coupons; but her aunt only smiled and remained dumb. James had been generous, too. His heavy baggage had arrived and from it he produced sarongs of gorgeous silk and jade earrings and quaint figures of ivory and pictures fashioned from butterflies' wings. The "opening ceremony" was in full swing, and everybody was talking at once when the door opened and Robert walked in laden with parcels like Santa Claus, parcels for every one — not forgetting Comfort. There was a pile of parcels for Robert on the sideboard, and he was invited to stay and open them.

Robert had come to bring his presents and also to invite them all to lunch with him at the Cock and Bull. Mrs. Herbert was preparing an elaborate feast, declared Robert, and would be desolated if nobody came to eat it. They accepted, of course, and Caroline arranged to have their own Christmas dinner in the evening. Robert would come and share it and they would play a game. This being settled, they got ready for church, and all walked down the hill together.

Caroline loved the little church. It was old and very beautiful, and she knew it so well that it had a comfortingly friendly atmosphere . . . and today it felt even more friendly than usual. The church was decorated with holly and white flowers;

it was warm and brightly lighted and the faces of the worshippers were peaceful and happy, for this was Christmas morning and they had all given and received tokens of goodwill. Perhaps it is better to give than to receive, but it is best to do both and to do it graciously in the Christmas spirit. Caroline had done both; her heart felt peaceful and it was full of gratitude for the safe return of her son. He stood beside her in the pew, the sleeve of his jacket brushed against her shoulder . . . God has been very good to me, she thought. Other things did not matter in comparison with the safety of James, they must be banished from her mind. She would banish them and be happy and grateful as she ought to be.

Most certainly she ought to be grateful. If she had known two months ago that James would be here beside her on Christmas Day she would have said she wanted nothing more, she would have been blissfully happy. Now her unruly heart wanted more — could anything be more ungrateful!

"When shepherds watched their flocks by night,

All seated on the ground;
An angel of the Lord appeared
And glory shone around . . ."

James was smiling down at her for this was his favourite hymn and, as she smiled back, the last vestige of her unhappiness vanished. I am happy, she thought. I am truly grateful. I don't want anything more.

Robert Shepperton had asked Sir Michael and Rhoda to join his lunch party, so they sat down eight to Mrs. Herbert's Christmas feast. They sat down informally, without arrangement, which was unfortunate — or so Caroline thought — she found herself between her host and Rhoda.

"Mrs. Dering, I've got a bone to pick with you!" exclaimed Rhoda. "I haven't had time to pick it before. I want to know why you were away when I came to see you, and I want to know what you meant by coming to town and never letting me know. I told you I would throw a party for you."

"That was why," declared Caroline, entering into the jest. "If you hadn't said you would throw a party I might have come."

"I throw very good parties — "

"Orgies," said Caroline gravely. "Mrs. Meldrum says they're orgies, so of course they must be."

"You always agree with Mrs. Meldrum, don't you?"

"Um — well — " said Caroline.

They both laughed.

Robert looked at Caroline several times but she continued to spar with Rhoda, so all he could see was a light-brown curl beneath the brim of her hat and a very pretty little ear with a pearl-stud in it. The stud went right through, it was not clipped on as were so many earrings nowadays. Robert had noticed this before, it was one of the first things he had noticed about Caroline. She wouldn't wear earrings at all if her ears were not pierced, thought Robert as he ate his turkey; clip-on earrings are artificial — well of course all earrings are artificial, but those with screws or clips are silly — and clothes should be simple, not fussed up with ornaments and frills and buttons that don't button into honest-to-goodness button-holes. It's the same kind of thing, thought Robert. Buttons that don't button and earrings that don't go right through — they're fakes — that's why Caroline doesn't wear them.

Robert had ample time to work out his theme, for Leda was sitting on his left. Leda did not like Robert and today she had even less use for him than usual. Sir Michael (who was next on her other side) was telling her all about Derek, and naturally the subject interested her profoundly. Rhoda had been to see Derek the day before and had found him cheerful and comfortable and exceedingly well looked after with a nurse in attendance. He was still at the Brights' house, but it was hoped to move him soon.

"I want him moved," declared Sir Michael. "The Brights have been very kind but we can't presume upon their hospitality. Rhoda agrees, she thinks he should be moved without delay, so I've written to the doctor and asked if Derek can be brought home in an ambulance."

"I wish I could see him!" exclaimed Leda.

"I know," agreed Sir Michael. "Of course you do — so do I, for that matter — but it's difficult when he's in the Brights' house. That's one of the reasons why he ought to be moved. We'll get him brought home, Leda. I've written to the doctor about it."

Leda smiled. She began to think Derek's accident was not such a tragedy as it had seemed, for if Derek came home to Ash House she could go there daily; she could take him books and talk to him — she might even be allowed to help the nurse to look after him. She could see Sir Michael was coming round. Sir Michael might possibly be wheedled into giving permission for them to be married quite soon.

Thinking thus, Leda was very charming to Sir Michael. She laid herself out to entertain him and never once glanced at her other neighbour.

Harriet smiled at Robert several times, but the table was large and round and Harriet was at the other side, hemmed in between her nephew and her younger niece, so she could do nothing to entertain her host . . . Robert could have kicked himself for the bad arrangement of his lunch-party, he ought to have thought it all out beforehand, of course.

28

WHEN the Christmas lunch-party was over, and every one had had as much as they could eat, it was decided to walk over to Vittoria Cottage and view the presents. Robert had seen the presents already, so instead of going in with the others he walked on. He was feeling rather miserable — everything seemed to be going wrong — and the indubitable fact that he had eaten too much did not help matters. He had eaten more than usual because he had had nobody to talk to during the meal . . . and the sensation was unfamiliar. Robert had lived on starvation diet for years, so he was not in training for Mrs. Herbert's idea of a Christmas feast.

He walked on to the Roman Well — which, although it was not Roman, was a pleasant place to go — and there he found Peter Podbury and Ted Mumper. The friendship which had started with Christmas carols and rabbit-snares had ripened considerably, and the two boys were delighted to see Mr. Shepperton. But Mr. Shepperton was not as cordial as usual — he was annoyed with Peter. It had come to his ears that the clock on the village hall had been altered again — though this time the trick had failed to deceive the driver of the Wandlebury bus.

"I thought you were going to turn over a new leaf, Peter," said Mr. Shepperton reproachfully. "You promised, didn't you? You said if I showed you how to set the snares you'd give up these idiotic pranks — and this prank was more idiotic than usual. You might have known you couldn't trick people a second time." (It was curious but true that Robert was almost as disappointed with Peter for doing such a foolish thing as for breaking his promise.)

"It wasn't us," said Peter.

"We didn't do it," said Ted.

"But you did it before!"

"That's why," returned Peter laconically.

"That's why!" echoed Mr. Shepperton in bewilderment. "I don't know what you mean."

"Peter don't like doing the same thing twice," explained Ted.

" 'Cos why?" said Peter. " 'Cos it's dull — an' silly. It's fun to do a thing once, but then it's over. 'Tisn't fun to keep on doing it."

Mr. Shepperton digested this information. He found it interesting. "I'm sorry," he said. "I shouldn't have jumped to the conclusion you and Ted had broken your promise."

"That's all right," declared Peter. "Everybody thinks it was us. We don't mind; we know who it was — see?"

"Tell him," urged Ted, poking his friend in the ribs. "Tell him — *you know what*, Peter."

"We want you to teach us navigation," said Peter obediently.

"Navigation!"

"We're going to be sailors — see?"

"It's true," declared Ted. "We've asked our dads an' they're finding out about it. We can go to a ship called *The Conway* when we're a bit older . . . but Peter an' me thought it 'u'd be a good idea to start learning about it right off."

"You will, won't you, Mr. Shepperton?" urged Peter.

Robert was amused and flattered at their

confidence in his powers. If they had wanted instruction in Persian they would have applied to him with equal confidence in his power to help them . . . fortunately he need not disappoint them for he had done some yachting in his youth and the art of navigation had always interested him; he knew enough about it to start them off in the right direction.

"So you want to be sailors?" he said.

"It would be a good idea, wouldn't it, Mr. Shepperton?"

Mr. Shepperton thought it would be an excellent idea. The Podburys were traditionally "stay-at-homes", but Peter was quite different from the other members of his family — Ashbridge was too small to hold Peter — he was full of initiative and resource, he was adventurous by nature . . . perhaps Peter was a throw-back to some dead and gone buccaneering Podbury who had sailed the Spanish Main. But whether that was the case or not, Robert Shepperton was quite sure that the discipline and ordered routine of a Naval Training School was exactly what Master Peter Podbury needed . . . and where he went Ted Mumper would follow blindly.

Meantime it would do them no harm to have a little mild instruction in seafaring matters, and it would be amusing — and useful — to undertake the task of instruction.

"You'll help, won't you?" urged Peter.

"All right, but you'll have to stick to it."

"We'll stick to it — like glue!" cried Peter joyously.

Robert Shepperton was feeling better and happier when he left the boys and continued his interrupted walk, for he had given happiness and intended to give more. It was not his way to do things by halves, and the boys had good stuff in them. He would speak to their fathers and see what he could do to help to arrange their future, to start them off in their career . . . it would make up a little for the loss of Philip if he took an interest in these two imps and could make plans for them.

Making plans for his new *protégés* filled Robert's mind so that he did not notice where he was going. He followed a rutty track across a field and presently found himself at the gate of a little cottage. It was a charming cottage, well kept and newly painted; there was a row of bee-hives in the little garden, and behind he could see a shed. Some hens were picking about in a wired enclosure — they were Rhode Island Reds, like Caroline's. Robert stood and looked at the cottage and thought what a delightful place it was; he wondered who lived here and whether they were happy people. Happiness was an odd thing, Robert thought. It depended upon so many small factors.

He was about to walk on when a girl came out of the cottage with a baby in her arms. The cottage was isolated and it seemed unfriendly not to greet a fellow-creature on Christmas Day, so he waved his hand and wished her good-afternoon.

The girl was glad to respond, she came down the path towards him. "A merry Christmas," she said. "It's a pity it isn't snow, isn't it?"

"Yes," said Robert, but he said it doubtfully for he was not particularly fond of snow . . . and it seemed to him that any one living here, so far from the amenities of civilisation, might find snow a nuisance rather than a pleasure.

"Not deep snow, of course," said the

girl. "Just a sprinkle like what you see on a Christmas card. It would be more Christmassy, wouldn't it?"

She was a pretty girl, Robert noticed, but she had "a delicate air" and the baby was tiny; it was the smallest morsel of humanity he had ever seen.

"Your baby looks very young," he told her.

"She *is* young," nodded the girl. "She's so young she didn't ought to have been born — or only just — but she's getting on nicely. She isn't pretty yet," continued her mother, who (privately) thought she was beautiful but had discovered that other people did not share her views. "She isn't pretty but she's good and very little bother. She's going to be christened soon."

"Have you decided what to call her?" Robert inquired.

"Caroline," said the girl, looking down at the tiny face with brightness in her own. "Caroline, her name is. It's the loveliest name I know."

"It is a beautiful name."

"You see," said Sue, looking up at him in her confiding way, "you see, Mrs. Dering is going to be her godmother — if it hadn't

been for Mrs. Dering she wouldn't b
here at all — so that's why Jim and me ar
calling her Caroline."

"I see," said Robert. It was not reall
true, of course, for he had no idea who th
girl was nor what she meant. Sue had th
advantage of him there; naturally she knew
who he was and all about him; for, althoug
Sue was living in an isolated spot, she wa
by no means cut off from her family and
there were few days when a Podbury o
some description — old or young, male o
female — did not visit her and bring he
all the village gossip. When Uncle Amo
came for gravel he always called at th
cottage for a cup of tea, and if he did no
appear Tom or Violet or little Amo
looked in, or her mother toiled up the hi
to see the baby. Cousins and aunts with
free hour walked up to see Sue, for it was
nice walk to the cottage and they wer
certain of a welcome.

"There's nobody like Mrs. Dering,"
continued Sue. "Jim and me both thin
that. There's nobody *in all the world* lik
Mrs. Dering."

"Yes," said Robert. "She is — very —
er — "

"She's a saint," said Sue, quite soberly. "I don't mean what people mean nowadays when they say a person's a saint; I mean like St. Francis and St. Catherine that did miracles long ago." She stopped suddenly for she knew she was a chatterbox and, if you had nobody to talk to all day, your tongue was apt to run away with you when you met somebody sympathetic — as this Mr. Shepperton was — and you suddenly found it saying things you didn't intend to say. Sue had decided she wasn't going to tell anybody about the strange, beautiful thing that had happened . . . not anybody at all, not Jim nor her mother, no, not anybody. It was a secret between her and Mrs. Dering and such a strange secret that even they had not spoken of it to one another. She would never forget it, of course; if she lived to be a hundred years old she would still remember that wonderful stream of peace and healing which had flowed into her through Mrs. Dering's hand and she would remember the sound of Mrs. Dering's voice when she had said, "Loving you. Shut your eyes, Sue."

"Miracles?" asked Robert Shepperton in surprise.

"There's a picture of St. Francis in church," Sue told him.

He was aware of this. It was a beautiful seventeenth century window and he admired it so much that he had changed his pew so that he could see it whenever he lifted his eyes . . . but that was not the point, and the girl knew it as well as he did. She was being stupid on purpose (it was the time-honoured defence of the peasant with a secret) but she need not have worried, for Robert was the last person to probe into matters which did not concern him. He gave the girl a present to buy something for little Caroline and walked on up the hill; but he had not gone far when he heard her running after him.

"P'raps you'd like to come to the christening," she said breathlessly. "It's Sunday week at two o'clock."

Robert was surprised and touched. Christenings were not much in his line (in fact Philip's christening was the only one he had attended, except presumably his own) but he realised the girl was offering him all she had to offer so he accepted gracefully.

29

CAROLINE was busy in the garden, sweeping up the leaves, when she saw the Admiral's Rolls stop at the gate. It was not an unusual sight these days for Sir Michael had begun to drop in quite frequently, and it was a welcome sight because Caroline had begun to like him very much indeed. There was something simple and boyish about the big man; he was sincere and kindly and straightforward. She waved her broom and went to meet him.

"Something's happened," he said as he came in at the gate.

"Heavens! Not — not Derek!"

"Yes, I've just seen him but I didn't get any satisfaction out of him — waste of petrol, that's all."

"You've been over to Oxford!" exclaimed Caroline, who now realised that Derek had not had a relapse and was neither dead nor dying.

"It seemed the only thing to do," he replied.

Caroline waited for more information but none was forthcoming. Sir Michael seemed tired and worried, he seemed unlike himself . . . and, unlike himself, he was looking at the ground as if he did not want to meet her eyes.

"Don't know how to tell you," he said at last. "Fact is . . . no, I'll give you the letter." He searched for the letter in all his pockets. "Got it this morning," he said. "It's from Bright and the only thing to do was to go straight over and see Derek; but I might have saved myself the trouble for all the good it did. Read it," he said, handing it to her. "Where are your glasses?"

"I don't need glasses," Caroline said.

She took the letter and was about to open it when Sir Michael took it out of her hand. "No," he said. "Wait a minute, Caroline."

"You're frightening me!"

"I know — I can't help it. We'll go indoors, shall we?"

They went into the drawing-room and Caroline sat down. She had said he was frightening her and it was true; but she was not really surprised.

"I suppose Derek wants to break the engagement," she said.

"How did you know?"

"I just — knew."

"That would be bad enough but this is worse," said Sir Michael and he handed her the letter for the second time.

She unfolded it. It was typewritten on thick, white, hand-made paper with a deckle edge and in spite of her worry and anxiety she could not help thinking how curious it looked and how badly typescript and hand-made paper went together:

BENDERSLEIGH MANOR,
near OXFORD.

DEAR SIR MICHAEL WARE,

I am informed that you are making arrangements for Derek's removal from my residence, but this is unnecessary as we are glad to have him here indefinitely. Derek has no desire to be moved, he is having the best attention money can provide and his progress is satisfactory. The fact is Valerie and Derek have taken a fancy to each other and Mrs. Bright and I have given permission to their engagement. As I have no son of my own I intend to take Derek into my business and train him for an executive post. I can assure you it is an excellent opening for a young man and there will be no need for you to give him financial assistance. He will have better prospects in BRIGHT'S LTD. than a degree in Law could give him. Derek has asked me to write and inform you of the new plans for his future welfare.

Believe me
Yours truly,
NATHANIEL BRIGHT.

The first time Caroline read it she could not believe her eyes, so she read it again. It was a most extraordinary letter, a horrible mixture of business jargon and vulgarity . . . and so smug and self-satisfied, so cruel. How could any father write to another father in such terms!

Sir Michael was standing at the window, gazing out. "I wouldn't have had this happen for anything," he said hoarsely. "I knew Derek was weak but I never thought he was a rotter. What would Alice have felt! You knew Alice; she was white all through."

"Yes," said Caroline. "Yes, she was — "

"Couldn't believe it at first," continued Sir Michael. "Thought there must be some mistake — some misunderstanding — so I went over in the car and saw Derek. Told him pretty straight what I thought of him. He pretended to be surprised, said he understood I didn't approve of his engagement to Leda and hadn't given my consent, so he didn't consider himself engaged to her. He said I'd made a fuss about the money, said he wouldn't need money from me now, said he thought I'd be pleased about *that*. He made it sound as if I grudged him his allowance. I never did — not for a moment — he's my only son and he had a right to the money. Of course, I had told him I was going to sell Betterlands Farm to get him started. I told him because I thought he ought to know. The place will be his when I'm dead, and if it's gradually shorn of all the best farms there won't be much of it left. I told him because I thought it would make him work harder and economise a bit, not because I grudged it. I told you, too," added Sir Michael. "You didn't think I grudged it, did you?"

"No," said Caroline. "I thought you were very generous, Sir Michael."

He was walking up and down now. "Well, anyhow, he put me in the wrong. He put me in the wrong over Leda, and he put me in the wrong over the money. I was wrong and he was the injured innocent! He had thought I'd be pleased . . . *pleased* mark you! He said I needn't sell Betterlands . . . and I shan't sell Betterlands," declared Sir Michael. "The place has been in the family since the year dot. I shall wire Stobbs and cancel the whole thing . . ."

Caroline let him run on. He was terribly upset and it was good for him to get it off his chest; he had nobody to talk to at home. She listened to him with half an ear while she thought of Leda and wondered how Leda would take it.

"But all that doesn't matter," said Sir Michael, stopping suddenly on the hearth rug and looking down at the fire. "That's all merely by the way. It's Leda we've got to think of. I don't know what to do — or say. I told him so. I said 'What about Leda? You seem to have forgotten Leda,' I said. So then he said Leda wouldn't mind. Apparently he and Leda had discussed the matter, they'd discussed Derek giving up Law and going into business and Leda wasn't in favour of it. Did you know that?"

"No," said Caroline. "Leda doesn't tell me much, I'm afraid."

"Well, they did," said Sir Michael. "They discussed it . . . and of course, Leda was right. Derek ought to take his degree. Leda appears to have some sense. Derek has none. Derek says she made rather a point of his sticking to Law. What d'you think about that, Caroline?"

She hesitated and then said, "Quite honestly, I don't think much of it. I'm afraid Leda will be terribly unhappy."

"It's damnable," he declared. "I wonder if we could say she'd broken it off. Could we?"

"I don't see how we could."

"No, perhaps not . . . silly idea of mine. It was just — well, I thought it might save her face a bit. It's hard for a girl. Caroline, I'm *terribly* sorry about this."

"You can't help it."

"I did all I could. If he'd been fit I could have said a lot more but the nurse came and turned me out — said his temperature was going up or something."

"You can't help it," she repeated. "You warned me, didn't you?"

"I wasn't too happy about it," admitted Sir Michael. "But I hoped it would be all right when it was settled — cut and dried. Derek hasn't any patience, that's the trouble. When he wants a thing he wants it at once — can't wait for it — quite different from Rhoda. It was the same when they were children, Derek always wanted things in a hurry and then got tired of them . . . but he won't get out of *this* in a hurry," said Sir Michael with a grim smile. "He's caught now, for better, for worse. I could see that quite clearly. The Brights have swallowed him whole."

Caroline nodded.

"Swallowed him whole," repeated Sir Michael. "He's in cotton-wool, pampered and cossetted, surrounded with hot-house flowers and picture papers. He's a prisoner in a gilded cage. I wonder how long it will be before he sees the bars."

There was a little silence.

"Well, that's that," said Sir Michael with a sigh. "I seem to have lost my son.

I suppose it's my own fault, I should have managed things better . . . I won't stay any longer, Caroline."

She rose and went to the door with him.

"Caroline," he said earnestly, "If there's anything I can do let me know, won't you? I'd be glad if there was something I could do."

"Yes, I will," said Caroline. She hesitated and then added, "Come and see us if you feel like it, Sir Michael."

"No ill-feeling?" he asked, taking her hand.

"Not towards you," she replied, trying to smile at him. "I can't say the same about Derek, I'm afraid."

"No, of course not — don't blame you."

She stood at the door for some minutes after he had gone.

30

CAROLINE decided that Leda must be told before the rest of the family and this meant she must bottle up the dreadful news until Leda returned from Wandlebury. She went upstairs to her bedroom and, sitting down in a chair near the window, she tried to compose her thoughts and to think of some way in which she could soften the blow. She had not been sitting there long when there was a knock on the door and James looked in.

"What did the Admiral want?" asked James. "I saw his car. You seemed to be having a terrific pow-wow so I didn't interrupt you."

Caroline hesitated.

"There's something wrong, I suppose," said James, looking at her.

It was no use trying to keep anything from James. They were too near one another; they understood one another too well . . . besides she wasn't going to tell

James a lie. "Something frightfully wrong," said Caroline miserably. "I don't know how I'm going to tell Leda."

"Derek, of course," said James.

"Yes, Derek. He's engaged to another girl — that Miss Bright."

"Engaged!" James exclaimed in amazement.

Caroline handed him the letter and he read it, standing beside her by the window. She noticed that he read it twice — as she had done — before he folded it up and returned it to the envelope.

"It's incredible," said James. "It's the most rotten thing I ever heard of. I had a feeling there was some funny business going on. Derek seemed a bit odd, somehow. I mean at the Ash House Party; he wasn't very — he didn't seem particularly *keen* on Leda — or so I thought. But this is beyond everything. This beats the band!"

"Sir Michael says they've swallowed him."

"So they have. You can see that from the letter."

"He's weak."

"Weak as water, but that doesn't excuse

him. Derek!" exclaimed James incredulously. "Derek . . . I've known Derek always!"

"Yes," agreed Caroline. They had both known Derek always.

"It's staggering," James declared. "People sometimes make mistakes — you can't help it sometimes — but surely he could have told Leda like a man! This is a rotten way to behave; it's cowardly."

It was cowardly, Caroline saw that. She saw, more or less, how the whole thing had happened, for she had the gift — which is often a doubtful blessing — of being able to see the other person's point of view, of being able to put herself in the other person's place. Derek had not wanted to go on with his studies (perhaps they bored him or perhaps he was doubtful of success in his exams) and Leda had not understood — nobody had understood. He was too cowardly, and too vain, to make a clean breast of it and to own up to his mistake; he had felt trapped and the Brights had offered him a pleasant, easy way out of all his difficulties.

James walked across the room and back. "He's a cad," said James.

"Yes," she agreed. It was an old-fashioned term, but it seemed to fit the case.

"What do we do, Mother?"

"What can we do?"

"No," he said thoughtfully. "No, nothing . . . but I feel as if I ought to take a hand in it . . . go after him with a horse-whip or something."

He looked so fierce, standing there with his hair ruffled and his eyes flashing that she could almost have laughed. "That's a bit out of date, I'm afraid," Caroline said.

"Pity! I'd like to, you know."

"You were born a hundred years too late for horse-whips, James."

"I don't even know what they look like," he admitted. "But they sound useful weapons. It must have been good when you could go after a fellow and beat him up without getting put in jail. Well, don't worry too much."

"No," said Caroline, with a sigh.

"I mean, she's well rid of him."

"Oh, yes. You might look out for her, James, and send her up to me when she comes in."

He nodded. "I don't envy you telling her. She'll take it hard," said James.

Leda took it hard. At first she would not believe that Derek wanted to break off the engagement. (Caroline had put it like this.) Somebody was trying to make mischief, declared Leda. She knew Derek She knew Derek loved her and wanted to marry her, he had said so time and again. It was just a plot to part her and Derek, because people didn't want them to be married . . . but the plot wouldn't succeed; she would go and see Derek herself and put everything right. Why should Derek have changed his mind suddenly? asked Leda.

Caroline told her about Valerie Bright.

"That girl!" exclaimed Leda scornfully. "That girl with her teeth on every poster! Derek wouldn't *look* at her."

It was necessary to show Leda the letter before she would be persuaded of the truth. Caroline had not meant to show Leda the letter — it was so bald and cruel and wounding — but what else could she do. The letter convinced Leda, of course . . . the colour faded from her cheeks as she read it and her face went set and hard.

"Leda, darling!" Caroline said. "I'm so sorry — so terribly sorry. It's dreadful for you!"

Looking back on the interview, when it was over and Leda had gone, Caroline realised that she had failed to get near her daughter. She had tried to comfort Leda, but everything she had said was wrong; she had opened her arms but Leda had remained outside, standing in the middle of the room, tearless and defiant.

"Why should this happen to *me*? What have I done?" she had exclaimed.

It was impossible to find any answer to this — or at least Caroline found it so.

Leda had led a sheltered life, her capacity for bearing suffering had never been tested, nothing serious had ever happened to her before. Her nature was arrogant (pride was the keystone of her nature) and this thrust had wounded her in a vital part. She felt disgraced — Derek had disgraced her — she could never hold up her head again. She could never go out and meet people, never again. She would know people were looking at her, pointing the finger of scorn. Some people would be glad with that strange unchristian gladness which glories in the downfall of others.

Caroline tried to reason with her and to point out that it was Derek who had behaved badly; he had disgraced *himself*, not Leda, by his behaviour. "People will be sorry," Caroline told her.

"I don't want their pity!" she cried. "I don't want sympathy. Of course, this *would* happen to *me* . . . other girls don't have frightful things like this to bear. Why should I have to bear it? I hate Derek — hate him! I hope he's terribly unhappy all his life."

Perhaps this was natural but it shocked Caroline for it was not merely an exclamation of distress. Leda really meant it seriously . . . and hatred is a terrible thing. Hatred hurts the hater far more than its object.

"Oh, Leda, don't hate him!" Caroline exclaimed and she tried to soften Leda's heart, tried to persuade her to accept her trouble in a different spirit but it was like talking to a stone.

"That's right, stand up for Derek," said Leda at last.

"I'm not standing up for Derek!"

exclaimed Caroline. "I think he's behaved abominably, but — "

Leda turned and went, pausing at the door to say, "You don't understand . . . and anyhow it's all your fault; if you'd been decent about it everything would have been all right."

"Oh, Leda!" cried Caroline in distress. "Leda — wait — "

But Leda was gone. She locked herself up in her room so that nobody could come in and offer her consolation.

Caroline had failed badly. She tried to think what she could have said or done. It was quite true that she did not understand Leda but it was not for want of trying. Leda had said, "Why should this happen to *me*?" and a few minutes later she had exclaimed bitterly, "Of course this *would* happen to *me*?" Of course one might exclaim thus in sudden grief — without really meaning anything — but Caroline realised that the words were not merely expressions of grief, they voiced a definite conviction. Arnold had said the same words over and over again when anything went wrong (things were always going wrong with Arnold) and Caroline had never been able to understand what they meant. She simply could not understand why people should claim special privileges from Providence (so that disasters might befall others but ought not to befall them) and yet, at the same time, should be convinced that Providence had a down on them and had singled them out — as Job was singled out — to bear the blasts of misfortune. In Caroline's opinion both these ideas were wrong and in addition they were incompatible.

Why can't I understand? wondered Caroline. If only I could understand Leda perhaps I could help (but she would never understand Leda because their natures were entirely different: Caroline was humble-hearted and Leda was proud).

31

BREAKFAST was late the following morning. Leda did not come down to breakfast nor would she open her door to let any one in her room with a tray. Caroline left the tray upon the table outside her door and came down feeling very unhappy.

"You would think someone had died," said Harriet looking up from her porridge.

"Harriet, what do you mean?"

"Nobody has died. Nothing serious has happened."

"Nothing serious has happened!" echoed Caroline in amazement.

"Nothing," said Harriet firmly. "Things like this happen every day and people go on living; they go on doing their work and eating their food and behaving like reasonable beings."

"But poor Leda —"

"Shucks!" exclaimed Harriet inelegantly. "There are as good fish in the sea as ever came out of it and Derek is only a sprat.

You know perfectly well you were never happy about the engagement'"

This was true of course, but still —

"You shouldn't encourage the child to make such a fuss," continued Harriet. " *'What can justify tears and lamentations.'* That's a Buddhist saying, and it's true. The more you see of the world the more you realise how few things can justify tears and lamentations. I'm wasting none over this."

"Yes," agreed Caroline doubtfully. "But all the same you must admit that it's a horrible thing to happen to a girl."

"It isn't what happens to you that matters, it's how you take it," replied Harriet with conviction.

They were silent for a few moments. Caroline was thinking it over, she realised that this was Harriet's creed. This was the conviction by which Harriet ruled her life. It accounted for many things which had puzzled Caroline.

"I've had some pretty severe knocks," continued Harriet. "Pass the marmalade, James . . . but I'm too proud to lie down and whimper. I don't let the world see my wounds. I bob up and laugh. Nobody can laugh at you if you laugh first; they laugh *with* you. That's different. That doesn't matter. Leda ought to put on her gayest hat and prance into the village . . . that's the way to take it."

"Aunt Harriet's right!" cried James.

Caroline thought so too, but she had no hopes of being able to convert Leda to Harriet's creed, especially through a locked door.

"If she can't do that she must go away," continued Harriet. "It isn't nearly so good, either for her reputation in the village or her own private character. People will talk far more if she goes away, and she's got to come back sometime, hasn't she? And it's bad to run away from things, it becomes a habit. But if she can't take it bravely she must go away. It's second best. She can go to my flat if she likes."

"Aunt Mamie would have her," suggested James.

"Third best," said Harriet thoughtfully. "Mamie would be far too kind and there would be nothing to do at Mureth."

When Caroline went upstairs to discuss matters with Leda she found the breakfast tray where she had left it but she was glad to note that the food had gone. She knocked at Leda's door but there was no answer and the door was locked.

"Let me in, Leda, I want to talk to you," Caroline said.

"Leave me alone," replied a muffled voice.

"But you can't stay here indefinitely. I want to discuss plans with you," Caroline explained.

"What plans?"

It seemed rather absurd to discuss plans through the keyhole, and Caroline (whose sense of humour could never be dormant for long) was reminded of the human wall in *Midsummer Night's Dream* and was tempted to say:

"I see a voice: now will I to the chink,
"To spy an I can hear my Thisby's face ..."

She resisted the temptation, however, and inquired whether Leda would like to go away for a little while.

"I don't care what I do," was the reply.

"But you must do something, darling," Caroline told her. "You must either come out and face things bravely or else go away.

Aunt Harrie says you can have her flat if you like."

"I'll go to Mureth," said Leda. "I'll go tomorrow morning. Aunt Harriet can drive me over to Wandlebury in her car."

"Tomorrow?" asked Caroline in surprise.

"Yes, tomorrow," said Leda firmly.

This was the third best course — according to Harriet — but as Leda refused to consider the other two courses it was decided to let her go to Mureth. Several long and complicated telegrams were exchanged with the Johnstones and the arrangements were completed. Caroline was by no means happy about it, for Leda was still hard and defiant and, although she allowed her mother to come into her room and pack her clothes, she would scarcely speak to her.

"You're sure you want to go?" Caroline asked. "You're *quite* sure? There's no need to go unless you want to."

"I've told you I want to go," replied Leda.

Caroline sighed. It seemed heartless to send her off like this — as if she were in disgrace — and without coming to an understanding with her. There were all sorts of things Caroline wanted to say, but she was afraid to say anything. She had said all the wrong things last night and would probably say them again so it was better to say nothing. Time would heal them again so it was better to say nothing. Time would heal Leda's wounds. Caroline was old enough to know this and patient enough to wait.

The morning was fine. Harriet brought her car to the gate and James carried out the luggage and stowed it away.

Caroline was waiting to say good-bye and when Leda came out she put her arms round her daughter and kissed her tenderly, but Leda did not respond. Leda neither pushed her mother aside, nor returned the embrace, she merely suffered it.

"You're sure you want to go?" Caroline asked anxiously.

"I don't care whether I go or not — nothing matters," replied Leda.

"Don't go, darling!" exclaimed Caroline. "It's still not too late — "

"How silly you are!" said Leda coldly as she got into the car and sat down.

Caroline was aware that she had been

silly — she felt silly. "You'll write, won't you?" she said.

"Oh, I suppose so," replied Leda impatiently.

The car drove away. Caroline's eyes were full of tears as she turned back into the house.

"You were a bit stony, weren't you?" said Harriet to her passenger. "What's the big idea? What has Caroline done to be treated like that?"

"It's all her fault," replied Leda.

"What's all her fault?"

"That we weren't married of course. If Mother and Sir Michael hadn't been so horrid we would have been married — "

"You must be mad!" Harriet exclaimed. "Any man who can behave like that is a rotter and you're well rid of him. For goodness sake have a little sense."

"You aren't very sympathetic — " began Leda.

"I thought you didn't want sympathy," interrupted her aunt. "Caroline offered sympathy and you wouldn't take it so I thought I'd offer something else."

"I wish you'd leave me alone. I'm miserable," Leda declared.

"I can see you're miserable," agreed Harriet. "The question is why are you miserable? You're well rid of Derek, you've had a lucky escape."

"Don't you understand — "

"I understand perfectly," said Harriet. "Your pride is hurt — that's what's the matter with you. Now just you listen to me," said Harriet and with that she opened out and told Leda a few things which she thought Leda ought to know. Leda would not have listened if she could have avoided it, but there was no escape. She could not get out of the swiftly moving car and walk away.

Meanwhile, Caroline took Harriet's advice. She blew her nose fiercely, put on her best hat and a little rouge and set off to the village to do the shopping.

She had not gone far when she was overtaken by James.

"I'm coming," said James, taking the basket from her. "You must never go down to the end of the town unless you go down with me!"

Caroline smiled for the quotation was apt; she and James had always loved the ittle poems in *When We were Very Young* and especially the one about James Morrison Weatherby George Dupree who took care of his mother and insisted on accompanying her on her shopping expeditions.

"All right," said Caroline. "I won't say I'm sorry to have your company."

"It would be extremely rude of you," said James sternly.

They walked on.

"I hope we shan't meet the Meldrums," Caroline remarked.

"I hope we shall," returned James. "We've got to meet them some time. This is the way to do it — the sooner the better. Aunt Harrie *knows*."

"Eve's Dilemma," said Caroline thoughtfully.

"Yes, she took that on the chin, didn't she? But I expect she's had other knocks too."

The village was full of people, as it always was on a Saturday morning, and Caroline had a feeling that everybody knew about Leda and Derek and was talking about them. Naturally people would talk, for Leda and Derek were so

351

well known in the district; their engagement had been the subject of conversation for days and the new development might prove an even more interesting topic. Mrs. Meldrum certainly knew. Caroline met her face to face coming out of the post office and the good lady started as if she had been stung by a wasp.

"Oh!" exclaimed Mrs. Meldrum. "Oh, Caroline! I didn't expect to see you this morning."

"Saturday morning?" said Caroline smiling. "Of course I had to come and do my shopping. I couldn't let the family starve just because Derek and Leda have decided not to be married, you know."

"Then it's true!"

"Oh, yes, perfectly true," nodded Caroline.

"*What* a pity! You must all be terribly upset."

"It is unfortunate, of course," Caroline replied. "But it isn't a major disaster. These things happen every day . . . young people are apt to rush into things and then find out their mistake."

"And I hear that Derek is going to marry Valerie Bright!"

"I heard that too. As a matter of fact, Sir Michael told me himself. I wonder where you heard about it."

"I heard — I mean — er — "

"Perhaps from your char?" suggested Caroline helpfully.

"How are Joan and Margaret?" asked James who had been standing by and had decided that the time had come for him to interfere (it was strange that his dear mother, usually so sweet and amiable, could not speak to Mrs. Meldrum for two minutes without getting into a wax). "I hope they're all right," said James earnestly. "None the worse of the party. Everybody thought their duologue was awfully good."

Mrs. Meldrum could not refuse this bait and the remainder of the conversation was concerned with the charms of her daughters and their astonishing cleverness.

"That's that," said James as they walked on. "It wasn't too bad, was it?"

"Thanks to you," replied Caroline. "I should have been rude to her in another minute if you hadn't chipped in."

"You were rude to her, darling," said

James. "I merely chipped in before you could be insulting."

Caroline had thought an encounter with Mrs. Meldrum would be the worst to endure but she found it was much harder to endure encounters with people she liked and respected — Mrs. Severn, for instance. Mrs. Severn was so kind and sympathetic, so upset by the news of the misfortune which had befallen her friend that she said all the wrong things one after another . . . and then, realising her *faux pas*, tried to retract and floundered deeper in the mire. Caroline felt quite shattered after her chat with Mrs. Severn and decided to go straight home without waiting for the fish, but she did not get home without further adventures. Old Mrs. Podbury waylaid her and said what a pity it was . . . "And it's funny, too, them knowing each other so well," said Old Mrs. Podbury. "I was just saying to Amos, you could 'ave understood it if they 'adn't known each other all their lives, I said . . ."

They met Robert Shepperton next, he came out of the Cock and Bull, just as they were passing the door. Peter and Ted were with him, for this was Saturday morning and they had just had their first lesson in the Art of Navigation.

"I'm sorry," said Robert, stopping and speaking in a low voice so that the boys should not hear. "Mrs. Herbert told me. I'm afraid Leda will be terribly upset. I'm *very* sorry, Caroline."

"Yes," said Caroline. "Yes, it is — unfortunate — "

There was no time to say more, for Mrs. Smart bore down upon them and, putting her arm through Caroline's, drew her aside and inquired for Leda in hushed accents as if Leda had just undergone a serious operation and her life was still hanging by a thread. How was the dear girl? Had she managed to get any sleep? Was she able to take any food? Caroline found herself saying that Leda was as well as could be expected — which was not only foolish but untrue.

32

SEVERAL days passed. News was received of Leda's safe arrival at Mureth. She was "bearing up wonderfully" wrote her sympathetic aunt. They were giving a little party to cheer her up and were taking her to Dumfries to see *Oliver Twist*.

"That ought to cheer her up like anything," remarked her less sympathetic aunt on reading Mamie's letter.

It was all very well for Harriet to treat the matter lightly, but Caroline could not do so. Caroline was still worried and unhappy about Leda. There are sorrows which add to a person's stature, but this was not one of them and, unless Leda could learn to bear it in the right spirit, it might embitter her for life. Caroline felt responsible for Leda — Harriet was not responsible in any way — therein lay the difference. So Caroline reread Mamie's letter and thought about it and wondered how to reply, and how to write to Leda . . . if she wrote to Leda cheerfully Leda would think her lacking in sympathy, if she wrote with sympathy she might undo all the good that Mamie's attempts at "cheering up" had accomplished.

Mamie was quite different from her sisters; she was not clever and amusing, like Harriet, nor capable and forthright, like Jean. Mamie had always been the dunce of the family — but how sweet, how innocent and good! Perhaps Mamie would be able to do for Leda what Caroline could not do. Caroline hoped so with all her heart.

Nothing had been seen or heard of the Wares since the breaking of the engagement, but one evening Sir Michael rang up and asked if James would like to shoot with him the following morning; he asked in a tentative and somewhat embarrassed manner and it was obvious that he was not very sure how the olive branch would be accepted.

James accepted it with alacrity, not only because he would enjoy shooting with the Admiral but also because they had all agreed it would be most uncomfortable and quite ridiculous to be on anything except friendly terms with the Wares.

The sins of the children were not to be visited upon the fathers, as Harriet put it.

"Fine!" said the Admiral. "There may not be much to shoot but we can't help that. It will be good exercise, anyhow. Rhoda's here and says she'll meet us for lunch."

James got out his gun and cleaned it carefully . . . and then he found he had no cartridges. He could ask the Admiral for some but he didn't want to do that. When you were asked to shoot you took your own cartridges, you didn't sponge on your host. Silas Podbury would have cartridges, of course — James had got them from him before — but by this time it was after eight o'clock and James wanted them early tomorrow morning. The difficulty might have seemed insurmountable to any one who had not been brought up from infancy in the village of Ashbridge, but James had had this advantage and he was aware that practically no obstacle of this nature was insurmountable if you gave your mind to it. He thought deeply and then rang up the telephone exchange on the chance that one of the operators might be a Podbury . . . and in a few moments later he was speaking to Violet Podbury who was a second cousin of Silas.

Violet was intelligent and caught on at once. "I'll send a message to Dad," said Violet. "Dad's sure to see Silas at the Cock and Bull. There's a darts competition on."

"Good!" said James. "The only thing is how shall I get them?"

"That'll be all right, Mr. James," replied Violet. "Uncle Amos is fetching a load of gravel for the vicar early tomorrow."

"Grand!" cried James. "Couldn't be better." He chatted to Violet for a minute or two, exchanging some gentle badinage and inquiring after some of her numerous relations and especially after her brother Luke who had sung with him in the choir when they were both trebles . . . and eventually he laid down the receiver secure in the comfortable conviction that the cartridges would be delivered at Vittoria Cottage round about eight tomorrow morning.

It was a lovely day. There had been a little frost during the night but the white rime was disappearing rapidly in the rays of the sun. James borrowed Bobbie's bike and armed with his gun and a good supply of ammunition he rode over to Ash House. Rhoda was not yet up, but Sir Michael was ready and waiting.

"I'm not late, am I, sir?" asked James, anxiously.

"You're early, my boy," replied Sir Michael. "It's a habit of mine to be ready too soon. Stupid habit, but can't break it, somehow. We'll get going straight off. I've got to get home for lunch, but you needn't. Rhoda is bringing lunch out; she'll meet you at the top of Cock Hill at one-thirty. That suit you?"

James said it suited him admirably, he was free as air.

"Nice feeling, isn't it?" said Sir Michael. "Grand to be free after being at every one's beck and call for years. I remember how much I enjoyed it when I left the Service."

James smiled to himself for this was the first time he had heard of an Admiral being at every one's beck and call . . . but he understood what Sir Michael meant all the same. It was the absence of responsibility that was so delightful, the feeling that nobody depended upon you, that you were no longer Time's slave.

They set off together at a good pace, through the garden and up the hill.

"How's Derek, sir?" inquired James, for he had made up his mind that the sooner he cleared this fence the better.

"Getting on," replied the Admiral. "He's up and about but still a bit lame. This has been a blow to me, James. Don't know what to say."

"Better not say anything, sir," suggested James.

"Better not to say anything," agreed the Admiral, but he was not used to bottling up his feelings so he went on to say a good deal. James heard exactly what the Admiral thought of his son's behaviour and the behaviour of his son's future in-laws; he learned that Derek was to be married shortly with great pomp and circumstance and as soon as he was fit he was to be given a post — with suitable emoluments — in the tooth-paste business.

"Tooth-paste!" exclaimed Sir Michael in disgust. "And his future wife's picture on every hoarding in the country. I call it indecent. I told Rhoda nothing would induce me to go to the wedding, but she's talked me round, so we're going — she and I. We're going to the wedding but not to the reception — I drew the line at that. Rhoda was asked to be a bridesmaid but she refused the honour and I don't blame her. Rhoda sees things straight — ought to have been a boy, I always said so."

"Well, I don't know about that," said James. "I mean — "

"Let's try this turnip-field first," said Sir Michael.

There was no more opportunity for conversation — or at any rate for conversation unconnected with the matter in hand — for the Admiral was a keen shot and there was room only for one idea in his head at a time. They tried the turnip field with moderate success and then swung on to the moor. James was enjoying himself immensely. He was not shooting well, but the day was fine and the air was fresh and bracing. It was odd to think of the last time he had had a gun in his hands . . . not a shot-gun of course . . . and the totally different feelings he had had in his heart.

Sir Michael was a pleasant companion;

he was unselfish and sporting and exceedingly tough for his age. James had expected that he would have to slow down his pace to suit his host but he found this was unnecessary. His host was always there and often there before him . . . and although Sir Michael was a very good shot himself he did not look for miracles from his less experienced guest.

"All right," said Sir Michael, when James apologised for missing a hare in the turnips. "Don't worry, James, you'd have got him plumb if he'd been a bandit. A hare's too small — eh?"

"An elephant would suit me best," declared James, grinning.

Once or twice the Admiral barked at James but James didn't mind. He was used to being barked at by superior officers and knew exactly how much barks were worth. There were barks *and* barks, thought James. These sort of barks had no threat of bite in them.

"It's a damn' nuisance I've got to go home," said Sir Michael at last, taking out his watch and looking at it regretfully. "Fact is old Stobbs is coming down to lunch — wants to talk to me about stocks, the old blighter! Sorry to leave you in the lurch like this."

"It doesn't matter at all, sir," James assured him.

"You go on, James. You may get a pheasant in the wood."

They parted with expressions of good-will. The Admiral stumped off across the moor . . . but after he had gone a few paces he turned . . .

"James!" he cried. "Hi, James — don't forget you're to meet Rhoda for lunch! She'll be disappointed if you don't turn up."

James assured him that there was no chance of Rhoda being disappointed.

" 'Hair such a wonder of flix and floss,
    Freshness and fragrance — floods of it,
        too!
    Gold, did I say ? Nay, gold's mere
        dross . . .' "

said James softly.

Rhoda turned her head and looked at him. "I didn't know you were a poet, James," she said.

"I'm not, but I like other men's poetry,"

he told her. "It sometimes says things you can't say yourself."

They were sitting on the very top of Cock Hill, eating sandwiches and drinking coffee from a thermos flask. Beside them lay James's gun and a bag which contained a hare and a pheasant and a brace of partridges. The fine morning had become a gorgeous day, the air was crisp and clear; there were a few — but only a very few — fleecy, white clouds floating serenely in the pale-blue sky.

"Browning likes golden hair almost as much as I do," continued James thoughtfully. "Most of his stuff might be written in Sanscrit for all the good it is to me, but some of his poems are quite easy to understand. For instance:

'If one could have that little head of hers
Painted upon a background of pale gold'

I like that," said James dreamily. "I'd like to see a bright gold head painted upon a pale gold background."

"Is that the poem where the man strangles the girl with her hair?" inquired Rhoda with academic interest.

James laughed. "No, that's another one . . . and anyhow I don't want to strangle you, just to kiss you." He put an arm round her shoulders and kissed her, very tenderly. "There," he said.

"Not again," said Rhoda, pushing him away and smiling.

"But Rhoda — "

"Once is enough. Listen, James — "

"Rhoda, please! Let me talk first. I want to marry you. I love you, love you, love you."

"You want to marry my hair."

"All of you," said James earnestly. "Your hair and your nose and your lovely neck and your eyes . . . and the you that lives inside your eyes. That most of all!"

"You're a darling, but I don't want to marry you," Rhoda said. She put her arms round her knees and looked away over the country which was spread out before them like a coloured map, or like country seen from an aeroplane. "I don't want to marry any one," she added.

"Never?" he exclaimed.

"Well, hardly ever," she replied with a little chuckle.

"I can wait," James told her. "I know

you're tremendously keen on your painting and of course I must get settled in a job before we could be married, but you do like me, Rhoda?"

"Yes," said Rhoda. "I do like you — I more than like you — but I couldn't give up my painting."

"Rhoda — "

"No, James, I know exactly what you're going to say, but I couldn't go on painting seriously if I were married; certainly not if I were married to you. Perhaps I might be able to if I married a man who was a painter himself, but the trouble with me is I don't like painters — not to marry. They're amusing as friends, of course."

"If I get a job in London — "

She put out her hand to stop him. "You see, James, I'm a good painter," said Rhoda gravely. "I really am . . . and I'm going to be very good. It means work and work and work, but I love it, James. I'm perfectly happy when I'm painting. It absorbs every bit of me."

"There's nobody else?"

"Just painting," she told him. "I expect it sounds silly."

"Not silly a bit," declared James. "I

understand exactly what you mean but lots of painters are married, aren't they? All the ones I can think of are married."

"Not the women. Men can be married and still go on with their work, but it's much harder for women and I know I couldn't. We might have babies; it wouldn't be right to be married and not have babies and I don't think I should like it, anyhow. It would be only half a marriage — a poor show."

"Rhoda, couldn't we — "

"No," said Rhoda. "No, we couldn't. You would want all of me, James, and I need all of me for painting. There's no room for marriage in my life."

He was silent. It was a blow of course, but not a knock-out blow. Rhoda more than liked him — she had said he was a darling — and there was nobody else.

"We'll go on being friends," declared Rhoda, smiling at him.

"Of course," he agreed.

"I shall see quite a lot of you when you come to London."

"But I'm not coming to London," James told her. "I'm going to Mureth to live with Uncle Jock and Aunt Mamie. I'm going to be a farmer. It's what I've always wanted (I mean really wanted at the bottom of my heart) but, of course, if you'd said yes it would have been different. I mean we would have talked it over and decided together, but — well, you haven't — so you see — "

"Yes, I see," said Rhoda doubtfully.

"I shall like it," he continued. "It's such a beautiful place, and life there is so free and friendly. It's quite a different sort of life and it just seems to fit me, if you know what I mean."

"What will you do with yourself when you aren't hoeing turnips?" inquired Rhoda with gentle sarcasm.

James laughed. "Oh, we don't do much turnip-hoeing. Mureth is a sheep farm. Of course Uncle Jock has a few cows as well, just enough to supply the house with cream and butter. He keeps pigs, too, so there's always plenty of bacon . . . and there's hunting and shooting and fishing, so I shan't be bored!"

"Opulent amusements!"

"Not opulent," James assured her. "That's what I like about Mureth. You get your sport at your door quite simply

and naturally without any fuss. The river
runs through the property, about two
hundred yards from the house, I caught a
twelve pound salmon in it last time I was
there. Uncle Jock hunts with the Buccleuch
— sometimes the meet is at Mureth — and
of course you can shoot all over the hills
wherever you like. Hunting, shooting,
fishing," said James, grinning at her.
"When you get tired of scrambling for
buses and eating *ersatz* food just send me a
wire and I'll come and fetch you."

"You're thinking of another poem,"
said Rhoda, smiling back at him:

"Goldilocks, Goldilocks, wilt thou be
    mine?
Thou shalt not wash dishes nor yet
    feed the swine.
Hunting and fishing thou shalt be
    taken
And feed upon butter and salmon and
    bacon."

They both burst out laughing.

"Yes," cried James. "Yes, but Rhoda
you are Goldilocks — look at your hair. So
that means — that means — "

"I suppose you think Goldilocks said yes?"

"Of course, she said yes!"

"How like a man! The poem doesn't say Goldilocks accepted the offer and I'm sure she didn't. The girl had more sense. She liked work."

"The poem doesn't say she refused the offer," James pointed out. He waited for a few moments but Rhoda said nothing. "Come on!" he added, leaping to his feet. "I want to go and look at the Roman Well and see if it's still there."

Rhoda got up at once and they went down the hill together.

33

VITTORIA COTTAGE settled down quite comfortably after all its excitements. Bobbie had taken Leda's place at Miss Penworthy's School; she went to Wandlebury every day and Miss Penworthy was more than satisfied with her change of assistants, for Bobbie, being little more than a child herself, got on very well with the children. Joss missed Bobbie, of course, but the other members of the family took him for walks and did their best to make up to him for his mistress's absence. Caroline, Harriet and James were very gay and had jokes together. Harriet was happy and she was not to know that her companions were less happy than herself but were merely endeavouring, with a good deal of success, to live up to the creed she had formulated.

There was one other truly happy person at Vittoria House. Comfort was happy, for at last the treatment was beginning to take effect and she was losing weight. Every few days she was weighed carefully and the progress noted. It was slow, of course — much too slow in the opinion of the patient — and the patient was anything but patient. She suggested to Caroline that she should take double the quantity of medicine and thus lose her burden at double pace. Caroline was so horrified at the idea that she kept Comfort's medicine locked up securely and carried the key with her wherever she went.

Comfort was losing weight, her waistbands were getting loose, and she was feeling grand.

"Oh, what a beautiful morning!
Oh, what a beautiful day!"

carolled Comfort as she went about her work.

"Don't you know any other song, Comfort?" asked James who was beginning to get a little tired of it.

"Well, of course, Mr. James. I used to sing in the choir — you know that as well as I do."

"Weary of life and laden with my fat," murmured James.

"Oh, Mr. James, you *are* awful," said Comfort, giggling. "That wouldn't do *nearly* so well. Fact is that song about it being a beauterful morning seems to keep on coming into my 'ead. 'Ev'rything's going my way' and so it is. You'd know what I feel if *you* was fat, an' *you* was beginning to get thinner, an' *your* waist-bands didn't nearly cut you in 'arf every time you stooped down. You're too thin, of course, Mr. James. You're trying to get fat — but that's different. People don't larf at thin people," said Comfort with a sigh.

It was eleven o'clock on a not very "beauterful morning" and James had come into the kitchen to get his milk. He was sitting on one end of the table sipping his milk and Comfort was standing at the other end preparing vegetables.

"Someday we'll meet," said James, sipping reflectively. "We'll meet at eleven stone, Comfort, and when that long awaited day arrives we'll go down to the Recreation Ground together and have some fun on the see-saw."

"Oh, Mr. James, you *are* awful!" Comfort cried. "Fancy you an' me on the see-saw! You don't 'arf make me larf!" And

374

Comfort "larfed" with her usual abandon, gasping like a fish and shaking like a jelly.

It was curious that when James came into the kitchen and sat on the table and chatted to Comfort (as he did nearly every morning at eleven o'clock) her English deteriorated and she spoke to him more or less as she spoke to her mother and other members of her family. Her aitches flew in all directions and she didn't bother to run after them. James had noticed this and it amused him a great deal, it interested him, too. Was it because he was a man and therefore not due the same respect as his mother and his aunt, or was it because Comfort felt more at ease with him? She liked him — he knew that — they understood one another and there was no silly nonsense about their relationship. He enjoyed teasing her and she enjoyed being teased. He had all sorts of jokes with Comfort.

One day James came back from the village with a large railway-poster upon which was inscribed:

STAGGERED HOLIDAYS FOR COMFORT

and he had pinned it up on the kitchen wall with drawing-pins. It had been a tremendous success — all the more amusing because Comfort had no idea what it meant. James had come in to find her standing in front of it with her hands on her hips gazing at it in bewilderment.

The poster still hung on the wall, Comfort wouldn't have parted with it for a good deal. She knew what it meant now, of course, because she had asked Mrs. Dering and Mrs. Dering had explained it to her.

"You won't get no work done today, it's too wet," remarked Comfort as she emptied her potatoes into a pan and dumped it on the stove. "I was telling Uncle Amos about that crazy path you're making, an' Uncle Amos said 'e could get you any amount of them there paving stones . . ."

James pricked up his ears, for he was running out of large, flat stones and had been wondering how he could get some more. He might have known that all he had to do was to mention his requirements to a Podbury.

"Tell him to call in next time he's up this

way," said James. "I'll talk to him about it."

The crazy path was Harriet's idea, Caroline had sanctioned it gladly and James was having a good time preparing the ground and fitting the stones together like a jig-saw puzzle. Robert Shepperton was interested in the work and spent hours in the garden helping James, and as the weather was fine and open, the path was lengthening daily.

Caroline looked out of her window and saw the two path-makers at work. There was something rather alike about them. They were both tall and spare with broad shoulders, and they both had light-brown hair. They worked very happily together, measuring and discussing, digging and lifting; sometimes they stood back and laughed heartily over some joke. Then they would come in and scrape their shoes at the garden-door and wash and tidy themselves before appearing in the drawing-room for tea. Men were very like little boys in some ways, Caroline thought.

In spite of the fact that Robert came quite often to the cottage Caroline had a feeling that the affair between him and

Harriet was hanging fire a little. She had made up her mind that Robert was to be her brother-in-law, and nothing else, but she still found it difficult to think of him in that light. She wished they would get things settled. If only he and Harriet were definitely engaged she would feel quite different, she would be able to accept the *fait accompli* and be happy in their happiness.

Meanwhile Caroline avoided Robert as much as possible. When she knew he was coming she found it necessary to go and see Mrs. Severn about material for the sewing circle or to walk up the hill to Sue's cottage with some oranges for the baby.

Harriet said nothing but it was obvious what her feelings were.

"The great Miss Harriet Fane is hooked at last," said James to his mother with a smile.

"It certainly looks like it," she replied, trying to make her words sound gay.

"Aren't you pleased about it?" inquired James. "He's an awfully good sort, you know . . . and it's high time Aunt Harrie was married if she doesn't want to get left on the shelf. I know you don't like him much," continued James, looking at her doubtfully. "I've often wondered why you don't like him . . . I should have thought he was just your sort, that's the funny thing."

"Of course I like him," said Caroline hastily. "It's just — I mean it's better to — to leave them alone as much as possible. That's why I go out when I know he's coming — and — well — that's the reason, James."

James was not entirely satisfied, he knew his mother too well, but he was occupied with his own troubles at the moment so he let the matter slide.

James had said that the great Miss Harriet Fane was hooked. It certainly looked like it. If Robert were expected to tea Harriet took the trouble to make a cake for his delectation. "That cake's stale," declared Harriet. "Besides, Robert likes chocolate cake better." (Caroline remembered Harriet saying to Leda, "It's a delightful task to cook delectable food for the man you love.") And Harriet was staying on at Vittoria Cottage much longer than she had intended; she had received numerous tempting invitations but had refused them all. She had been asked to stay with friends in Leicestershire for a Hunt Ball; she had been invited to a big house-party at Bath; Marcus Rome had written beseeching her to come to town for a few days and go with him to a charity matinee at which the Duke and Duchess of Edinburgh were to be present.

"I can't be bothered," Harriet had said with an elaborate show of indifference. "If you and James can put up with me I'd rather stay on a bit longer."

James winked at his mother mischievously.

Harriet's "creed" helped Caroline a good deal. *It isn't what happens to you that matters, it's how you take it* . . . and after all what had happened? Nothing, except that she had been foolish enough to allow herself to fall in love with Robert. Quite silly at your age, Caroline told herself. The sooner you get over it the better.

Taking it thus, in the spirit of Harriet's creed, Caroline began to get over it. She began to feel happier — or at least less unhappy — and to envisage the future more cheerfully. She loved her house and garden. She could be perfectly happy living at Vittoria Cottage with Leda and Bobbie; James would come for an occasional visit, and she could go up to Mureth whenever she felt inclined and have a look at James . . . she saw herself getting older, but still continuing to run the Dramatic Club, still trying to maintain peace with Mrs. Meldrum in the Women's Institute and helping Mrs. Burnard with the Girl Guides. There was plenty to do, that was one comfort, you need never be idle in a village like Ashbridge.

Caroline was thinking of all this as she walked down to the little church on Sunday afternoon to attend her godchild's christening. It was a fine, dry, blustery day; the trees were swaying in the wind, their delicate tracery of bare, black twigs and branches seemed to be sweeping the pale-blue sky. It was winter still, but there was a feeling of spring in the air; the wind, though boisterous, was less nipping and more genial. The wind whipped her hair about her face, it disturbed the dead leaves and sent them flying about like flocks of little brown birds. It was an exhilarating day and when Caroline reached the shelter of the church-porch her cheeks were pink and her eyes were sparkling. She waited for a moment or two, trying to tidy her hair and to attain a proper decorum and then she unlatched the door and entered the dim, quiet church.

The christening party was already there, grouped round the font, waiting for Mr. Severn; Sue was sitting on a chair holding the baby, and Jim was standing beside her looking grave and unfamiliar in his Sunday clothes. They were flanked by Sue's family, her mother and father and masses of brothers and sisters and aunts and cousins — the Podbury family had turned out in force — and behind them at a little distance stood Robert Shepperton.

Robert! What was he doing here? Caroline felt quite angry with him. She was trying to stop thinking about him and to tear him out of her heart; but oh, how much easier it would be if she did not have to see him! Fortunately there was no need to speak to Robert, no need to look at him . . . Caroline went forward and smiled at Sue and took little Caroline in her arms; and, Mr. Severn arriving from the vestry at that moment, the service began.

Caroline had always felt that a christening should be a beautiful, simple service for it was a beautiful, simple idea: the acceptance of a tiny innocent human being into God's church. But the service (in Caroline's opinion) was neither beautiful nor simple. She had always found it slightly absurd. Today's service was no exception to the rule and, as she renounced the Devil and all his Works, the Vain Pomp and Glory of the World and the Sinful Desires of the Flesh on behalf of her small god-daughter, she found it very difficult to maintain a becoming gravity. Most certainly she would keep an eye on little Caroline and do all she could for her — that went without saying — but she could not do what she was promising to do, nobody could. And it was quite unnecessary and ridiculous (Caroline thought) to pray that all Evil Desires of the Flesh might die in little Caroline, for they had never lived in her. Little Caroline was as innocent of evil as a lamb . . . what right had any sinful grown-up person to impute sin to this innocent?

Little Caroline was very good. She was wide-awake and her misty, blue eyes looked up at her godmother with a bewildered expression. Her relations stood round in a circle with their prayer-books in their hands. It was obvious that they saw nothing the least funny in the proceedings; their faces were awe-struck, their gravity was profound, it was not disturbed even when little Caroline developed an attack of hiccups and hiccupped loudly and cheerfully all through the closing prayers.

34

WHEN they came out of church the wind was still blowing as strongly as ever, the leaves were whirling madly and the sky was full of torn clouds. Caroline said good-bye to the Podburys and started off home . . . it was still early afternoon, and if she were quick there would be time to make scones for tea. James and Bobbie had gone to spend the day at Ash House, but Harriet would be home for tea and Harriet liked scones.

Caroline was hastening up the hill when she heard footsteps behind her; she knew it was Robert without looking round.

"Caroline!" he exclaimed.

She waited for him and they walked on together.

"You didn't see me in church," Robert said. "Young Mrs. Widgeon asked me to come; it was nice of her, I thought."

"Yes," said Caroline.

"They're so friendly and kind. I've got to know a lot of people in Ashbridge now.

Sometimes in the evenings I go into the bar-room and play darts or chat to the older men, and I've learnt a great deal from them not only about the district but about human nature. There's an Elizabethan flavour about these people, they are simple-minded and brave. I find them very lovable."

Caroline agreed. She, too, had found the Ashbridge people easy to love.

Robert continued to talk about the people and of his contacts with them until they reached the gate of Vittoria Cottage.

"May I come in?" he asked.

Caroline hesitated. "The others are out," she told him. "Harriet has taken Joss for a walk up the hill. If you go on towards the gravel-pit you'll meet her coming back."

"I'd rather come in, if it isn't a bother."

"I'm going to make scones but you can come in and watch me if you like," said Caroline. It sounded ungracious — and she felt ungracious — couldn't he see that she was offering him a heaven-sent opportunity?

Robert hesitated. "I'd like to, if you don't mind," he said diffidently. "I want to see you. I want to talk to you for a few minutes."

A little while ago Robert would have come in without asking, sure of his welcome, but things had changed and he and Caroline were not comfortable with each other any more.

"Come in, by all means," Caroline told him.

He followed her into the kitchen. "I haven't seen you properly for weeks," he said. "You always seem to be busy."

"There's more cooking to do — with James here, and Harriet — I like to do most of the cooking myself. Comfort is all right, but she needs a good deal of supervision."

Caroline had thrown off her hat and coat and put on an apron. She was standing at the table measuring out the ingredients for her scones. She could feel that Robert was watching her and she felt uneasy and embarrassed.

"Caroline," he said at last. "I don't know what to do. I can't go on like this, it's getting me down. I feel cut off from you. Have I done anything to hurt you? Are you annoyed with me?"

"Of course not!" she exclaimed.

"I feel cut off," he repeated. "I feel as if you had withdrawn your — your friendship from me. Do tell me what's the matter."

"It's nothing — honestly — you're imagining things."

He walked to the window and looked out. "No," he said. "I'm not imagining things. There's something wrong between you and me, Caroline."

"Robert, there isn't — "

"I can't bear it! If it mattered less I could let things drift and hope for them to come right of themselves. I thought at first that was the best way — not to bother you, just to go on waiting for things to come right — but, instead of coming right, things are getting worse; you're drifting farther and farther away every day."

Caroline had begun to mix the dough, but her hands were shaking so that she had to stop. "Don't, Robert," she said in a low voice. "Don't say any more."

"But I must!" he exclaimed. "I must get to the bottom of it. Surely you can tell me what I've done to offend you!

It isn't fair to cast me off without telling me what I've done — without giving me a chance to explain."

"You haven't — offended me. How could you think so!"

He was silent for a few moments and then he sighed. "I suppose it's hopeless," he said. "I was afraid it was hopeless but I couldn't go away without trying to put things right."

"You're going away!"

He nodded. "I can't stay here. I must find something to do, some sort of work. I can't stay in Ashbridge."

"But, Robert — surely — I mean you aren't going away *now*!" cried Caroline in horror-stricken tones.

"Don't you want me to go?"

"No, of course not."

"Then there *is* hope," he said eagerly. "You don't absolutely dislike me, Caroline? Oh, my dear, I love you so tenderly. I'll wait and go on waiting if there's the slightest hope."

"Robert!" she cried in dismay.

"I thought at one time you were beginning to be fond of me," he continued. "I didn't want to rush you. I thought I would let you get to know me better. I thought I would go slowly."

"Robert — no!"

"You knew I loved you?"

"No, this — this amazes me!" she cried. "You don't mean it, Robert!"

"Of course I mean it. I thought you knew. I thought you understood what I felt."

"No," said Caroline. "No, I never thought — "

"But, Caroline, you *must* have known. How could you *not* know?" asked Robert in bewilderment. "I kept on coming here, trying to see you . . . surely you must have realised it was because I couldn't stay away!"

She did not answer that.

"Well, you know now," he told her. "It was because I couldn't stay away, because I went on hoping to see you and talk to you as we used to talk when I first came to Ashbridge."

"But, Robert, I thought — "

"You thought what?" he asked.

"I thought you came to see — the others," she murmured.

"Well — of course," he agreed. "I like

all your family. James is a grand fellow and Harriet is one of the best . . . but there's only one you. I want to marry you, Caroline."

"I couldn't *think* of it!" she exclaimed.

"Please think of it. We were such friends — we got on so well together. I know you liked me at one time. Some stupid little thing has come between us — I'd give anything to know what it was." He looked at her appealingly, but she said nothing.

"I won't ask for love," he continued. "I love you dearly, but I can do without your love if you will give me your friendship — your companionship. We're both rather lonely people, aren't we? I know we could be happy together — "

"It's impossible," said Caroline in a low voice "You've made a mistake — a frightful mistake."

"You mean you don't like me at all?"

"Of course I like you, Robert."

"Then it isn't absolutely hopeless."

"Yes, it's hopeless," she declared. "I've made up my mind not to marry again. There's so much to do . . . I have to think of the children . . ." She was floundering about, trying to find words; she was so amazed, so taken aback that she scarcely knew what she was saying. It all sounded foolish and unreal. "I like you immensely," she repeated. "I've thought of you as my friend. I should like you as a brother, that's how I've thought of you . . . I couldn't . . . couldn't change . . . I couldn't think of it."

"Then there's no hope at all?" asked Robert sadly. He hesitated for a few moments, looking at her, but she did not reply; indeed she could not reply for there was a lump in her throat that almost choked her and her eyes were stinging with tears.

"Don't worry about it," he said. "I won't bother you any more."

It was at this moment, when they were still standing there, that Harriet looked in at the window. "We've had a lovely walk," she cried gaily. "Joss caught a rabbit — wasn't it clever of him? We can have it for supper instead of cod. How I hate cod! Hallo, Robert, are you helping Caroline to make scones?"

"Hindering her, I'm afraid," returned Robert, trying to speak naturally.

"You can come and help me," she told him. "You can dry Joss — it's a man's job — he went into the bog after the rabbit. I think we should start by putting him through the mangle."

Robert was glad of the excuse to leave the kitchen. He went out, and Caroline heard them talking together over their task. Her thoughts were in confusion, she felt quite dazed. She had been so sure that Robert and Harriet were fond of each other. She was still quite sure that Harriet was fond of Robert. What a frightful mess! thought Caroline. And there was no way out of it as far as she could see. She had turned deliberately from Robert, withdrawing inside herself and erecting a barrier so that nobody should see her heart . . . and it was all a terrible mistake. She had handed Robert to Harriet and had encouraged Harriet to think of him — not encouraged her openly, of course, but in all sorts of little ways — so how could she take him back? In any case she couldn't, for she had refused him irrevocably.

What would happen now? Robert would go away and neither she nor Harriet would ever see him again. *Harriet*, thought Caroline in dismay. Harriet, who had refused a dozen offers and now had fallen in love! What ought I to do, wondered Caroline. Should I say something to Harriet? But what could I say?

She was still dazed by all that had happened when Harriet came in with Joss jumping round her.

"Robert wouldn't stay to tea," said Harriet. "We'll have it cosily by ourselves. Are the scones ready?"

"No," said Caroline. "I didn't make them after all."

"Of course you made them," declared Harriet, laughing. She walked across the kitchen and opened the oven door. "And here they are!" she added.

"I must have made them without noticing," said Caroline.

"Are you feeling all right?" asked Harriet in alarm.

"Yes — at least I've got a little headache, that's all. We'll have tea, shall we?"

"I'll make it, darling. You go and sit down in the drawing-room. I'll do everything," declared Harriet, beginning to bustle about. "You've been doing too much, that's what's the matter. You must let me do more to help you."

35

THE evening seemed extraordinarily long. Caroline sat by the fire and turned over the pages of a book while the others played a game . . . she was aware that she was not living up to Harriet's creed but she felt so shattered by what had happened that she could not disguise her suffering. Harriet and James and Bobbie were full of sympathy and kept on inquiring if her headache were any better, and finally they decided she must go to bed.

"If you aren't better in the morning I shall ring up Dr. Smart," said James firmly.

"Nonsense," declared Caroline. "It's a headache, that's all. I shall be perfectly well in the morning, there's no need to worry."

Harriet was just as worried as James. She pursued Caroline to her room and dosed her with aspirin and tucked her up in bed . . . and these kind attentions made

Caroline feel worse than ever, made her feel like a murderess.

"If you're ill in the night you'll come for me, won't you?" said Harriet, looking at her patient anxiously.

"I'm very fond of you," declared Caroline. "You know that, don't you? I'd do anything for you, Harrie."

"Yes, of course," agreed her sister in some alarm. "Of course, darling, and so would I for you."

"Remember that, won't you? Sometimes one can't do anything — and sometimes one tries to do something and it all goes wrong. I'm rather silly, I'm afraid, but I do love you, Harrie."

"I think I'd better take your temperature!"

"No," said Caroline, pulling herself together. "No, I'm not a bit feverish. Don't worry about me, I shall be all right in the morning."

Oddly enough, Caroline slept quite well, perhaps this was due to the aspirin or perhaps it was because she felt it was no good worrying. The situation was so complicated that it was utterly beyond her. I shall do nothing about it, she thought as she shut her eyes . . . and in a few moments she was asleep.

The morning was fine and sunny and the wind had gone down. Caroline felt much better, she came down to breakfast as usual and endeavoured to reassure her relations as to her health.

"I'm perfectly well," she told them. "I don't know what was the matter — perhaps something disagreed with me, or I may have got a little chill. I shall go out for a good walk this morning. That will complete the cure."

"If you're quite sure you're fit for it," said Harriet doubtfully.

Caroline was quite sure — there was nothing like a walk to clear the brain and blow the cobwebs away. So, after she had made a shepherd's-pie (from the scanty remains of yesterday's dinner), she put it in the oven and went to get her coat.

"Are you coming, Harriet?" she asked, looking in at the drawing-room door.

"No, I've got a letter to write," replied Harriet. "Take Joss — and don't go too far, will you?"

"Just up to the gravel-pit," nodded Caroline.

Harriet watched her walk down the path to the gate and turn up the hill. She seemed all right this morning, but all the same Harriet was worried about her. What on earth had been the matter with Caroline last night! She had been quite confused — almost tearful at times — she had seemed almost delirious. Harriet had been so alarmed about her that she had gone in twice during the night, but had found her patient sleeping as peacefully as a child. All the same, it was most unlike Caroline to rave like that . . . *I'd do anything for you*, she had said. *Remember that, won't you. Sometimes when one tries to do something it all goes wrong.* That's what she had said — or words to that effect — but what on earth had she meant? Then she had added, *I'm rather silly, I'm afraid, but I do love you, Harrie,* and that was out of character too, for, although they were devoted to one another, Caroline and Harriet never mentioned the fact — it simply was not necessary.

Harriet had come to the conclusion that the whole thing was a mystery (and would remain a mystery unless Caroline explained it), when the telephone bell rang. Harriet answered it — she was sure it was Robert, and it was.

"Is that Harriet?" asked Robert. "Yes, I thought it was you. I just wondered if you would be in this morning. The fact is I want to see you — I want to ask you something."

"Yes, I shall be here," she replied.

"You aren't going out? I could come this afternoon if that will suit you better."

"I shall be in all morning," Harriet assured him.

She smiled as she laid down the receiver . . . of course she would be in! She would be here, waiting for him. Robert need not be so diffident, surely he knew that. Meanwhile she must write that letter and it would not be an easy letter to write.

Harriet had received a long communication (it was more than a letter, really) from Marcus Rome on Saturday and she had not answered it yet. She had put off the task of answering it, not because there was any doubt in her mind as to what she was going to say, but because she did not know how to say it. The answer was in the negative, but she must write a nice, long, chatty letter to poor Marcus and try to soften the blow — it would be a bitter blow but she could not help that. Marcus would have to bear it.

Harriet sat down on the window-seat, from whence she could keep an eye on the gate, and took out Marcus's letter. His writing was thick and well-marked, it looked as if it had been formed with a paint-brush . . . Harriet had often teased poor old Marcus about his writing; she knew he was rather proud of it. The letter ran as follows:

"Harriet darling, have you eaten enough grass? There must be cobwebs all over you by this time. Of course you wanted a rest — we all did after Eve's decline and fall — but now you've had it and you simply must come back. Really, darling, you simply must. Now listen to me and I will a tale unfold. I saw Teddy Minden yesterday at the Ivy and the Great Man called me over to his table and asked me where you were — all mysterious like — he had been ringing up your flat until the wire was hot but had got no answer. I said why did he think I would know where you were and he said

401

he had an idea we were buddies, so I said,
well, perhaps I did know, but what did he
want you for, and he said he just wanted to
see you, and I said of course you were nice
to look at, and he said he couldn't agree
more. So then after a good deal of humming
and hawing he said there was no great
secret about it but I wasn't to mention it to
a living soul — except you of course — and
I said I promised faithfully not to divulge
it to a dead haddock — except you of
course — and then at long last he came to
the point and spilt the beans good and
proper. Did I think you'd be interested in
an American Tour — Shakespeare, my
dear! Not the big plays but one or two of
the lighter and lesser known. He mentioned *The Tempest* (Did I say that he
wants me too? No, I didn't, but he does!).
My dear, it would be absolute heaven!
You, as Miranda — 'What is't? A spirit?
Lord, how it looks about! Believe me, sir,
it carries a brave form! — but 'tis a spirit
. . . I might call him a thing divine, for
nothing natural I ever saw so noble.'
That's what you say about me, darling, and
I should swoon with delight to be so com-
mended by you; "Admir'd Miranda! In-

leed the top of admiration, Worth what's dearest in the world!' Yes, dear Harriet, of course I went straight home and read it — spent all night reading it if the truth be told! What marvellous theatre it is! What fine brave poetry it is! Better than slick dialogue about a rocking-horse. Harriet, why can't people write like that nowadays? The rhythm is ringing in my ears like a bell . . . and the clothes, my dear! We could let ourselves go — we could spread ourselves. Teddy does things well and he's all agog over this, so no expense will be spared. He hasn't fixed on a second play but spoke vaguely of *The Winter's Tale* and said some students of Shakespeare considered it had never had a proper showing (you would have laughed at Teddy gone all high-brow) so if you have any ideas for or against playing Perdita you had better come and see Teddy before he gets *his* ideas firmly fixed. My dear, think of America! We've dreamed about an American Tour so often and wondered how it could be wangled . . . and here it is on a plate . . . and, talking of plates, think of the food. Do, please, think of the food, darling. Are you thinking about it? Tenderloin steaks, Maryland chicken, ice-cream made with real, live cream instead of paper-hanger's paste . . . and if that doesn't bring you to town helter-skelter, what will . . ."

Nothing would, thought Harriet; she must write to Marcus and refuse the offer as kindly and tactfully as possible. *Nothing* would take her to London now, for she had made up her mind that if Robert Shepperton asked her to marry him she would say yes, and she was certain that he intended to ask her this very morning.

Harriet had thought at first (when she first came to Ashbridge) that Robert and Caroline . . . but then she had seen that there was nothing in that. Caroline didn't even *like* Robert very much. Sometimes it seemed as if she actively disliked him, for she was cool and impersonal towards him; she was less than herself when Robert was there. So there was no need to worry about that, and it was just as well, for Harriet was in love. She had been in love before, several times, but never in love with a man she could respect and admire. People had said Harriet Fane was cold and hard-hearted . . . but how glad she was that she had not wasted herself and frittered herself away on stupid little love affairs as so many of her friends had done and were doing all the time! She had kept herself to herself; she had been waiting for the right man and the right man was here. Harriet had a core of hard sense: she knew that love was all very well but it didn't last unless there were other things behind it, unless you had the same values, unless you saw the same jokes and enjoyed doing the same kind of things. Robert was all she wanted and she loved him . . . and he had rung up to ask if she would be in this morning because he wanted to ask her something.

Harriet was still sitting on the window-seat and had just got out her writing-pad; she was wondering how she would begin her letter to Marcus — whether it would hurt him less if she wrote in a light, teasing vein or quite seriously and firmly — when she heard the click of the front gate and saw Robert coming up the path.

He waved when he saw her and Harriet signalled to him to come straight in. She stood up and waited for him.

"Is everybody out?" he asked, looking round the room.

"Yes," said Harriet. "Everybody except me."

"Good," said Robert, nodding. "I wanted to see you alone."

"Sit down, Robert. Have a cigarette," she said. She was annoyed to find her hands were trembling; they were so shaky that she could not risk trying to light a match so she handed him the box.

"Thank you," he said, taking it.

There was a little silence while he lighted the cigarette and shook out the match. Then he leaned forward.

"We're friends, aren't we, Harriet?" said Robert, smiling confidingly. "We're real honest-to-goodness friends. I've always felt *that* from the very first moment I saw you — at the Wares' party — do you remember? We decided we could have carried out the perfect crime together. You do remember, don't you?"

"Yes, of course, Robert."

"So now I'm going to ask you something." He hesitated for a moment or two but Harriet did not speak. "I want your advice," he added.

"My advice!"

"It's about Caroline, of course. I'm

desperately fond of Caroline — you knew that, didn't you? I believe you knew I was in love with Caroline before I knew it myself."

Robert paused and looked at her but she did not answer.

"Some time ago," continued Robert, turning his head and looking out of the window, "about two months ago I thought there was quite a lot of hope. I didn't want to rush her, of course, but I was sure she was fond of me. There was one day especially . . . and then gradually she seemed to withdraw. She was still *there* but I couldn't get near her; she became unapproachable. Of course she was busy — I knew that — and she was worried about Leda. At first I put it down to that and I decided to wait patiently. But I found things were becoming worse instead of better . . . and I could never get her alone — never, for a single moment — that was odd, wasn't it?"

"Yes," said Harriet. "Yes, it seems — odd."

"She avoided me. I'm sure of it. What do you think it could be?"

Harriet thought of several things it could

be but principally of two things: either Caroline didn't like him at all, or else — or else liked him too much.

"What do you think it could be?" repeated Robert. "Could I have done something to offend her? You don't know of anything, I suppose? I mean Caroline hasn't said anything to you?"

"Caroline and I are tremendous friends but we have — reticences," said Harriet in a strained voice.

He sighed. "I was hoping you might know," he said hopelessly. "I thought perhaps you could advise me what to do; whether it's any good to stay on and try to win her round, or whether I should go away and try to forget about her."

"Whether you should go away?"

"What's the use of staying?"

Harriet got up. She couldn't sit there any longer . . . she couldn't face him.

"Why don't you ask her, Robert?" Harriet said.

"I *did* ask her — yesterday afternoon. It was the first time I had seen her alone for weeks. I asked her if I had done anything to hurt her. She said no, nothing . . . but somehow I had a feeling that it wasn't quite true. Then I asked her to marry me. I suppose it was foolish to ask her then, but one thing led to another and I — I asked her."

"What did she say?"

"She seemed absolutely amazed. She said it was a mistake and that I didn't mean it. She said she liked me immensely but she had made up her mind not to marry again because there was so much to do."

"Because there was so much to do!" echoed Harriet in amazement. It was the most extraordinary reason for refusing an offer of matrimony that Harriet had ever heard.

"That's what she said," nodded Robert.

"What else did she say?"

"Nothing much — except that she would like me as a brother."

"She said that!" exclaimed Harriet.

"It's the sort of thing a woman says when she wants to let you down lightly," said Robert with a rueful smile.

Harriet disagreed with him. She did not think Caroline had said it to let him down lightly. Caroline had too much sense. It was the sort of absurd request made by early Victorian heroines to their disappointed swains. "Be a brother to me!" It was a downright silly thing to say . . . unless, of course, you meant it literally. . . .

There was quite a long silence while Harriet thought about this, and about other things . . . about the way Caroline had avoided Robert and her strange behaviour last night and the odd things she had said . . . *one tries to do something and then it all goes wrong . . . I'm rather silly, but I do love you. Harrie.*

Robert had got up, he was standing looking out of the window. He was waiting for Harriet to speak.

"Ask her again," said Harriet at last.

"Ask her again!" exclaimed Robert. "I can't do that. She was absolutely definite."

"Ask her."

"No — honestly. She left no loop-hole at all."

"Robert, you must ask her again."

"I can't!" he cried. "I asked her and she said no. I promised I wouldn't bother her any more. I might try again later, perhaps, but — "

"Ask her today."

"Harriet, listen — "

"Go after her *now*," said Harriet urgently. "She's gone up to the gravel-pit. Go after her and find her and say, 'Caroline, please marry me. I can't do without you.' Tell her all you've told me — everything. Then, if she still says no . . ." Harriet paused.

"What then?" asked Robert with dawning hope.

"Then say, 'Harriet told me to go on asking you until you say yes.' "

"But, Harriet, why — "

"That's all," said Harriet firmly.

He rose and went without further ado — somehow he had acquired the habit of doing what Harriet told him.

Harriet called to him as he ran down the path, "Robert, tell her I'm looking after the pie!"

Robert waved his hand and ran on. The gate slammed behind him. Harriet stood quite still and listened to the sound of his footsteps until she could hear them no longer. Her eyes were blurred with tears.

"Idiot!" she said, blinking them away. "What are you whimpering for! You know perfectly well you'll adore playing Miranda to American audiences — it'll be a whole lot of fun."